CHERUB

Robert Muchamore is a London-based private investigator. *CHERUB: Maximum Security* is his third novel.

For more information on Robert and his work, visit www.cherubcampus.com.

Praise for the CHERUB series:
'Punchy, exciting, glamorous and, what's more, you'll completely wish it was true.' *Sunday Express*

'An excellent start to a promising series. It is every boy's wish to be a spy, and this book will enthrall every single one of them.' *The Bookseller*

'No kidding, this is the funniest book I have ever read . . . this book is excellent from the first page to the last!' Christopher, age 12

'Excellent book! I just couldn't put it down. (They're a thieving bunch in my house.)' Charlie, age 12

'One of the best books I've ever read.' Chase, age 11

'I think that your book was brilliant!' Callum, age 10

'This book is exciting all the way through.' Victoria, age 10

Also from Robert Muchamore:

CHERUB: The Recruit
CHERUB: Class A

And coming soon . . .

CHERUB: The Killing

Other titles available from Hodder Children's Books:

Acceleration
Graham McNamee

Silverwing
Sunwing
Firewing
Airborn
Kenneth Oppel

Superhuman
Boy Kills Man
Matt Whyman

MAXIMUM
SECURITY
Robert Muchamore

*Hodder
Children's
Books*

A division of Hodder Headline Limited

A Catalogue record for this book is available
from the British Library

ISBN 0 340 88435 5

Typeset in Goudy by Avon DataSet Ltd,
Bidford-on-Avon, Warwickshire

Printed and bound in Great Britain by
Bookmarque Ltd, Croydon, Surrey

The paper and board used in this paperback by
Hodder Children's Books are natural recyclable products
made from wood grown in sustainable forests.
The manufacturing processes conform to the
environmental regulations of the country of origin.

Hodder Children's Books
a division of Hodder Headline Limited
338 Euston Road
London NW1 3BH

WHAT IS CHERUB?

CHERUB is a branch of British Intelligence. Its agents are aged between ten and seventeen years. Cherubs are mainly orphans who have been taken out of care homes and trained to work undercover. They live on CHERUB campus, a secret facility hidden in the English countryside.

WHAT USE ARE KIDS?

Quite a lot. Nobody realises kids do undercover missions, which means they can get away with all kinds of stuff that adults can't.

WHO ARE THEY?

About three hundred children live on CHERUB campus. JAMES ADAMS is our thirteen-year-old hero. He's a well-respected CHERUB agent, with two successful missions under his belt; although he does have an unfortunate habit of getting himself in trouble.

James' younger sister, LAUREN ADAMS, is now nearing

the end of her CHERUB basic training. If she passes the course, she'll be qualified to work undercover. KERRY CHANG is a Hong Kong-born Karate champion and James' girlfriend.

Amongst James' closest friends on campus are BRUCE NORRIS, GABRIELLE O'BRIEN and the twins CALLUM and CONNOR REILLY. His best friend is KYLE BLUEMAN, who is fifteen.

AND THE T-SHIRTS?

Cherubs are ranked according to the colour of the T-shirts they wear on campus. ORANGE is for visitors. RED is for kids who live on CHERUB campus, but are too young to qualify as agents. BLUE is for kids undergoing CHERUB's tough 100-day basic training regime. A GREY T-shirt means you're qualified for missions. NAVY – the T-shirt James wears – is a reward for outstanding performance on a single mission. If you do well, you'll end your CHERUB career wearing a BLACK T-shirt, the ultimate recognition for outstanding achievement over a number of missions. When you retire, you get the WHITE T-shirt, which is also worn by staff.

1. COLD

Before you entered basic training, you probably heard stories from qualified CHERUB agents about the nature of this one-hundred-day course. Although every basic training course is designed to teach the same core abilities of physical fitness and extreme mental endurance, you can expect your training to differ from that of your predecessors in order to retain the element of surprise.

(Excerpt from the CHERUB Basic Training Manual)

It looked the same in every direction. The sunlight blazing off the field of snow made it impossible for the two ten-year-old girls to see more than twenty metres into the distance, despite the heavily tinted snow goggles over their eyes.

'How far to the checkpoint?' Lauren Adams shouted, breaking her stride to stare at the global positioning unit strapped around her best friend's wrist.

'Only two and a half kilometres,' Bethany Parker shouted back. 'If the ground stays flat, we should be at the shelter in forty minutes.'

The girls had to shout for their voices to override the

howling wind and the three layers of clothing protecting their ears.

'That's cutting it close to sundown,' Lauren yelled. 'We'd better get a move on.'

They'd set off at dawn, dragging lightweight sleds that could be hooked over their shoulders and carried as backpacks on difficult terrain. The good news was, the two CHERUB trainees had the whole day to trek fifteen kilometres across the Alaskan snowfield to their next checkpoint. The bad news was that at this time in April, the daylight lasted just four hours and wading through half a metre of powdery snow put enormous strain on their thighs and ankles. Every step was painful.

Lauren heard a howling noise rising up in the distance. 'It's gonna to be another big one,' she shouted.

The girls crouched down, pulled their sleds in close and wrapped their arms tightly around each other's waists. Just as you can hear waves approaching a beach, out here in the Alaskan snowfields you could hear a strong gust stirring up in the distance.

They were both dressed for extreme cold. Lauren's normal underwear was covered with a long sleeved thermal vest and long johns. The next layer was a zip-up suit made from polar fleece that covered her whole body, except for a slit around the eyes. The second fleece was designed to trap body heat. It looked like a baggy Easter bunny suit, minus the pom-pom tail and sticking up ears. Then came more gloves, another balaclava, snow goggles and waterproof outer gloves that went all the way up to Lauren's elbows, ending in a tightly fitting elastic cuff. Finally, on the outside was a thickly padded snowsuit and snow boots with spiked bottoms.

The clothing was enough to keep them comfortable as they walked, despite the temperature being minus eighteen centigrade, but this dropped another fifteen degrees whenever a strong gust hit. The wind pushed the insulating layers of warm air between the girls' clothes into all the places where it wasn't needed, leaving nothing but a couple of centimetres of synthetic fibre between their skin and the ferociously cold air. Each blast ripped into their bodies, delivering searing pain to any exposed area.

Lauren and Bethany used their sleds as windbreaks when the gust hit. A spike of cold air punched through the tightly fitting rim of Lauren's goggles. She pushed her face against Bethany's suit and squeezed her eyes shut, as snow and ice pounded deafeningly against her hood.

When the gust passed and the snow had settled, Lauren brushed the dusting of powder off her suit and stumbled back to her feet.

'Everything OK?' Bethany shouted.

Lauren stuck up her thumbs. 'Ninety-nine days down, one to go,' she shouted.

*

Lauren and Bethany's home for the night was a metal container painted in an high visibility shade of orange. It was the kind of container you'd normally expect to pass on the motorway, mounted on the back of an articulated truck. There was a radio mast and a shattered flagpole lashed to the roof.

The girls had beaten the darkness. The sun's distant face was already touching the horizon and the light it sent through the mist of falling snow gave the whole landscape a powdery yellow hue. The girls were too exhausted to appreciate its beauty; all they cared about was getting warm.

It took a few minutes to dig out the snow from around the two metal doors that formed one end of the container. Once they were open, Lauren dragged the two sleds inside, while Bethany searched along a wooden shelf until she found a gas lamp. Lauren closed the metal doors, creating a boom that would have been deafening if the girls' ears hadn't been shielded by their outdoor clothes.

'We've got even less fuel tonight,' Lauren shouted, as the lamp erupted in an unsteady blue glow. She looked at the single bottle of gas as she peeled off her goggles and outermost set of gloves. Her hands were freezing, but it was impossible to manipulate anything with three sets of gloves on.

On the first night of their week in the Alaskan wilderness, the girls had found two large bottles of gas in their shelter. They'd heated the room until it was toasty, cooked lavishly and warmed up water to wash with. The fun ended abruptly when the gas ran out in the middle of the night and the indoor temperature rapidly dropped back below freezing. After this harsh lesson, the girls took pains to ration their energy supply.

Bethany fixed a hose from the gas bottle to a small heater and lit just one of its three chambers. This would slowly bring the temperature inside their container above freezing. Until it did, the girls would keep as many of their outdoor clothes on as the task at hand allowed.

They spent the next few minutes rummaging through the supplies that had been left for them. There were plenty of high-energy foods, such as tinned meats, flapjacks, instant noodles, chocolate bars and glucose powder. They also found their mission briefings, clean underwear, fresh boot liners and floor mats. Combined with the pots, utensils and sleeping bags packed in their sleds, it would be enough to make the nineteen hours until the sun returned reasonably comfortable.

Once the girls had ensured that they had all the basics, Lauren couldn't help wondering what was under the tarpaulin at the back of the container.

'That's got to be something to do with our mission for tomorrow,' Bethany said.

They stepped across and dragged the tarp off a giant cardboard box. It was over two metres long and almost up to Lauren's shoulders. Scraping at the layer of frost over the cardboard revealed a Yamaha logo and an outline drawing of a snowmobile.

'Cool,' Bethany said. 'I don't think my legs could handle another day trudging through that snow.'

'Have you ever driven one?' Lauren asked.

'Nah,' Bethany said, shaking her head excitedly. 'But it can't be much different from the quad bikes we drove last summer at the hostel . . . Let's open our briefings and work out what we've got to do tomorrow.'

'We'd better take our temperatures and radio base camp first,' Lauren said.

There was a radio set already linked up to the aerial on the roof. Its battery was cold and it took several seconds for the orange frequency display on the front panel to light up. While they waited, the girls took turns measuring their body temperatures with a small plastic strip that you tucked under your armpit.

The indicator lit up between the thirty-five and thirty-six degree marks on both of them. It meant the girls were running slightly below normal body temperature, which is exactly what you'd expect for two people who'd just spent several hours in extreme cold. Another hour would have been enough for them to develop early symptoms of hypothermia.

Lauren grabbed the microphone and keyed up. 'This is unit three calling instructor Large. Over.'

'Instructor Large receiving . . . Greetings, my little sugar plums.'

It was reassuring hearing a human voice other than Bethany's for the first time in twenty-four hours, even if it was that of Mr Large, CHERUB's head training instructor. Large was a nasty piece of work. Pushing kids through tough training courses wasn't just part of his job; he actually enjoyed making them suffer.

'Just reporting in to say that everything is fine with me and unit four,' Lauren said. 'Over.'

'Why aren't you using the coded frequency? Over,' Mr Large asked angrily.

Lauren realised her instructor was right and hurriedly flipped the scramble switch on the front of the receiver.

'Oh . . . Sorry. Over.'

'You will be tomorrow morning when I get my hands on you,' Large snapped. 'Minus ten house points for Hufflepuff. Over and out.'

'Over and out,' Lauren said bitterly. She put down the

microphone and kicked out at the side of the metal container. 'God, I *really* hate that man's guts.'

Bethany laughed a little. 'Not as much as he hates you for knocking him head first into that muddy hole with a spade.'

'True,' Lauren said, allowing herself a grin as she recalled the event that had brought her first attempt at basic training to an abrupt end. 'I suppose we'd better get cracking. You start translating the briefing. I'll go outside and bring in some snow to melt for drinking water.'

Lauren found a bucket and grabbed the torch out of her sled. She pushed the metal door of the container and squeezed herself and the bucket through a small gap, so as not to let out too much heat.

The sun was gone and only the tiny shaft of light from inside the container enabled Lauren to notice the giant white outline in the snow. Half convinced that she was overtired and imagining things, Lauren flicked on her torch.

What Lauren saw left her in no doubt. She screamed as she scrambled back inside the container and swiftly pulled up the metal door.

'What's the matter?' Bethany asked, turning sharply from her mission briefing.

'Polar bear!' Lauren gasped. 'Lying in the snow right outside the door. Luckily it seemed to be resting; another few steps and I would have trodden on it.'

'It *can't* be,' Bethany said.

Lauren waved the torch in her training partner's face. 'Here, take this. Stick your head out and look for yourself.'

It only took the briefest of glances to confirm it. The mat of white fur, with plumes of hot breath steaming out of its nostrils, lay less than five metres from the entrance to the container.

*

Once Lauren recovered from her near-death experience, the girls thought things through and decided that the situation wasn't too serious.

They could get all the drinking water they needed by leaning out of the metal doors and scooping up the snow around the entrance. Once they'd got enough snow, they decided to leave the giant bear in peace. It seemed unlikely the animal would leave itself exposed to the cold all night. Surely it would move away to find shelter before the sun came back up.

The inside of the container had now warmed up enough for the girls not to be able to see their breath curling in front of their faces. After their day in the cold, it seemed toasty. They stepped out of their boots and outer suits, hanging them on a line in the warm air above the gas heater, so that the moisture in them would evaporate overnight.

The metal floor of the container was cold to touch, so they put on trainers and laid out insulating foam mats retrieved from their sleds. They turned the heater up and lined icy tins of corned beef and fruit in front of it, as Bethany melted a saucepan of snow over a portable stove.

It took an hour to read the briefings for the final twenty-four hours of their course, under the flickering light of two gas lamps. The briefings only ran to five pages, but were written in languages with non-European alphabets that the girls had only started learning at the beginning of the course: Russian for Bethany and Greek for Lauren.

The gist of the briefings was simple. The girls had to unpack the snowmobile from its shipping crate and prepare it for first use: a task that involved screwing various bits together, lubricating the drive track and engine and filling the tank with petrol. From sun-up, they'd have two hours to make a thirty-five-kilometre journey by snowmobile to a checkpoint where they would liaise with the four other trainees for something the briefing ominously described as the 'Ultimate test of physical courage in an extreme weather environment'.

'Well,' Lauren said, as she dug her spoon into a can of corned beef that was warm and greasy on the outside but rock hard in the centre, 'at least the instructions for the snowmobile are in English.'

2. BOWLING

James Adams had been looking forward to spending Saturday night in town at the bowling alley, but now he was here he'd got himself in a mood. The four other CHERUB agents on the lane seemed to be having far more fun than he was.

Kyle was in great form, lording it over everyone, buying them hotdogs and Cokes with the small fortune he'd made burning pirate DVDs for half the kids on campus. Kyle always had some dodgy money-making scheme going on, but as far as James could work out this was the first one that had ever earned decent money.

The identical twins, Callum and Connor, were also enjoying themselves, despite their stupid bet with each other that one of them could get off with Gabrielle before the night was out. James had told the twins they were dreaming: they might be nice guys, but Gabrielle was thirteen and totally fit. If Gabrielle wanted a boyfriend – which as far as anyone could tell she didn't – she could do better than pick between two gangly twelve-year-olds with dishevelled blond hair and a gap the size of a Mars bar between their crooked front teeth.

'*Strike* . . .' Gabrielle shouted, as ten pins rattled off in different directions. She flailed her arms and jiggled her bum about, doing a kind of freaky war dance. 'You're up, Kyle,' she whooped.

Gabrielle turned away from the scene of her triumph to see Callum and Connor grinning at her from their plastic chairs, either side of where she'd been sitting before she bowled.

'Great shot,' Callum beamed.

'Didn't I say you'd bowl better if you swung your arm back a little less?' Connor interrupted, as he shot an evil glance at his identical twin. 'Your balance is much better now.'

Gabrielle remembered the advice, but she hadn't bowled any differently to normal. The strike had been down to luck. She looked at her plastic seat and realised she couldn't handle another second of the two boys fawning over her. She reached under her chair and grabbed her bag.

'Where are you going?' Callum asked apprehensively. 'What's the matter?'

'James looks a bit down in the dumps,' Gabrielle explained. 'I'm gonna sit with him for a minute and see if I can cheer him up.'

'Good idea,' Connor grinned. 'I'll come with you.'

'No,' Gabrielle said stiffly. 'You two are gonna stay *right* there.'

'But . . .' Connor said, half standing up before sitting down again.

'Look,' Gabrielle said. 'I don't mean to be rude, but you two are acting seriously weird and it's getting on my nerves. Can't you let me have five minutes' peace?'

Gabrielle felt bad as she reached over and pulled her jacket off the back of her chair. Both twins had the exact same expression: like toddlers whose mother had punished them by confiscating their favourite toy.

James was in a daze, staring down at the floor between his legs. Gabrielle tapped him on the knee. 'What's up, misery guts?' she asked, as she took the seat next to him. 'Still thinking about Miami?' The previous summer, James had got into a bad situation and ended up shooting a man to save his own life. He still had nightmares about it.

'I guess,' James shrugged. 'And I kind of miss Kerry. I haven't heard from her in over a week.'

'Neither have I,' Gabrielle said. 'But the last message I got said she'd arrived in Japan and was going deep undercover, so it's hardly surprising.'

James nodded. 'I spoke to her mission controller on the phone. He says everything's fine and hopefully Kerry will be home in a month or so.'

'What about Lauren?' Gabrielle asked. 'How's she getting on with basic training?'

'You know how it is,' James said, 'you only ever hear rumours, but I think she's doing OK.'

Gabrielle started to laugh. 'Remember when we were in training? Me and Kerry locked all you guys out on that hotel balcony and made you grovel to get back in?'

James allowed himself to smile a little. 'Yeah, we never got you back for that.'

Something cold touched the back of James' neck. He looked around and realised he and Gabrielle had been splashed with Coke and ice by the gang of sixteen- and seventeen-year-old boys who were playing the next lane. They were acting rowdy, rucking and throwing stuff around.

'Oi,' Gabrielle stormed, as she scowled over her shoulder at a mass of acne in a Tottenham Hotspur shirt. 'Do you mind?'

'Sorry,' the kid said, grinning mischievously at the ice in the bottom of his cardboard cup. Gabrielle got the impression he wasn't sorry at all.

'James,' Kyle shouted. 'Your frame.'

James got out of his seat and grabbed a bowling ball off the rack. He'd picked up a coupon and taken a couple of free bowling lessons, so when James was on form he looked the business: delivering the ball in a powerful arc and racking up respectable scores. But not tonight. In fact, James' mood had nothing to do with missing Kerry, or worrying if Lauren would pass basic training. James was feeling down because he couldn't aim a bowling ball to save his life.

He lined up, holding the heavy ball under his chin. He took a good smooth swing. The ball crashed nicely into the front three pins, and for a second James thought he'd scored his first strike in ages. But pin seven, at the back on the far left, merely wobbled and number ten on the extreme right didn't even have the decency to do that. James couldn't believe his rotten luck.

'Seven-ten split,' Kyle shouted, slapping his thighs deliriously. 'You're going *down* again, Adams.'

James glanced up at the scoreboard. When they bowled in a group, James usually fought Kyle for first place and won more than he lost. But he'd already lost two matches tonight and was thirty points behind Kyle in this one, with four frames left to play. James thought Kyle rubbing in the misery was harsh, conveniently forgetting he would have acted exactly the same if it had been Kyle having a bad night.

James grabbed his ball as soon as it clattered on to the rack and stopped spinning. He lined up to take his second shot, glowering at the two pins standing on opposite sides of the lane.

To make a seven-ten split, you need to hit one pin so hard that it bounces against the wall behind, then spins out and knocks down the pin on the opposite side. The shot requires a hefty chunk of luck and even a world championship standard bowler wouldn't expect to make it often.

'You'll never hit both in a million years,' Kyle goaded.

James turned back and smirked at Kyle, struggling to fake an air of confidence. 'Sit your butt down and watch the master at work.'

James swung the ball as hard as he could, but when you bowl fast you lose control. The ball did a little bobble as James let go. It had plenty of pace, but James knew straight away that it wasn't right.

'Turn back,' James gasped desperately, as the ball edged closer to the gutter. 'Come on*nnnnnn baby* . . .'

The ball thunked into the gutter a couple of metres shy of the pin. James put his hands over his eyes and cursed under his breath. He almost couldn't bear turning away, knowing he'd catch sight of Kyle's smug face.

'Eight points and a gutter ball,' Kyle said happily. 'Maybe you should wander down to the bumper lanes and ask the supervisor if you can play with the little red-shirt kids.'

James huffed as he slumped back into his seat next to

Gabrielle. 'The way I'm going tonight, I reckon the little kids would beat me.'

'You're doing better than Callum and Connor, though,' Gabrielle said sympathetically, pointing up at the TV screen with the scores on it.

'Some consolation that is. Those two are hopeless.'

Gabrielle smiled and brushed the back of her hand against James' leg. 'Just not your night, I guess.'

As she said it, both their backs got sprayed with more Coke. They turned quickly to see two beefy looking guys in football shirts wrestling in a puddle on the floor. James waited until they broke apart before having a go at them.

'What are you two retards playing at?' James barked furiously. 'I'm bloody soaked.'

'My top's all marked,' Gabrielle said, looking anxiously down her back and wondering if the stains would come out.

The two lads were giggling as they got to their feet. 'We're just having a laugh,' the one in the Tottenham shirt said.

The other lad looked less sympathetic. 'There's loads of empty seats over there,' he grunted. 'Why don't you just move?'

'Because this is *our* rink,' Gabrielle said. 'I don't want to walk five miles every time I take my shot.'

'Yeah,' James agreed. 'Why should we move, just because you want to roll around the floor with your boyfriend?'

The kid jabbed James in the back. 'Are you calling me a queer?'

James and Gabrielle stood up and turned around to face the two lads, who towered over them.

'I didn't come here for a row,' James said.

'Nor did I,' the tough guy said. 'But you're going the right way about getting into one; so why don't you just take your little *wog* girlfriend off and sit somewhere else?'

The tough guy had twenty-five centimetres and fifteen kilos on Gabrielle, so he never expected what happened next. Gabrielle, who was a second-dan Karate black belt, launched a high kick over the row of plastic seats. Her bowling shoe slammed into the thug's kidney and by the time he'd got his breath back, he was pinned to the ground with a bloody nose and an orange painted thumbnail digging into his cheek.

'Call me that again,' Gabrielle screamed, as she bunched up her fist. 'Go on . . . I dare you.'

Her voice echoed across the bowling alley's metal roof as a hundred sets of stunned eyes turned towards her. The whole place went quiet, except for the sound of a couple of squealing toddlers and the blipping of arcade machines.

James quickly straddled over the rows of seats and rested his palm on Gabrielle's shoulder. 'Come on, Gabrielle,' he said soothingly. 'Cool it. It's not worth getting upset over the likes of *him*.'

Gabrielle released her hand from her victim's face and stood up. James thought he'd defused the situation, but then he realised four other lads were moving in to surround them. As he stepped forward to walk back to his lane, a clumsy punch glanced across the side of his head.

James instinctively swung back with his elbow to take out his assailant, catching him full in the face and deftly sweeping away his opponent's legs as he stumbled backwards. The other three lads didn't like this one bit. Two lunged at James, while the guy in the Tottenham shirt tried to take down Gabrielle by jumping on her back.

CHERUB had trained James to handle himself in a fight, but there's a limit to what you can do against three significantly larger opponents at close range. Luckily, the other cherubs were rushing to his defence.

Kyle, Connor and Callum all piled over or around the seats and launched themselves at the thugs. James caught a second punch and his bowling shoe squealed as he lost his balance on the polished wooden floor.

He tried to get back on his feet, but found himself trapped on the ground, while a tangle of limbs waged war overhead. He caught sight of Kyle's knee hitting someone in the guts and Tottenham-shirt guy getting pulled into a painful arm-lock by the twins.

By the time a group of adults – including the two CHERUB supervisors looking after the younger kids in the bumper lane – charged in to break up the fight, there was no doubt about the result. The five yobs were crawling around on the floor in varying degrees of pain, with a ring of steely-faced CHERUB agents surrounding them, defying them to make another move.

James rolled on to his back and took a big gasp of air. He got a little rush from being on the winning side, even though his main contribution had been getting thumped in the head and falling over. He reckoned the older kids deserved what they'd got; the way they'd started on Gabrielle was totally out of order.

But James' mood darkened as he levered himself up on to the plastic seats. His head hurt, his clothes were filthy and there were going to be consequences when they got back to campus.

*

Dr Terence McAfferty, usually known as Mac, stared at the five kids lined up in front of his big oak desk, wondering exactly how many times he'd faced similar line-ups of worried faces in the thirteen years since he'd been appointed chairman of CHERUB. He was sure the number ran into thousands.

'So,' Mac said wearily, 'what caused the fight at the bowling alley earlier this evening?'

'This guy on the next rink had a go at Gabrielle,' Kyle explained, stepping forward and taking the lead role because he was the oldest. 'They were chucking their drinks around and acting like idiots. We all kind of lost our temper and piled into them.'

'You all *simultaneously* decided to pile in,' Mac said, clearly not finding this explanation likely. 'And I suppose none of you is any more to blame than anyone else?'

'That's right,' Kyle lied.

The rest of the line-up nodded. They'd huddled together and sorted out their cover story on the mini-bus ride back to campus. Gabrielle had started the punch-up, of course, but she'd been racially abused and none of the other kids thought she deserved to cop all the blame.

'I understand,' Mac said reluctantly. 'If that's the way you want me to deal with this, so be it. But I spoke to the staff members who were at the scene and I think I have a pretty accurate idea of what *really* happened.'

As he said this, Mac cast deliberate glances at Gabrielle and James.

'I shouldn't have to tell you how serious this incident could have been,' Mac continued. 'It's been drilled into you all time and again. What is the number one priority for groups of CHERUB agents when they're off campus?'

The line-up droned the answer, at different speeds and with varying degrees of gusto: 'Keep a low profile.'

'A *low* profile,' Mac nodded. 'CHERUB is a secret organisation. The safety of your colleagues who are currently away on undercover missions depends upon the fact that nobody knows we exist. When you're off campus, I expect you to behave in a manner that doesn't attract undue attention. I expect you to avoid trouble at all costs, even under extreme provocation. Is that clearly understood?'

'Yes sir,' everyone nodded sombrely.

'A whole bunch of people saw your little display of fighting skills at the bowling alley this evening. Don't you think they're going to be extremely curious about who you are and how a group of youngsters might come by advanced martial arts skills like that? Can you imagine the fuss that would have been caused if one of the boys you assaulted had been seriously injured? I know you're all trained in unarmed combat and had the good sense to use minimal force, but freak accidents can still happen.

'On top of that, you can count yourselves extremely lucky that I have connections at the local police station. I had to use all my leverage to ensure that the five of you aren't sitting in a police cell at this very moment facing criminal charges. So, your punishments.'

It was midnight. The kids had been tired and fidgety while they listened to the lecture, but they snapped to attention at the mention of punishments, anxious to know what they were going to get.

'First of all, you're all banned from going into town for the next four months,' Mac announced. 'Secondly, we're always short of pupils at CHERUB and right now we're getting desperate for new blood . . .'

Mac reached into his desk drawer and pulled out a pad of pre-printed mission briefings. James let out a little groan as he realised he was about to be sent off to some strange children's home to recruit a new CHERUB agent. James had never been on a recruitment mission before, but everyone he knew who had said they were a complete nightmare.

3. WILDLIFE

It was near midnight when Lauren and Bethany finished readying the snowmobile for its journey the next morning. The vehicle was designed to be taken from its packing crate and assembled, lubricated and fuelled by anyone who could follow basic instructions.

The girls zipped their sleeping bags together and snuggled up. If you believed the cold weather survival manual, sleeping in individual bags was warmer. But textbooks don't take into account the comfort factor of falling asleep beside your best friend, even when the fleece-covered arm she wraps around your back stinks of petrol.

*

A few streaks of light penetrated the container when the first sun crept over the horizon, despite the bits of cardboard the girls had pushed into the gaps around the metal doors to keep out the draught.

Lauren and Bethany were sleeping heavily when their wristwatch alarms began bleeping, just a few seconds apart. The girls were taking no chances. They'd set two alarms in case one of them made a mistake, or one of the watches went wrong. Any kind of error could lead to them missing the final checkpoint and their ninety-nine days of suffering would all be for nothing. They tried keeping thoughts of failure out of their minds, but it was like being trapped in a burning building and trying not to think about the flames creeping towards you.

Lauren pulled back the zip and slid out of her sleeping bag, then stood up and lit one of the gas lamps. The floor of the container was freezing cold on her socked feet. Bethany was always a slow starter and like every other day since training began, it took a nudge from Lauren to get her moving.

'Come on, lazy head,' Lauren said. 'You start packing up our equipment, I'll make the porridge. It'll be safest if we get going the second it's light enough.'

As she said this, Lauren squatted over a metal bucket in the middle of the floor and began the undignified process of peeling off the outer fleece suit and thermal underwear she'd slept in.

'Why couldn't I have been a boy?' Lauren asked rhetorically, as Bethany sat up on the sleeping bag and pushed the detachable linings into her boots. 'A penis would make this lark *so* much easier.'

'Imagine what our brothers are doing right now,' Bethany said. 'With the time difference, it's bedtime over there. I bet they're sitting in front of their TVs, with hot drinks and chocolate biscuits.'

Lauren laughed. 'Knowing James, he's out on the athletics track running punishment laps.'

'Probably alongside Jake,' Bethany grinned. 'My brother's almost as bad as yours.'

'You want to use the bucket before I sling this lot outside?' Lauren asked, as she adjusted her underwear and pulled up the zip on her fleece suit.

'Yeah. Hand it over, I'm busting,' Bethany said. 'I hope that bear's gone.'

Lauren smiled. 'If not, he's about to get woken up by having a bucket of pee chucked over his head.'

After Bethany had peed, Lauren cautiously pushed the metal door open with her shoulder. It was hard to shift because half a metre of snow had blown against it during the night. The cold air stung her uncovered hands and face. She slung out the contents of the steaming bucket and glanced through the sleet.

'Dammit,' Lauren said anxiously. 'It's still out there.'

The sleeping bear was now blanketed in the overnight snowfall, except for a patch around its snout that had been melted by the breath rising out of its nose.

'Look at the size of him,' Lauren said. 'I bet he could kill us both in one swipe. It's going to be too dangerous dragging the snowmobile out before he's gone. We'll have to shoo him off.'

'We should do it now,' Bethany said, as she crept up to the crack in the container door beside Lauren. 'That way he'll be long gone by the time we have to leave.'

Lauren nodded in agreement. 'Those TV shows always say that even big animals are easily scared, so it shouldn't be that hard.'

She pushed the metal bucket through the doors and whacked it as hard as she could against the container door. The girls had to bury their ears in their hands to dull the eardrum-shattering clang. The bear, on the other hand, didn't move a millimetre.

'Stupid creature,' Lauren snapped.

'Maybe we should lob something at it,' Bethany suggested.

The open door was letting out the heat and the girls were underdressed. They retreated inside to put on gloves and balaclavas. Bethany rummaged around for a good throwing object, while Lauren poured porridge oats, powdered milk and water into a tin and set it over the camping stove so that their breakfast was warming while they dealt with the wildlife problem.

Bethany approached the doors holding two saucepans, the only items amongst their lightweight camping equipment that seemed sufficiently hefty to rouse a polar bear.

'I'll have to get close to make sure I don't miss,' Bethany said. 'But it might charge at me, so you hold the door and be ready to pull it shut the second I come back through.'

Bethany's heart drummed as she crept to within three metres of the bear, holding a saucepan in each hand. She hurled both saucepans, before spinning around and charging back to the container in a flurry of white powder.

Lauren slammed the doors of their metal cage. Bethany's momentum carried her forward over Lauren's sled and she ended up sprawled out on the floor beyond it.

'Are you OK?' Lauren asked.

'I'll live,' Bethany gasped, as she rolled on to her back. 'Did it work?'

Lauren's main concern had been Bethany's safety. She hadn't seen the bear's reaction through the clouds of snow.

She pushed the door back open a couple of centimetres and took a peek.

'I do *not* believe it,' Lauren gasped.

Bethany poked her head through the gap between the doors and didn't believe it either. The bear still hadn't moved. All that had changed was that there was now a saucepan on the ground in front of its snout and another buried in the snow over its midsection, swelling up and down with each breath.

'It had to happen this morning, didn't it?' Lauren said, sounding stressed out. 'We should have eaten breakfast, packed up and dragged the snowmobile outside by now.'

'Think, girl!' Bethany said, pounding her gloved hand against her thigh. 'There *must* be a way to make it move.'

'Maybe it's deaf or something,' Lauren said.

'Think, think, think...' Bethany repeated. 'What if we loaded everything on the snowmobile and pushed it outside quietly? It wouldn't catch up with us once we're moving.'

'Too risky,' Lauren said. 'What if we disturbed it at the wrong moment and it went after one of us? We wouldn't stand a chance.'

'True,' Bethany said. 'But looking at that dozy lump, I'd say you'd have to shove a firework up its butt for it to budge.'

'That's *it*,' Lauren gasped. 'Bethany, you're a genius.'

'What?' Bethany asked. 'We don't have a firework. We do have our distress flare, but if we set that off the rescue helicopter will come for us and we'll fail training.'

'Not a firework,' Lauren explained. 'But we can make fire. Animals are scared of fire.'

Feeling that she couldn't spare time to explain, Lauren plunged into the wreckage of the snowmobile packaging at the back of the container. She grabbed one of the long pieces of cardboard and tore off a ragged section, thirty centimetres wide and three metres long. Then she rolled it into a tube.

'Tie this off with some of that tape,' Lauren ordered.

Bethany picked up the strong plastic binding strip they'd cut off the outside of the snowmobile box before opening it. She wound it around the tube, tying knots as she went.

'Are we gonna poke it with this?' Bethany asked.

'Uh-huh,' Lauren nodded, as she gathered up the bits of oily rag they'd used when they were working on the snowmobile and stuffed them into one end of the tube.

'The oil on these rags will burn easily,' Lauren explained. 'It won't stick around long enough to feel any more than a quick lick of flame.'

'Good thinking,' Bethany said admiringly.

Bethany found some waterproof matches in her sled, as Lauren moved up to the door with the long cardboard tube.

'Be ready to pull up the door after me,' Lauren said. 'He's not going to like this one bit.'

Bethany went up on tiptoes with a match in her hand. The oiled rags instantly erupted in blue flames. Lauren pushed the burning tube through the doorway, hoping that the freezing wind wouldn't snuff out the flame.

The fire turned orange as Lauren tilted the tube forward and the cardboard caught light. Her second crunching step through the snow took the flaming end to within half a metre of the bear's head. When the flame was almost touching its nose, Lauren lowered the tube on to the snow and rolled it towards the bear's face. Certain that the bear would rear up the instant the flame touched it, she scrambled desperately back towards the container and Bethany clanged the door shut behind her.

The girls caught their breath for a moment, before cracking the door back open. They were expecting to find a four-hundred-kilogram bear with a burned snout on the rampage, but what they saw was more shocking: the bear's head was in flames and its eye socket had sunk down through its skull into its head.

'We killed it,' Bethany shrieked. 'The poor thing must have been old, or sick.'

But Lauren wasn't buying it. She'd noticed the grey wisps of smoke venting out the back of the mound in the snow. Lauren didn't know much about the anatomy of polar bears, but she was certain their insides weren't hollow.

'It's fake,' Lauren announced.

Lauren plunged into the snow towards the smouldering bear and leaned over it. Although it was smoky, she got a reasonable view inside the cavity where the head had melted. The bear was made of nylon fur, stretched over a frame shaped out of chicken wire. Inside, she could see the plastic bellows, rubber tubing, car battery and electric pump that had made it breathe.

'We should have known,' Bethany stormed, angrily kicking up a flurry of snow. 'After all the tricks the instructors have played on us.'

Lauren looked at her watch. 'I reckon we've lost fifteen minutes of daylight. Let's get breakfast down our necks and get out of here.'

The porridge was bubbling over the side of its tin when they got back inside the container. Lauren laced the porridge with a heavy dose of glucose powder and a slow-release energy supplement designed for long-distance runners. The girls' bodies would need every calorie of this high-energy food to keep warm on their thirty-five-kilometre snowmobile journey. When it was all mixed in, the porridge had a gritty texture and the grey pallor of cement, but the girls barely considered this as they half spooned and half drank the soggy mixture.

'I hope there's no more tricks,' Lauren said, as she wiped a dribble of porridge from the corner of her mouth.

Bethany spoke with her mouth full. 'If we can just keep our heads together for four more hours . . .'

4. SUNDAY

Kids who live on CHERUB campus miss a lot of school when they're away on missions. One of the ways they catch up is by having lessons on Saturday mornings. James thought this was cruel, because it left Sunday as the only time when he got a chance to lie in.

It was nearly eleven when he decided to untangle himself from his duvet. Dressed only in boxers and a grubby CHERUB T-shirt, he glanced through the slats in his blind and saw that it was a typical April morning, with a light frost on the grass and a drizzle of rain. A football match was being played on the pitches beyond the tennis courts. The players were a bunch of muddy eight- and nine-year-olds, mostly boys.

James wandered across to his laptop, flipped up the screen and tapped on the navigation pad to check his e-mail. He was hoping for a message from Kerry, but all he had was spam from a company offering him a *Free online personality test that could change your WHOLE life!!!* and a schedule notification from the mission controller Zara Asker:

James,
Please ensure you attend the mission preparation building,
room 31, at 1530 this afternoon, where you will be briefed on
your upcoming recruitment mission.
Zara Asker (Mission Controller)

James thought about sending an e-mail to Kerry, but he'd
sent her three since she'd last replied and the only news he
had was about the fight at the bowling alley, which he didn't
feel like going into.

He felt too lazy to go down to the canteen, so James
flicked on Sky Sports News, poured himself a bowl of cereal
and got milk and orange juice from his miniature fridge.
There was a knock on the door while he ate.

'Not locked,' James munched.

Kyle and Bruce came in, both dressed in shorts and
trainers and holding carrier bags with a towel and a change
of clothes in them.

'Aren't you ready?' Kyle asked.

James looked at the clock on his bedside table. 'Sorry,' he
said, 'I never realised it was time.'

James went to the fitness training session with Kyle and
Bruce every Sunday morning. Most boys preferred playing
football or rugby, but after thirteen years of missing open
goals, tripping in the mud and getting smacked in the face by
balls that came out of nowhere, he'd reluctantly accepted
that ball games were not his forte.

'I'll get some clothes on,' James said, as he sat on the edge
of his bed and grabbed one of the crusty sports socks
scattered over his floor.

'Way to go at the bowling alley last night, James,' Bruce sneered.

'You would have been involved if you hadn't *already* been on punishment detail in the kitchens,' James sneered back.

'Yeah well,' Bruce smiled, 'better spending a couple of hours down on my knees cleaning out the ovens, than a month stuck in some god-awful children's home. Mind you, it's always a shame to miss a punch-up, whatever the consequences.'

'You know what?' James said, as he pulled on a white sock that didn't match the first one. 'I don't see what all this fuss is about recruitment missions. It can't be *that* bad being sent off to some children's home to try and get another kid to join CHERUB.'

Kyle, who'd been on five recruitment missions for his many sins, nodded. 'They're not awful. They're just really boring and a lot of the kids you meet in those places are complete scumbags; nicking your stuff and that. One time I got sent to this place in Newcastle. I had guys starting on me every five minutes. I was there for three weeks and I must have been in a row every day.'

'Did you recruit anyone?'

Kyle nodded. 'Those two blonde twins with the Geordie accents. Remember I pointed them out to you? They were only seven at the time, but they had more brains than all the other kids in that dump combined.'

*

There were three gymnasiums on CHERUB campus. Fitness training was taught in the oldest of them, which was still known as the Boys' Gym, from the days when physical education was a single-sex affair. James had a soft spot for this dilapidated building, with its mahogany wall clock permanently stuck at a quarter to five, dim light bulbs suspended from long wires and shrunken floorboards that creaked underfoot. His favourite feature was the hand-painted sign hanging over the entrance:

> *Any boy bringing in mud or dirt on*
> *his plimsolls will be thrashed.*
> P.T. Bivott (Sports Master)

Today's teacher was Meryl Spencer, a retired Olympic sprinter, who could think of a couple of kids she wouldn't have minded thrashing if corporal punishment at CHERUB hadn't been banned more than twenty years earlier.

The gym had been laid out with forty stations. Some were as simple as a foam mat with a laminated card on it saying *Push Ups*. Others were more complex: traffic cones set out for shuttle runs, a chest-press machine, a chin-up bar.

The thirty kids in the class picked a station to start at. They worked it for two minutes, after which Meryl would blast her whistle and the kids would run to the next. The whole circuit took eighty minutes and the only relief from exhaustion came at the two rest stops along the way. Anyone who looked slack found Meryl or her assistant yelling in their face, calling them soft and threatening them with *a good boot up the backside*.

Eight boys piled into the showers when the session ended. James towelled off and put on clean jeans, then flexed his chest muscles and biceps in front of the steamed-up mirror.

He'd sprouted eight centimetres in the last three months and packed on muscle since starting regular strength training.

Bruce flicked James' back with his towel. 'You little poser,' Bruce grinned. 'Stop poncing about.'

James turned away and grinned as he rolled deodorant under his arms. 'You're just jealous because I'm looking so beefy these days,' he said. 'It's hardly surprising that half the girls on campus are chasing after me.'

'You reckon, do you?' Bruce huffed.

Kyle spotted a golden opportunity for one of his trademark wind-ups. 'I think you're right, actually,' he said, stepping forward and putting his hand on James' bum. 'I think you're hot stuff.'

James leapt half a metre in the air and screamed. 'Cut that gay shit out, Kyle.'

After a great deal of persuasion from Kerry and a few others, James had eventually decided that there was nothing wrong with his friend Kyle being gay. Sometimes it still gave him the creeps though. He spun around and furiously shoved Kyle away, his face burning with rage as Bruce and the other boys started laughing. James realised the only way to save face was to outdo Kyle at his own game. He quickly balled up all the saliva he could muster, grabbed Kyle around the back of the neck and planted a massive soggy kiss on his cheek. Kyle recoiled in horror, with a glistening trail of James' spit rolling down his face.

'You filthy *little* . . .' Kyle shouted, as he scoured his wet face on his towel.

'What's the matter?' James asked sweetly. 'Come on, baby. Won't you give us a snog?'

Bruce and the others were killing themselves laughing, as Kyle bundled up his clothes and scrambled to the opposite end of the changing room.

*

Sunday lunch was an occasion on campus. It was the only meal of the week when the individual tables in the dining-room were pushed together. Table cloths were laid and places set with the good cutlery. The traditional Sunday roast with all the trimmings was James' favourite meal of the week, but the atmosphere at his table was miserable, because everyone except Bruce was being briefed for their recruitment missions later that afternoon. Even the banter riding back and forth about James and Kyle fancying each other didn't do much to lighten the mood.

Kyle, James and Gabrielle shared the first appointment with Zara. They strolled through the drizzle without speaking, their bloated stomachs deadening their progress.

The brand new mission preparation building was a kilometre away from the main building, where they'd eaten lunch. The banana-shaped construction looked impressive as you approached: a hundred metres of reflective glass, bristling with satellite dishes and aerials. Impressions took a turn for the worse when you got close and realised that the paths up to the building comprised wooden boards laid over mud. There were still wheelbarrows, cement mixers and building materials everywhere and the high-tech entry system that was supposed to identify you by scanning the lattice of blood vessels in the back of your eye had a soggy *Out Of Order* notice drooped over it.

The three kids passed along a corridor that smelled of

new carpet tiles. The offices all had the names of CHERUB mission controllers printed on the locked doors.

Zara Asker was one of the most senior mission controllers. She had a big office at the end of the corridor, with a semi-circle of floor-to-ceiling windows and some rather swish-looking furniture with lots of curving wood and flashy chrome trim. She struggled out of her seat as the kids walked through her open door, revealing a set of baggy dungarees stretched over an almost nine-month-pregnant belly.

'Well, well, well,' Zara grinned, nodding at James and Kyle. 'Dr McAfferty told me it wouldn't take long to find a few bodies to send on recruitment missions. I can't say I'm surprised to see you two hooligans here . . . And you must be Gabrielle, I don't believe we've had the pleasure.'

As Gabrielle and Zara shook hands, James couldn't help smiling guiltily. Zara had been one of the controllers on his last mission and he'd got on well with her.

'How's Joshua these days?' James asked.

Zara broke into a smile. 'He's grown a lot since you last saw him. His back teeth are pushing through and he's driving me and Ewart crazy. As a matter of fact, any time you fancy coming over to the staff quarters to baby-sit . . .'

James laughed. 'I'll give that offer a miss, thanks.'

'OK,' Zara said, returning to business. 'I take it you all know what a recruitment mission entails? We've put together a background scenario and false identity for each of you and you can expect to be sent off to a children's home within the next week. As with any other CHERUB mission, you have an absolute right to refuse to undertake it. However, if you refuse in this instance, I expect Dr McAfferty will issue you with an alternative punishment, which you can expect to be a lot less pleasant than a few weeks in local authority care.

'When you arrive at the children's home, your job is to check everyone out. You're looking for a potential CHERUB recruit, which means a smart, physically fit kid. Family ties are a big no-no. Foreign language skills and identical twins will be looked upon very favourably. It's all in the mission briefing.'

Zara leaned across her desk and handed James, Kyle and Gabrielle a photocopy of the standard briefing for recruitment missions.

'Good candidates can get shipped off to foster homes in no time,' Zara continued. 'So if you spot someone who looks the business, get on to me or one of the assistant mission controllers straight away and we'll arrange to have the kid drugged and brought here to undertake the recruitment tests . . .'

There was a gentle knock on Zara's open door.

'John,' Zara said, breaking into a smile. 'Good to see I'm not the only mission controller who comes in on Sunday afternoons.'

James turned around and instantly recognised the silver-rimmed glasses and pale, bald head of John Jones. John had only just taken a job as a CHERUB mission controller, but James had worked with John the year before when he was still employed by MI5, the adult branch of British intelligence.

'I thought I spotted James in here,' John said awkwardly. 'You're not sending him out are you?'

'He got himself in *another* spot of bother,' Zara explained. 'Mac wants him to go on a recruitment mission, but I'm sure he'll yield if you've got James pencilled in for something important.'

James' heart leapt at the prospect of escape.

John Jones nodded. 'Perhaps I could have a quick word, in confidence?'

Zara looked at the kids. 'Sorry,' she said. 'Would you step out into the corridor for a jiffy?'

As soon as James shut Zara's office door, Kyle glowered at him.

'I can't believe you're gonna weasel your way out of this, James,' he said indignantly.

James folded his arms and broke into a smug grin.

It was ten minutes before Zara pulled her door open and the three kids filed back in. 'Well, James,' Zara said. 'I just rang Dr McAfferty and you're off the hook, provided you accept the mission John is going to offer you at a briefing later this evening.'

'*So jammy,*' Kyle whispered under his breath.

James couldn't help smiling.

'I wouldn't look so satisfied if I was you,' John Jones said. 'You might decide you'd prefer the recruitment mission when you see what I've got lined up for you.'

5. ROPE

Eleven kids had started basic training three months earlier. Lauren stood to attention in the snow with the five others who'd made it to the final checkpoint on their snowmobiles. Mr Large, the head instructor, was eyeballing her.

'Can anybody here tell this young lady what polar bears do in the winter?' he shouted.

A couple of kids grumbled a response: 'Hibernate.'

'That's right, Miss Thicko,' Large grinned. 'They dig a big hole under the ice and they drift off to snoozy land until the daffodils pop up in springtime. If you'd *bothered* to study the training manual, you'd also have seen that bears eat fish and live on the ice floes near the coast. Not out here, over a hundred kilometres inland. Is that understood?'

'Yes, sir,' Lauren said meekly.

'And the radio. Why did you forget to switch on the encryption device?'

'I was cold and tired, and . . .' Lauren saw Mr Large's eyes bulge out behind his snow goggles and realised she was giving the wrong answer. 'Sorry, sir . . . No excuse, sir,' she said sharply.

Mr Large shoved Lauren to the ground and plunged his size-fifteen boots into the snow on either side of her head.

'When I woke up this morning, Lauren *Adams*,' Large spat, 'my back hurt. It hurt the same way it's hurt every *single* morning since a nasty little girl hit me with a spade five months back. Can you remind me who it was that did that?'

'Me, sir?' Lauren inquired innocently.

'If I'd had my way, you would have been permanently excluded from CHERUB.'

Lauren had been surprised that Mr Large hadn't made training harder for her from day one. Now she had the horrible realisation that he'd saved up his revenge for the very end.

'And *so*,' Mr Large said, 'to the ultimate test of courage that was mentioned in all of your mission briefings. There's been a slight change of plan. The briefing should now read, *Ultimate test of* Lauren's *courage*.'

Lauren felt a tear welling up behind her snow goggles as the icy ground chilled her back. She didn't reckon she could face a third attempt at basic training. Failure now would be the end of her CHERUB career.

Mr Large crushed Lauren's knuckles as he tugged her back to her feet.

'Who's the best swimmer out of you six trainees?' Mr Large asked, eyeballing Lauren again.

'Me, I suppose,' Lauren said.

'That's *riiiiight*, isn't it?' Mr Large said cockily. 'Quite the little mermaid, I recall ... So if one of you had to swim across a fast-flowing river, grab six lovely grey CHERUB

T-shirts and then swim back again, you'd be the ideal candidate. Wouldn't you?'

'Yes sir,' Lauren barked, trying desperately not to show Mr Large how upset she was. He absolutely loved it when he made a trainee cry.

Mr Large took a step back and addressed the whole line-up. 'I'd suggest that all of you do what you can to help Lauren out; because if she doesn't come back with the T-shirts, I'll make each of you swim across individually and fetch your own. The river is four hundred metres away, over the brow of the next hill. I'd suggest you get moving if you want to be indoors by sundown.'

Lauren led the row of kids scrambling uphill through the deep snow, dragging their equipment sleds behind them. Mr Large and the two assistant training instructors, Mr Speaks and Miss Smoke, followed them.

The rushing water made a roar that overpowered all but the most persistent howls of wind. The river would have been over a hundred metres wide in the summer, but the banks were iced up, cutting Lauren's swim to less than sixty.

Miss Smoke, a woman who was butch even by the standards of retired kickboxing champions, pointed her muscular arm at the opposite embankment. 'Your grey T-shirts are in a waterproof backpack behind that traffic cone,' she rumbled.

The six trainees huddled up and pulled their balaclavas away from their mouths, so they could hear each other speak. As their steaming breath mingled, nobody could look Lauren in the eye. They felt sorry for her, but at the same time it was a relief not to be suffering alongside her.

'It could have been worse,' Lauren said, trying to sound cheerful and break the silence. 'I'll have to go in naked. If I'm wearing clothes, they'll freeze solid the second I step out of the water and I'll never get them off.'

A twelve-year-old Kurdish boy called Aram replied. 'We've all got Vaseline in our first-aid packs. It will act as insulation if Lauren smears it on.'

'That'll help keep me warm,' Lauren nodded.

'What if we tie our rescue ropes together and knot them under Lauren's arms?' Bethany suggested. 'It should be long enough to reach across the river and we can haul her in if she gets in trouble.'

'Good idea,' Lauren grinned. 'I'll still have to swim out, but you guys can pull me back with the rope.'

'Do you think you can make it over?' Aram asked.

'It's gonna be cold and the current looks vicious,' Lauren said. 'But the distance is only a bit more than one length of a swimming pool.'

The six trainees tied their rescue ropes together. Lauren double-checked all the knots, then the kids burrowed inside their sleds and grabbed their tubs of Vaseline.

Bethany led the way out to the riverbank and began helping Lauren unzip her outer layers of clothing. The kids knew from their survival manuals that any water flowing in these parts would be a couple of degrees above freezing. You wouldn't swim in it out of choice, but it was survivable. Lauren's real problem was the air outside the water, which was more than fifteen degrees *below* freezing. A few minutes' exposure to temperatures this low would blister Lauren's bare skin, as surely as if she'd jumped into a bath of boiling water.

Two of the boys laid a foam-insulating mat on the snow and weighted down the ends with sleds to stop it blowing away.

'OK,' Lauren said. 'Does everyone know what their job is? I don't want any hold-ups.'

After a line of nods had satisfied Lauren, she sat on the foam mat and two of the boys started tugging at her snow boots. Once they were off, Lauren stood up, and stepped out of her snowsuit and outer fleece layer in a single frenzied movement. Next, she peeled away the tightly fitting inner fleece, followed by her socks and underwear. Bethany gathered up the inner layers of clothing as they were cast off and pushed them inside her snowsuit so they didn't freeze up.

As soon as Lauren had hurled her knickers away, she dived on to the foam mat and the boys threw a couple of sleeping bags on top of her.

Bethany leaned in and yelled, 'Are you OK?', forgetting that Lauren no longer had three hats covering her ears.

Lauren shuddered as she poked her head from under the sleeping bags and nodded. 'Give me the grease.'

Aram and his younger brother, Milar, began passing Lauren the tubs of Vaseline. She sunk her numb fingers into each tub and smeared it thickly over her body, trying not to wriggle too much because she didn't want any grease wasted by rubbing off on to the sleeping bags.

When Lauren was well slathered, Bethany pushed one end of the nylon climbing rope under the sleeping bags. Lauren wound the rope under her arms and tied it into a bowknot, like a shoelace. That way she could pull on the bow and release herself easily if the rope became snagged.

'All ready?' Aram asked.

'As ready as I'll ever be.'

Bethany and Aram each grabbed a corner of the insulated mat and dragged it on to the ice at the edge of the river, with Lauren curled up under the sleeping bags. They stopped a couple of metres shy of the water's edge where the ice looked dangerously thin.

Miss Smoke was waiting for them. She pulled back the sleeping bags and tested the knot in the rope under Lauren's arms.

'Remember, the air is much colder than the water,' Smoke said gruffly. 'Keep your head under, except when you have to breathe, and don't hang around when you get to the other side.'

With no sleeping bags over her top half, Lauren was shivering too badly to speak, but she managed a nod.

'OK,' Smoke said. 'Get going.'

Bethany whipped the sleeping bags away from Lauren's legs. As Lauren sprang up, Aram gave her a quick inspection, before moving in with a Vaseline-smeared glove and patching up a few areas where the coating looked thin.

Lauren had too much on her mind to give a damn about everyone seeing her naked. She took three quick tiptoe leaps over the thin ice and took a huge breath as she speared into the water. Because Lauren had acclimatised to a temperature nineteen degrees colder than the water, a sense of calm passed over her as she began to swim. It almost felt warm.

She set off in a powerful front crawl, turning her head to breathe whenever the choppy water allowed her to. After two minutes' swimming flat out, Lauren thought she must have almost reached the opposite bank. She raised her head out of the water to get a look. A blast of sleet pounded her face, but she managed to keep her eyes open long enough to see that she was barely halfway across.

Lauren felt crushed as she dived back under, swimming at a diagonal into the fierce current; pushing as hard as her aching body would allow. She now had serious doubts about her ability to make it across. The next minutes were the most agonising of Lauren's life. Her skin felt numb and she was fighting a stitch down her left side.

Finally, more than four shattering minutes after setting off, Lauren spotted the orange cone less than five metres from her face. Touching the ice sheet on the embankment was a relief, but getting out of the water was another challenge.

Lauren's fingers were numb and the ice gave her nothing to grip on to. Her first three goes at climbing out of the water failed and she started getting desperate. At the fourth attempt, a wave pushed her at exactly the right moment and she managed to lift a knee on to the ice.

The danger now was of her bare skin freezing to the ice beneath the snow. The only way to prevent this was not to let any part of her body touch the ground for more than a fraction of a second.

Shivering so violently that she could barely control her movements, Lauren quickly smeared the soles of her feet through some extra thick grease on her ankles. By the time she'd done this, a few dozen drips of water that hadn't been repelled by the Vaseline had frozen to the skin on her back. Every bead felt like a nail drilling her flesh.

Lauren stood up to an eruption of encouraging screams from the opposite embankment. She took four quick leaps towards the orange cone and plucked the small backpack out of the snow behind it. When she'd hooked it over her shoulders, Lauren allowed herself a moment of triumph, turning to the other trainees and raising a thumb in the air.

The first step back towards the water made Lauren scream out, as a layer of skin tore from the ball of her foot. The grease had rubbed away and her damp sole had taken less than two seconds to freeze to the ground. She glanced back at the trail of blood in the snow, then took three painful steps and dived into the water.

As soon as Lauren hit the water, she felt the rope dig into the joints under her arms as the other trainees began hauling it. She thought about trying to swim, but she was being dragged through the water too fast for it to make any difference. In fact, Lauren thought the five kids standing on the embankment were overdoing it. The rope felt like it was tearing her arms out of their sockets and it was a struggle getting her head above the water for long enough to take a proper breath.

At least the return journey was fast. Within sixty seconds, Lauren found herself being lifted out of the water and on to a sleeping bag by the two Kurdish boys. Once they'd dragged her away from the thin ice, they grabbed the soggy backpack off Lauren's shoulders, while the other three trainees descended on her with towels. They rubbed off as much water as they could, before rolling Lauren's gasping body on to the foam sleeping mat and throwing all their sleeping bags on top of her.

Lauren felt her vision go out of focus as Bethany waved a thermal vest under her nose.

'Snap out of it,' Bethany shouted. 'You've got to get your clothes back on before . . .'

*

When Lauren came around, she got a sniff of the grease still smeared over her body and shots of pain from the dressing over her foot and the rope burns under her arms.

'Hey,' Bethany said gently. 'Welcome back, partner.'

Lauren realised she was on the floor, at the base camp where they'd set off on their Alaskan trek five days earlier. The building was fantastically warm, with electric light and proper central heating. The other trainees were scattered around the carpet on giant floor cushions, dressed in shorts and grey CHERUB T-shirts. Their hair was wet and mussed, like they'd towelled off after a shower. Most of them held steaming mugs.

'How long . . .?' Lauren asked, erupting into a coughing fit before she could finish her sentence.

Bethany looked at her watch. 'You've been out for about forty minutes. Miss Smoke says you're suffering from mild hypothermia and exhaustion. She reckons you'll be fine after a few hours' rest and some hot food and drink. And you'll be pleased to know that you making it across that river put Mr Large in a stinking mood.'

'Where's my grey T-shirt?' Lauren asked drowsily.

Bethany smirked. 'You're holding it in your hand. I didn't take it out of its packet in case you got grease over it.'

Lauren's fingers still felt numb, but now she realised the T-shirt was in her hand, she pulled the polythene-wrapped square up to her face and stared at the grey fabric with the CHERUB logo on it.

'No more training,' Lauren grinned.

'Yeah,' Bethany smiled. 'Undercover missions here we come.'

6. MISSILES

John Jones showed James into his office. It wasn't as nice as Zara's, but it was a decent size with three computers, a giant LCD television hanging on the wall and a long suede-covered sofa. It was dark outside and the floor-to-ceiling window overlooked moonlit trees.

A sixteen-year-old wearing a black CHERUB T-shirt was sprawled over the sofa. James got excited when he realised it was Dave Moss. Dave was a legend. He'd earned his navy CHERUB T-shirt at eleven and his black T-shirt at thirteen, on a mission that brought down half the Ukrainian mafia. He spoke five languages and had won every CHERUB Karate and judo tournament he'd ever entered.

There were lots of talented kids at CHERUB, but Dave was one of the ones who managed to pull it off without everyone thinking he was a swot. His looks helped. Dave was tall and muscular: handsome in a grungy sort of way, with bright green eyes and long blond hair. His girlfriends were always the hottest on campus and there was even a rumour he'd got one of them pregnant. James had pretended to be appalled when Kerry told him; but as far as all the guys were concerned, the whiff of sex made Dave seem even cooler than he was already.

'Do you know David Moss?' John Jones asked.

'No, I don't,' James said nervously, as he reached out and shook Dave's hand. 'Pleased to meet you, David.'

'Call me Dave,' Dave smiled.

James felt like a tit. Who introduced themselves to someone like Dave Moss by saying *Pleased to meet you*? It was the kind of thing you'd say to an old granny at a funeral.

'David is highly regarded amongst the mission preparation staff,' John Jones explained, 'and we're looking for two good agents to work alongside him on one of the most important missions CHERUB has ever undertaken.'

James couldn't stop himself from grinning. 'I knew it was big,' he stuttered. 'I mean . . . Everyone knows Dave's reputation. You're not going to send him on some piddly little mission.'

'You've not done badly yourself, James,' Dave said reassuringly. 'I've read your personnel file. You've only been on two missions, but what you lack in quantity you more than make up for in quality.'

'Cheers,' James grinned. The compliment made him feel a little more relaxed in the company of the campus hero. 'So what's this mission about?'

Dave looked at John Jones. 'Can I show him now, boss?'

John nodded. 'I'll just make it clear to James before you do: whether or not you choose to accept this mission, everything you hear from now on *must* stay within these walls.'

James nodded. 'Of course, same as always.'

Dave reached down the arm of the sofa and picked up a fat aluminium tube with a shoulder stock and trigger hanging underneath it.

'Do you know what one of these is?'

'It looks like a missile,' James said.

'Got it in one,' Dave said. 'You rest it on your shoulder and aim it at a tank, helicopter, whatever. You get one shot, then you throw the launch module away. This one is the latest model. The missile has a solid-fuel rocket engine with a ten-kilometre range and more brainpower than a roomful of nerds.'

John went into detail. 'Around the time you were born, James, the Americans used Tomahawk cruise missiles in the first Gulf War. Until then, everyone dropped unguided bombs out of aeroplanes five kilometres up in the sky and crossed their fingers. You'd count yourself lucky if one bomb out of twenty hit the spot, and unlucky if you happened to live anywhere near a target. Then the Tomahawk missile came along. Suddenly, you could sit in a control room five hundred kilometres from a war zone and send off a missile accurate enough smack the target on the nose ninety-nine times out of a hundred. This kind of accuracy gave the Americans a big tactical advantage, but it didn't come cheap: every Tomahawk cost half a million dollars. They were spending two billion dollars on missiles every day the Gulf War lasted and even the Yanks don't have that sort of cash to throw around.'

Dave passed the missile across to James for a look.

'So,' John continued, 'the big challenge for the boffins wasn't to make precision-guided missiles bigger, or to give them longer range, or more accuracy. The challenge was to make them cheap. The weapon you're holding in your hand is the result of fifteen years' development. Its official acronym is PGSLM: Precision Guided Shoulder Launched Missile, but everyone calls it a Buddy missile. It's built using off-the-shelf components, like those you might find inside computers, or in-car navigation systems. You can program in targeting data using any laptop computer or handheld device capable of running an internet browser, or you can download live data on a moving target such as a car or ship, via a satellite link. Then, all you have to do is move within ten kilometres of your target, either on the ground or from a helicopter. You point the dangerous end at the sky, press the trigger and the missile weaves its merry way to the target.'

James admiringly turned the metal tube over in his hands. 'So how much does this cost?' he asked.

'That one's a mock-up,' John said. 'But the real deal comes in at under fifteen thousand dollars a shot. Of course, the Americans will only sell this kind of technology to their closest allies.'

'Safe,' James said, as he pulled on the trigger and made a *ka-pow* noise. 'I'll start saving up.'

John smiled. 'As a matter of fact, James, we're hoping you'll be able to get your hands on some real ones.'

'I thought the Americans were our allies. Won't they sell them to us?'

John smiled uneasily. 'The manufacturers gave the British army thirty-five pre-production samples for field trials. A little under three weeks ago, we sent a Royal Air Force freighter aircraft to pick them up from a military base in Nevada. The truck carrying the missiles never showed up.'

'You mean somebody nicked them?' James gasped.

'Precisely,' John nodded. 'The only consolation is that we think we know who took them.'

'Terrorists?' James asked.

'No; at least not directly. US intelligence thinks they were stolen on behalf of an illegal weapons dealer called Jane Oxford. These missiles are worth millions to the right buyer. We think she'll be holding on to them until some terrorist group or tin-pot dictatorship is able to raise a very significant sum of money to buy them. Assuming we're right about this, Jane Oxford's greed will buy us time.'

'How much damage could one of these missiles do?' James asked.

'They're not big enough to pack an enormous explosive punch,' John explained. 'But you don't need it with a weapon this accurate. Imagine a terrorist pointing a Buddy missile out of a bedroom window in a London suburb and blasting Her Majesty out of bed at Buckingham Palace. That's the kind of capability we're talking about here.'

'Is there anything you can do to defend against the missile once it's fired?'

'Not a lot,' John said. 'The Americans are looking at protecting their president by fitting a rapid firing anti-missile Phalanx gun on to a flatbed truck. But you're talking about a weapon designed for use on ships, that rips off a thousand twenty-millimetre shells every minute. It's not the kind of thing you want going off accidentally in the middle of a presidential motorcade.'

'Definitely not,' James grinned. 'So where does CHERUB fit into getting these missiles back?'

'A decision was taken at cabinet level on both sides of the Atlantic not to release any information to the public about the stolen missiles, because of the panic it was likely to cause,' John said.

Dave interrupted. '*And* because it would make a lot of politicians who claim to be winning the war on terrorism look dumb.'

'The trouble is,' John continued, 'law enforcement and intelligence agencies on both sides of the Atlantic have been trying to track down Jane Oxford and other members of her organisation since the early 1980s. They've got no more reason to believe they can catch her now than at any other time in the last thirty years. However, the Americans have one highly unusual lead. Only someone your age would be able to pursue it.'

'Don't the Americans have their own version of CHERUB?' James asked.

John shook his head as he pulled a mission briefing out of his desk drawer and threw it into James' lap. 'You'd better read this.'

7. BRIEFING

CLASSIFIED
MISSION BRIEFING FOR JAMES ADAMS
THIS DOCUMENT IS PROTECTED WITH A RADIO
FREQUENCY IDENTIFICATION TAG. <u>ANY</u> ATTEMPT
TO REMOVE IT FROM THE MISSION PREPARATION
BUILDING WILL SET OFF AN ALARM
DO <u>NOT</u> PHOTOCOPY OR MAKE NOTES

JANE OXFORD (FORMERLY JANE HAMMOND) – EARLY YEARS
Jane Hammond was born on a United States Army base in
Hampshire, England, in 1950. She was the daughter of Captain
Marcus Hammond, a US Army logistics specialist and his wife
Frances, a British citizen he'd met and married while based in the
United Kingdom.

Jane spent her early years living at various military installations
around the world. She was a bright girl with a rebellious streak.
At fifteen, while living in Germany, Jane ran away with a nineteen-
year-old private in the US Marines. They surrendered themselves
to the Parisian police three weeks later, when they ran out of
money.

By this time Jane's father, Marcus Hammond, had risen to the rank of General and was close to retirement. He requested a final military posting near to his birthplace in California, believing that a return to the United States would help Jane settle down and gain qualifications to attend college.

General Hammond was posted to Oakland naval base in California. He was put in charge of the supply chain, shipping troops and equipment across the Pacific to the escalating war in Vietnam.

Jane, meanwhile, did not buckle down to her education as her father had hoped. She began to skip school regularly and hang out with a group of hippies. Photographs from this era show a grubby-looking girl with long braided hair, strings of beads around her neck and flared jeans with holes over the knees.

Jane became interested in anti-Vietnam war issues through a boyfriend called Fowler Wood. Twenty-year-old Fowler was a dropout from the nearby University of California and the chairman of a radical anti-Vietnam war protest group.

Fowler became fascinated with General Hammond's job. He'd been searching for a non-violent way to blunt the American war effort and came up with the idea of sabotaging weapons passing through Oakland docks. Jane began digging into the papers her father brought home each night. She even broke into his office and took blank security passes for the wharves where the goods were being loaded on to ships.

Jane learned about a regular shipment of assault rifles. Fowler and his anti-war movement colleagues hatched a plan. It involved using stolen security passes to bring a truckload of caustic lime into the docks. The protestors planned to break open the weapon crates and shovel powdered lime over the guns. By the time the guns arrived in Vietnam, the lime would have corroded the metal, making them useless.

Two nights before the raid was set to take place, Fowler's peace group took a vote and decided that the guerrilla action was too risky. Or as Jane put it, 'The little wimps chickened out.' She immediately broke up with Fowler. She stole his car and her mother's chequebook and headed south, paying her way towards Mexico with bad cheques.

JANE HAMMOND MEETS KURT OXFORD

Jane got as far as San Diego, which borders on to the Mexican town of Tijuana. She found a room in a cheap motel and began scouring the local bars, looking for someone who could sell her the fake passport and driver's licence she needed to cross the border. Instead, she found Kurt Oxford.

Kurt was a mountainous twenty-eight-year-old outlaw biker, complete with beard, tattoos and a prison record for violent behaviour and armed robbery. He'd co-founded a motorcycle club called the Brigands. At the time it was the second largest motorcycle gang in California and a bitter rival of the internationally famous Hell's Angels. Jane took up the offer of a room in Kurt's house, which also served as a clubhouse for the Brigands.

The Brigands were suspected of paying for their lifestyle by smuggling drugs across the border from Mexico and Kurt's house was under twenty-four-hour police surveillance. Archived photographs show Jane making a rapid transformation from hippy to leather- and denim-clad biker. Police didn't bother enquiring as to who Jane was or where she had come from, because of the notoriously low status of women within the biker subculture (*according to the rule book of the Brigand Motorcycle Club, women were not allowed to join the gang as full members, ride motorcycles except as pillion passengers, engage in any criminal activity, or speak at official club meetings except to offer food or drink to the men*).

Kurt became excited when he heard Jane's story about the stolen security passes and the cases of guns at Oakland navy base, but he was no peace protestor. His plan was to steal two truckloads of guns and sell them on the black market to a drug dealing acquaintance in Mexico, who would in turn sell the weapons on to rebel and terrorist groups in Africa and South America.

Jane had attended dozens of anti-war demonstrations while living in Oakland. Despite this, she readily agreed to Kurt's gun-smuggling plan. Criminal psychologists have described Jane's behaviour as a textbook example of an extreme thrill seeker: a person with few moral scruples, who finds everyday life boring and constantly craves dangerous relationships and activities.

The Rise and Fall of Kurt & Jane Oxford

Kurt Oxford and Jane Hammond robbed the docks at Oakland navy base on three separate occasions, earning themselves over $25,000 (equivalent to $145,000 at today's prices). Jane did some research and realised that every military supply depot in the United States used identical, easy-to-fake, security paperwork. Over the next two years, Kurt and Jane staged over eighty robberies on United States military facilities.

Jane had stolen reference books from her father that showed where different kinds of military supplies were stored. She would place an order over the phone, pretending to be the assistant of a senior officer in the logistics corps. The next day, a clean-shaven Kurt would arrive at the supply depot in an army surplus truck, wearing uniform and carrying a set of authentic-looking paperwork that Jane had typed up in her motel room the night before. The truck would be loaded up and Kurt would drive out laden with weapons. The Mexican arms dealer would then ship the load to South America.

The beauty of this scheme was that the robberies went unnoticed; at least to begin with. With a quarter of a million troops on duty in Vietnam, thousands of US military trucks were moving weapons and ammunition around the country. The paper-based stock control system made keeping an up-to-date tally on every movement impossible. Even when someone checked the paperwork and noticed that a truckload of guns had vanished, it would be several months after the event and everyone would assume it was a clerical error rather than a robbery.

By 1968, Kurt and Jane were earning over $20,000 (2005 equivalent – $110,000) a month from their illegal weapons business. With over half a million dollars stashed in overseas bank accounts, they had started flying first class and staying in five-star hotels. They also stopped doing robberies themselves and began relying on members of the Brigands motorcycle gang to do their dirty work.

On 26 December 1968, Kurt Oxford and Jane Hammond landed in Las Vegas and booked a suite at the Desert Inn resort and casino. Kurt purchased a two-carat diamond ring and the next morning, he took his eighteen-year-old girlfriend on a limousine ride to a wedding chapel. After the ceremony, Kurt and Jane changed into swimwear, got drunk at the poolside and began losing heavily at a floating blackjack table.

Kurt took offence when another blackjack player called him a fool. Kurt punched the man out and ended up being hauled into a back room by casino security. He was taken to the local police station, where the Las Vegas police ran a routine check. They found that Kurt had skipped bail on a Nevada assault charge five years earlier, following a fight between rival motorcycle gangs in Reno.

Less than six hours after getting married, Kurt was locked up in Las Vegas county jail, facing a three- to five-year sentence. Jane pledged to stand by her husband, but was then shocked to discover that her husband had violated his California parole and that police there wanted to question him about an unsolved murder.

Kurt Oxford was extradited to California. On 24 January 1969, five days before his trial for murder was due to begin, Kurt became involved in a fight in the prison exercise yard. A guard fired a warning shot, but the fight continued and Kurt received a shotgun blast in his chest. He died of his wounds in the prison hospital eleven days later.

JANE OXFORD – INTERNATIONAL ARMS DEALER
By the time she turned nineteen, Jane Oxford had run away from her family, amassed a half-million-dollar fortune (equivalent to $2.6 million today), got married and seen her husband die in prison. Jane had no police record, apart from a missing persons report filed by her father in Oakland. Fearing a public scandal, General Hammond had honoured the bad cheques and compensated Fowler Wood for his stolen car.

Some people might have quit while they were ahead, but Jane Oxford spent the 1970s transforming herself from a thief into a big-time black-market weapons dealer. The business of stealing from the US military thrived. When the army launched an investigation into the large amount of missing equipment and tightened up security, Jane developed more sophisticated techniques for relieving the US military of its weapons. Every American base had its share of bored, broke and homesick servicemen who were willing to turn a blind eye, or drive a truck off-base in return for a car, or enough cash to put down a deposit on a home.

The next step in developing the business was for Jane to bypass her Mexican connection and deal directly with people who wanted to buy the stolen weapons. She travelled the world using a variety of aliases and disguises, making contacts with terrorist groups, drug tsars, local warlords and dictators. Jane brokered deals to sell weapons from all over the world, but most of her profits continued to stem from her unique web of corrupt contacts within the US military.

The Ghost

In 1982, a retired member of the Brigands bike gang called Michael Smith was arrested at the gates of an army base in Kentucky, after attempting to pass a security check with a truckload of mortars. Smith had lost the paperwork given to him by an associate of Jane Oxford and stupidly tried to carry out the robbery using crudely altered paperwork from a previous raid.

Smith had been involved in dozens of military supply thefts over the preceding decade. He offered to give the US military police information on Jane Oxford and her organisation, in return for a light prison sentence. Smith was stunned by the answer the US military police gave him: not only was nobody looking for Jane Oxford, they'd never even heard of her.

Following Michael Smith's tip-off, Jane Oxford went from being an unknown to a spot on the FBI's most wanted list. The FBI, CIA and US military police set up a two-hundred-person taskforce to bring Jane Oxford to justice. The trouble was, almost nothing was known about her.

After fourteen years of successfully stealing American weapons, Jane had put distance between herself and the day-to-day operation of her organisation. Nobody knew who her deputies were, what country she lived in, if she'd married again or had children. Jane had made no contact with her parents since leaving home sixteen years earlier and the nearest thing to an up-to-date picture was the photograph found in the uncollected personal effects of the late Kurt Oxford. It had been taken in the Las Vegas wedding chapel in 1969 and to this day it remains the most recent photograph of Jane Oxford on FBI records. After numerous stings, surveillance operations, attempts at infiltration and twenty million hours of police work, Jane Oxford is still at large. The FBI task force chasing after Jane call her The Ghost.

CURRENT STATUS OF JANE OXFORD'S ORGANISATION
The world is now awash with cheap, illegal weapons produced in former communist countries. Consequently, it is impossible to turn a profit stealing everyday weapons from the American military. Nowadays, it is America's high-tech weapons that are of interest to black-market weapons dealers.

Since 1998, it is believed Jane Oxford has orchestrated more than twenty carefully planned thefts of high-tech equipment from the US military. Stolen items have included night-vision sights for sniper rifles, unmanned miniature surveillance aircraft, radar-jamming equipment, plasma-injecting anti-tank shells and surface-to-air missiles. These relatively compact loads are easily smuggled across the US/Mexican border and each one is worth millions of dollars to the right customer.

The latest and most serious act was the theft of 35 PGSLM Buddy missiles, which were crossing the Nevada desert en-route to a British military cargo aircraft. After this theft, Jane Oxford was promoted to second place on the FBI's list of most wanted criminals.

AN UNEXPECTED BREAKTHROUGH

In May 2004 a troubled fourteen-year-old boy named Curtis Key escaped the night curfew at an Arizona military boarding school and ploughed through a set of locked gates in his commandant's car. He parked up at a nearby liquor store, picked up a bottle of Coke and asked the clerk for vodka from behind the counter. When the clerk asked for proof of age, Curtis Key produced a handgun and shot the clerk through the heart. He calmly emptied half the bottle of Coke on to the floor, topped up the bottle with vodka and took a long drink. CCTV cameras inside the store filmed the entire event.

On the way out, Curtis spotted a man getting out of a Jaguar. After shooting the driver and his girlfriend dead, Curtis took the Jaguar and drove more than twenty miles at high speed, slugging the mixture of vodka and Coke the whole time. When he heard the sirens of three chasing police cars, Curtis – by now paralytically drunk – pulled up at the roadside. He picked his gun off the passenger seat, pushed the muzzle against his head and pulled the trigger. The bullet jammed in the chamber.

Under Arizona state law, anyone aged fourteen or over, charged with a serious offence such as murder, can be tried and sentenced to the same prison term as an adult. In October 2004, Curtis Key was deemed mentally fit and given life without parole. This sentence means Curtis will spend the rest of his life in prison. He is currently one of the 270 offenders serving time in the specially built young offenders unit at Arizona Maximum Security Prison, known by its staff and inmates as Arizona Max.

Bizarrely, Curtis' parents did not come forward after his arrest. The home address registered at the military school turned out not to exist and Curtis' school fees had been paid from an untraceable bank account in the Seychelles. Curtis claimed that he had lost his memory and remembered nothing about his mother and father.

Arizona police suspected Curtis was protecting a parent or parents who were wanted criminals and sent his DNA profile to the FBI. The profile showed there was a 99% chance that Curtis was a descendant of General Marcus Hammond, who had agreed to give a DNA sample to the FBI team trying to locate his daughter.

There was only one possible explanation: Curtis Key was the son of Jane Oxford.

WHAT USE IS CURTIS OXFORD?

The FBI were delighted. The unearthing of Curtis Key was the biggest breakthrough in the twenty-two-year hunt for Jane Oxford. The FBI didn't let on that they'd uncovered Curtis' true lineage and mounted close surveillance on him. They sent an officer into Arizona Max to work as a guard on Curtis' young offender unit and carefully monitored all his communications, both with other prisoners and with the outside world in the form of letters and telephone calls.

Jane Oxford was clearly working behind the scenes. Her connections within the biker community put out word inside Arizona Max that Curtis was untouchable. Anyone trying to bully, extort money, or otherwise harm Curtis could expect both themselves and their families on the outside to face savage retribution. Two prison officers on Curtis' unit also reported to their superiors that they had been approached by a mysterious biker, offering them $1,500 a month if they agreed to look out for Curtis and occasionally smuggle items into his cell.

While Jane Oxford was doing all she could to look after her son, the FBI's hopes that she would stick her neck out and try to visit Curtis were never realised. Apart from his lawyer, the only people on Curtis Key's list of approved telephone contacts and visitors were two men from Las Vegas who claimed to be Curtis' uncles. Covert DNA tests carried out on the men showed that they were not blood relatives of Curtis. Despite this, the men were put on the approved contacts list and the conversations that took place during their visits were bugged.

Curtis seemed to know his visitors well and they clearly had contacts with his mother. The men are still under FBI surveillance. Unfortunately, this surveillance has yet to yield any useful information on the activities or whereabouts of Jane Oxford.

As Curtis' first months in prison passed by, the FBI became convinced that their big breakthrough had turned into a damp squib. To minimise the already slight chance that anyone would dare to harm Curtis, his visitors informed the prison authorities that his real name was Curtis Oxford, and told Curtis to reveal his true identity to fellow inmates. Once this secret was out, the FBI realised that the chances of Jane ever visiting her son had shrunk to zero.

If Jane Oxford wasn't planning to visit her son in prison, the next best thing would be if Curtis got out and someone could follow him back to his mother. The FBI studied a number of options for getting Curtis out of prison. They looked for legal loopholes that would get Curtis off the hook and considered a scheme where the Arizona police miraculously discovered new evidence that would make Curtis look innocent.

The problem was, clear video footage showed Curtis shooting the clerk in the off-licence; he had pleaded guilty in court and the feelings of the families of his three victims also had to be taken into consideration. Besides, Jane Oxford has spent the last thirty years sniffing out FBI stings. If her son was miraculously released from prison, she would undoubtedly smell a giant rat.

The FBI realised that Jane would be less suspicious if her son escaped from prison. They devised an elaborate plan that they called 'Escape and Infiltrate'. It involved sending undercover agents into Arizona Max as prisoners. The agents would win Curtis' trust and then announce that they had found an escape route. They would offer Curtis a chance of escape; in return, they would ask Curtis to get Jane Oxford to protect them and set them up with false identities in another country.

Jane Oxford might be suspicious, but the FBI reckoned that if every detail of Curtis' escape was made to look absolutely real, including the faked murder of a prison guard and a full police alert to recapture the escapees, she might just buy it.

If the agents managed to pull off their escape and hold Jane and Curtis up to their end of the bargain, they would gain unprecedented access to Jane Oxford's organisation and perhaps even make contact with Oxford herself.

The FBI agreed that it was a risky plan. They rated the chances of success at less than one half, and the undercover agents would be at serious risk of death or injury at the hands of other law enforcement agencies that would be out trying to recapture them. But the biggest stumbling block was that under Arizona law, juveniles may be tried as adults and held inside adult prisons, but they cannot be held 'within sight or sound' of adult prisoners. If the FBI want to get undercover agents to befriend Curtis Oxford, they will have to wait until he turns eighteen and is moved into the adult population of Arizona Max. This is not due to happen until 2009.

THE ROLE OF BRITISH INTELLIGENCE & CHERUB

Although Jane Oxford was known to British intelligence, she had never stolen British military equipment and was regarded as an American problem until the theft of the thirty-five Buddy missiles in March 2005. The British began an investigation, to see if anyone on their side of the Atlantic had leaked details about the movement of the Royal Air Force cargo aircraft sent across the Atlantic to collect the missiles. They also sent a senior British intelligence officer to America to work alongside the FBI team investigating the theft.

The MI5 officer sent a top-secret briefing back to Britain. It included details of the FBI's long-term plan to send undercover agents into Arizona Max and escape with Curtis Oxford. When the chairman of CHERUB read this briefing, he realised that the FBI's ambitious 'Escape and Infiltrate' plan could be carried out immediately if underage CHERUB agents were sent into the juvenile unit at Arizona Max. An escape carried out by people too young to be employed by law enforcement agencies would also make it easier to convince Jane Oxford that the escape is genuine.

John Jones has been selected as Mission Controller and has begun working out exact details of a plan that will send two CHERUB agents into Arizona Max, with a third CHERUB agent aiding the escape on the outside.

NOTE: THE CHERUB ETHICS COMMITTEE PASSED THIS MISSION BRIEFING, ON CONDITION THAT ALL AGENTS UNDERSTAND THE FOLLOWING:

This mission has been classified HIGH RISK. All agents are reminded of their right to refuse to undertake this mission and to withdraw from it at any time. The mission will involve incarceration in a dangerous prison environment and pursuit by armed prison guards and police. For security reasons, only a tiny number of senior law enforcement officials will be aware that CHERUB and the FBI have set up the escape.

While every possible step will be taken to ensure your safety, the agents deployed on this mission are urged to consider the dangers carefully before accepting their role.

*

'Wow,' James said, when he put the briefing down on John Jones' desk. 'That whole breaking-out-of-prison deal sounds *berserk*.'

'I'm not asking for an instant decision,' John said. 'But this is our only half-decent shot at getting hold of Jane Oxford and the Buddy missiles. How about you think it through and come and see me in the morning?'

James shook his head. 'I'm not *scared*,' he said firmly. 'I'll do it.'

John smiled. 'I'd be much happier if you slept on it before making a final decision. I'll even allow you to discuss it with Meryl Spencer if you want.'

'Whatever,' James said dismissively. 'I take it me and Dave are the two people going into Arizona Max?'

John nodded. 'You're only a few months younger than Curtis Oxford and roughly the same physical size. You're a perfect candidate to make friends with him. For the purposes of the mission, Dave will be your older brother. We need a big guy like him to protect you on the inside and to dress up as a guard during the escape. He's also got lots of high-speed driving experience.'

'So who's the third person on the mission?' James asked. 'The one who's going to help our escape from outside the prison.'

'We want someone who would pass as a sibling or cousin to you and Dave,' John explained. 'But we're having a tricky time finding the right person.'

'What about my sister, Lauren?' James asked. 'Today's her last day of basic training. If she gets through she'd be eligible to come.'

John smiled. 'Lauren's a good kid, James. But I'm really looking for someone more experienced.'

8. WARMER

James caught a glimpse as the mini-bus driven by Mr Large passed the window of his classroom. He leapt noisily out of his chair, making his maths teacher turn away from the whiteboard in mid-sentence.

'They're back from training,' James explained excitedly, grabbing the olive-coloured combat coat off the back of his chair. 'Can I go meet my sister?'

Luckily, maths was James' best subject and he was on good terms with Mrs Brennan. She handed James his homework assignment, which he stuffed inside his backpack as he jogged down the corridor between the classrooms and out through a set of double doors into the cold.

James stopped for a moment to zip up his coat and hook his backpack over both shoulders so it didn't slide off as he ran. As James did this, Bethany's eight-year-old brother burst out of the doors behind him. Jake was a cute kid, with big brown eyes and spiky hair.

'You going over to meet them as they leave the training compound?' Jake asked.

'Course,' James nodded.

'I hope they passed training,' Jake said.

'Didn't Bethany call you or anything?' James asked, surprised. 'I was out at a mission briefing, but there was a voicemail on my mobile when I got back. Lauren was in the terminal at Toronto airport, waiting for a flight to London. She said she'd hurt her foot, but everyone had made it through.'

'Safe,' Jake grinned. 'I'll race you.'

Jake belted off across the grass with his backpack rattling up and down. James jogged after him at a steady pace. There was no reason to run flat out; Mr Large would make the trainees pack up all their stuff and tidy the training compound before he let them go.

When Jake got a hundred metres ahead, he stopped running and turned back towards James with a wounded look. 'Are you racing or not?' he shouted.

James was looking forward to seeing his sister and Jake's enthusiasm was contagious. 'I'm just giving you a start,' he jeered, as he broke into a full sprint. 'You'll need it.'

Jake squealed and started running again. It took James a couple of hundred metres to close the gap, by which time the two boys were running across a couple of muddy football pitches. The wire fence around the training compound was visible in the distance.

Instead of sprinting past, James decided it would be funny if he ran up behind Jake and gave him a friendly shove in the back. Jake stumbled forwards and ploughed into the soft ground.

'Enjoy the mud, El-Squirto,' James hooted.

He started to think he'd overdone it when Jake made no

attempt to get back up. He stopped running and walked back towards the little ball rolled up on the grass.

James leaned over nervously. 'Are you OK?'

'I think you broke my arm,' Jake whimpered.

James felt a queasy sensation rise up from his guts. There'd be no easy way to talk himself out of hurting an eight-year-old, even though it was an accident. Jake might end up in hospital, he'd be in trouble and it would ruin Lauren and Bethany's return from training.

'I'm sorry,' James said, gently rubbing Jake's shoulder. 'Can you move your arm at all? Do you really think it's broken?'

Jake's expression changed to a grin as his muddy hand tightened around James' wrist. The eight-year-old yanked James' arm forward, while simultaneously hooking his foot around James' ankle and sweeping his boot from under him.

James overbalanced, ending up sprawled out on the soggy ground alongside Jake. The younger boy quickly scooped up a clod of mud, splatted it against James' cheek and then combed his mucky fingers upwards through James' blond hair.

While James lay on the floor, stunned by the icy brown water trickling down his neck, Jake exuberantly sprang to his feet.

'I'm in *so* much pain,' Jake sneered. '*Suck-ahhh.*'

Jake jogged the last stretch towards the gates of the training compound, flailing his arms in the air and bowing to an imaginary crowd. James staggered to his feet and did the best he could to wipe the water out of his ear with a crinkled-up tissue.

'Cheating little git,' James shouted bitterly, as it occurred to him that he should have known better: every kid at CHERUB did Karate and judo training and even little guys like Jake knew some smart moves.

James saw the funny side once the shock wore off. When he got up to the gate of the training compound, joining siblings and close friends of the other trainees, he pulled out the chocolate bar he'd been saving for morning break and gave Jake two squares to make it clear there were no hard feelings.

'I'll have to get you back for that,' James said.

'Can try if you like,' Jake shrugged confidently, as he crammed the rectangle of chocolate into his mouth with his grubby fingers.

James got excited as soon as he saw the trainees in their grey T-shirts. The first four jogged down the concrete path from the compound, but Lauren was limping slightly. She had her bandaged foot in an unlaced trainer and Bethany loyally at her side.

James didn't like Bethany much. He was happy that Lauren had found a close friend, but when the two girls were together they drove him mad with their girlie talk and half-hour giggling fits over the lamest jokes.

Jake got scooped into his big sister's arms, as James wrapped Lauren in a tight hug and kissed her cheek. Lauren looked taller and her shoulders seemed more muscular than before. James felt a twinge of sadness at the passing of the chubby-faced little sister he'd had when their mum died eighteen months earlier.

'You look so grown up,' James sniffled happily. 'Congratulations . . . I'm so proud of you.'

'I missed you,' Lauren sniffed back.

Lauren's mood evaporated when she saw the dirty brown marks James had smeared over her uniform.

'For *god's* sake,' she gasped, as she backed away. 'Where have you been? What happened to your hair?'

'Me and Jake had a race on the way over here,' James explained. 'It got a bit out of hand.'

'And *I* won,' Jake interrupted.

'Rolling in the mud with an eight-year-old,' Lauren sneered, as she smudged a tear off her cheek. 'That sounds about your level . . . We had to wait five hours when we changed planes at Toronto airport. I got you a present in the gift shop.'

Lauren pulled a brown paper bag out of her jacket and handed it to James. He opened it up, revealing a fleece hat with yellow and blue tassels dangling off either end.

'Cheers,' James grinned, as he stretched it over his muddy hair. 'It's in Arsenal away colours.'

Bethany had bought an identical hat for Jake and the two boys headed back towards the main building, hats on, listening to their sisters rabbiting about stuff that had happened during training.

*

James wasn't sure if his teachers would let him off the rest of the day's lessons to hang out with Lauren. He got around this thorny issue by not bothering to ask. He decided if he got pulled up, he'd act emotional about Lauren's return and get off with a few punishment laps at worst.

Lauren had been allocated one of the newly converted rooms on the eighth floor, where the old mission preparation suites had been. She wouldn't let James cross the threshold until he'd washed his hair and put on clean uniform.

The layout was the same as the room James had two floors below. There was a double bed, ensuite bathroom, laptop, mini fridge, microwave and a little lounge area by the door with a two-seat sofa, where you could watch TV or play video games.

James was a bit jealous: he'd inherited his room from another kid, whereas everything in Lauren's room was spanking new. The rooms at the front of the building also had sliding glass doors and balconies that overlooked gardens, rather than the windows overlooking the muddy football pitches you got at the back.

It took three round trips in an electric golf buggy to bring Lauren's stuff over from her old room in the junior building, followed by a dozen rides carrying boxes up to the eighth floor in the lift. It was lunchtime by the time James and Lauren were through.

Lauren hobbled down to the storeroom on the fourth floor and got a ton of junk food to stock up her fridge: drinks, snacks and chocolate. She also grabbed two Snickers ice creams and two microwave burritos out of the freezer for their lunch.

The microwave meals were supposed to be for kids who'd arrived back from a mission, or training, after the canteen closed in the evening. James would have preferred the proper food being served downstairs, but Lauren wanted to zap something in her new microwave.

When they'd finished the burritos, James and Lauren opened the balcony doors to let out the stink and sprawled out next to each other on the double bed, too stuffed to bother getting on with the unpacking.

'Man,' Lauren said, rubbing her tummy and doing a little burp. 'At least I've got a week off before I have to restart lessons. I'm so whacked after training, I'm gonna sleep till noon every day, then steam in the bath all afternoon, reading books and stuffing my face.'

'Sounds good to me,' James smirked. 'I'm only gonna be around for a couple more days. I'm off on some mission in America. I tried to get you on it, but John Jones didn't sound keen. He thinks you're too inexperienced.'

'What's the mission all about?' Lauren asked.

Before James got to answer, he had a mental jolt. 'Oh shit . . .' he gasped. 'John's gonna kill me.'

Lauren sat up anxiously. 'Why? What have you done?'

'It's like, a *massive*, important mission and I was supposed to give him my final decision about going on it this morning.'

James dived off Lauren's bed, grabbed her telephone and dialled John Jones' extension. It got picked up straight away.

'James,' John said tersely. 'Where have you been? I've been to your room, I've been round all your teachers, I've been asking all your friends if they've seen you and I've even left messages on your mobile.'

'I'm *really* sorry,' James grovelled. 'My mobile's flat and the mission totally went out of my head when Lauren got out of training this morning. I started helping her unpack and—'

'Are you with us on this mission or not?' John interrupted.

'Sure,' James said. 'You knew there was never any doubt in my mind.'

'I'd like to speak with Lauren too,' John said.

'You said she was too young.'

'I've thought it through,' John said. 'Time is tight and we don't have a lot of suitable candidates for the third spot. If we tweak things slightly, the cute little girl factor might even work in our favour when you're on the run.'

'I don't know if she's up to it, John. She's got a bad foot and she's wiped out from training.'

Lauren realised she was being talked about. She scrambled excitedly across the bed and whispered in her brother's ear, 'I'm not *that* tired.'

James moved the earpiece away from Lauren, so he could hear what John was saying:

'Her part of the mission wouldn't start until after you escape from Arizona Max, so she'll have a few days to relax.'

'She seems quite keen,' James said, as his sister nodded frantically.

'Good,' John replied. 'Now, stop whatever you're doing and get over here sharpish.'

'One day out of training and I've already got my first mission,' Lauren squealed, as James put the phone down.

'*Bloody* hell,' James moaned, as he pulled his ringing head away from his sister. 'Did you have to shout that right down my ear?'

'Sorry,' Lauren giggled. 'I'm just excited. Bethany's gonna be *hell* jealous.'

9. BACKGROUND

John Jones was concerned by Lauren's eagerness to go on the mission before she'd even read the briefing. He sent James and Dave Moss out of his office and sat on a corner of his desk, telling Lauren about the dangers she might face and trying to satisfy himself that a ten-year-old would be able to handle them.

John had spent the previous eighteen years working for the adult branch of the intelligence service. He'd been in charge of undercover missions in all parts of the world and had seen operatives killed, imprisoned and badly injured. John could get his head around boys like James and Dave going undercover – they were teenagers and their unarmed combat training meant they could handle themselves against most adults – but Lauren made him uncomfortable.

Part of John's problem was that his own daughter was a few months older than Lauren. He worried about her crossing two main roads on her way to school, and whether she was being properly looked after when she went off on camping trips with her youth group. John's gut instinct told him something was deeply wrong about sitting with a girl of the same age, discussing jail breaks and the best thing to do when the cops start shooting at you.

But Lauren was well trained. Her answers to John's questions showed she was intelligent enough to understand the risks she was being asked to take and the reasons why they were worth taking. After an hour going through every detail of the mission, John had stopped worrying about Lauren and started asking himself what his own daughter might be capable of if she'd been pushed through CHERUB training, instead of spending her days being chauffeured between piano lessons, drama club and friends' houses in his ex-wife's car.

*

A CIA officer based at the American embassy in London worked into the early hours of Tuesday morning, creating identification documents in the names of James Rose, Lauren Rose and David Rose. Lauren and Dave's dates of birth were their real ones, but James' had been put back exactly one year to make him fourteen: old enough to be sentenced to Arizona Max.

A motorcycle messenger drove through the night. He arrived at CHERUB campus at 6 a.m., with a sealed pouch containing three American passports and four sets of diplomatic paperwork. This paperwork gave John Jones and the three young agents immunity from American laws for the duration of the mission.

It was dark outside, but James was already up. He'd showered, packed his bag and received a call from Lauren, who sounded like she'd worked herself into a state.

'I don't know what to pack,' Lauren said, when James got

upstairs to her room. 'And I can't find half the stuff I do want.'

James put it down to first-mission jitters. Once he'd calmed Lauren down, he helped her go through all the unpacked boxes and find the clothes and equipment she needed for the mission.

'You usually get a list of what to pack,' James explained, as he rummaged through a cardboard box, searching for the spare battery and charger for Lauren's digital camera. 'But this has all been put together at the last minute. I guess John didn't have time.'

When Lauren was satisfied that everything she needed was packed, both kids put their in-flight packs over their backs and wheeled their suitcases along the corridor to the lift.

Downstairs in the canteen, John and Dave were at a table together. They had their luggage standing beside their chairs and their cooked breakfasts were already half eaten.

John glanced at his watch. 'Cutting it a bit fine, aren't we?'

'My fault,' James said. 'Alarm didn't go off.'

Lauren gave James a smile as they grabbed plates at the breakfast buffet. 'Thanks for taking the blame.'

*

According to the background story John had devised for the mission in conjunction with the FBI, James and Dave were presently being held in a Nebraska prison, awaiting transfer back to Arizona where they were about to be tried for murder. This ruled out flying into Arizona aboard a commercial jet, in case one of the four hundred other passengers had links with Arizona law enforcement or prisons.

They were flying from a Royal Air Force base fifteen minutes drive from campus. The CHERUB driver pulled up the mini-bus on a taxiway, beside the wingtip of a small passenger jet. The RAF pilot and co-pilot loaded the luggage into the cargo hold, while a customs official shook John Jones' hand and took a cursory glance at the four American passports.

John and the kids went up six metal steps. Everyone except Lauren had to duck as they passed through the door into the aircraft. The cabin was cramped, but luxuriously fitted out with deep pile carpet, a spray of fresh cut flowers, walnut trim and four leather armchairs down each side that faced each other so you could hold a meeting.

By the time James had done up his seatbelt and kicked off his trainers, the co-pilot had pulled the steps in and was shutting the cabin door. Thirty seconds later, the aircraft began taxiing towards the runway.

'Cool,' James said to Lauren, who was sitting opposite. 'Beats arriving at the airport three hours before check-in.'

The co-pilot stood in the middle of the cabin, with his neck stooped to avoid the ceiling. 'Welcome aboard the Royal Air Force's high-speed taxi service,' he grinned. 'Make sure your seatbelts are on for takeoff. We're going to be flying higher and faster than the commercial jets you might be used to, so we should make it to Arizona in around seven and a half hours, including our refuelling stop. The toilet is in the back and there's a fridge stocked with sandwiches and things. There's also a microwave and hot-drinks machine up there, so feel free to tuck in whenever you get the munchies.'

The co-pilot stumbled through the juddering aircraft to his seat in the cockpit and belted himself in as the plane stopped moving at the end of the runway. James noticed Lauren's fingernails digging into the arms of her leather chair.

'Still not keen on flying?' James grinned.

'Shut your face,' Lauren said stiffly.

The engines opened up and the pilot's voice came over the intercom. 'All passengers, prepare for takeoff.'

'These little planes crash all the time,' James shouted, as his body was pushed against the arm of his seat by the rapid acceleration. 'They're really dangerous.'

Lauren booted James in the shin as the nose-wheel lifted off the runway.

*

Once the plane levelled off, John Jones got everyone hot drinks and biscuits, including the two pilots. When they'd finished drinking, he closed the cockpit door so the pilots couldn't overhear.

'How are you all getting on with memorising your mission details and background stories for your characters?' he asked.

'I'm getting there,' Lauren said.

James and Dave didn't look so confident.

'So let's test you out,' John said. 'Lauren first, what accent are you going to speak in?'

'My normal English accent.'

John nodded. 'Good. Why is that?'

'Because it's impossible to keep up a false accent over a long mission, particularly when you're under stress.'

'No, no,' John said. 'I wasn't asking why we try and avoid

using accents generally. I mean how do you explain your English accent if someone asks why you speak that way during the mission?'

'Right, sorry,' Lauren said. 'Our father was Robert Rose, a businessman who worked in London. We grew up there, but moved back to live with our uncle in Arizona three years ago, after our father died of throat cancer.'

'Excellent,' John said. 'James' turn. What was your first criminal offence?'

'I got picked up by Arizona police after Dave and me ram-raided a branch of PC Planet. We stole fifteen thousand dollars' worth of digital cameras and made a clean getaway, but we got busted a month later when we tried to sell them on E-Bay.'

'What sentence did you receive?'

'Twelve months' suspended prison sentence and two hundred hours' community service.'

'*Fifty* hours,' John said tersely. 'You need to know your background story like it's your own life, James. Tell me how you got the alarm codes to break into the car dealership?'

'Dave and I were pretty lonely. We didn't have any friends in Arizona, so we started getting into computer hacking. Dave drove around Phoenix, while I sat in the passenger seat using a laptop computer and sniffer software to find unsecured wireless networks. We were hoping to get someone's credit card number, or details of company bank accounts. When we hacked into the network at a second-hand-car dealership, we found a document on the hard drive that had all the staff burglar-alarm codes.

'I hid in the boot of a BMW on the car lot, climbed out

after closing time and turned off the alarms. We stole eight thousand dollars in cash and drove away from the scene in an almost new Lexus RX300. During our getaway, the car veered up on to the sidewalk and killed a homeless woman who was sleeping there. This robbery and the death of the homeless woman were reported in local newspapers at the time, so we're covered if Jane Oxford wants to check our story out.'

'What if they find the people who really robbed the car dealership?' Lauren asked.

'The FBI frequently send officers into prisons to work undercover, either to wheedle information out of suspects or uncover drug trafficking and gang activities,' John explained. 'A realistic background story is essential for the officer's safety inside prison, so the FBI create so-called *ghost crimes*. Ghost crimes are set up by FBI officers and reported to local police and media as if they're for real.'

'But what about the homeless woman?' Lauren asked.

John shrugged. 'I expect they found a homeless woman who died of a heart attack and changed the details on her death certificate so that it looked like she'd been hit by a car. The FBI like to have a few unsolved ghost crimes in every state, so that they can rapidly infiltrate any prison in the country.'

Lauren nodded. 'That's clever.'

'So, Dave,' John said, 'what happened after you ran the old lady over?'

Dave cleared his throat before he spoke. 'James and I got out of the car to see what I'd hit. When I realised it was a person, we panicked and drove home. We grabbed our money and stuff, left a note for Lauren and our uncle John and headed north. We spent two days on the run in the Lexus, before we got into another traffic accident in Nebraska. I got some head injuries that match up with a real scar I got in a skiing accident last year. James escaped unhurt and got caught by police after a brief chase on foot.'

'OK,' John said. 'James, take the story from there.'

'The police busted us and put us in a remand home. We got taken to Omaha juvenile court and sentenced to six months.'

'Why didn't any other prisoners see you when you were in Nebraska?'

James looked blank. Lauren stuck her finger in the air and started rocking from side to side. 'I know,' she said excitably.

'This is *not* good, James,' John said, shaking his head. 'You should have remembered basic details like this by now. If necessary, we're going to spend this entire flight going over this story, until all three of you can recite it backwards, forwards and inside out . . . Go on, Lauren; tell your brother why no other prisoners saw James and Dave during their six months in Nebraska.'

'Because they nearly escaped,' Lauren said. 'Dave managed to pocket some handcuff keys in the Nebraska courthouse. James and Dave released each other and got as far as the lawn in front of the courthouse, before a police officer spotted their orange prison uniforms and pulled a gun on them. Because they were an escape risk, James and Dave were locked up in single cells, with no privileges and no contact with the rest of the prison population.'

John explained. 'The idea behind having this escape in

your back story is that it will make your plan to get out of Arizona Max seem much more credible when you're trying to make Curtis Oxford believe that he has a realistic chance of escaping with you.'

10. ARIZONA

They cleared customs at a United States Air Force base in Wisconsin. The opportunity to stretch their legs at the side of the runway while the jet was refuelled turned into a snowball fight. By the time they touched down at another USAF base in Arizona three hours later, John and the kids were sick of being cooped up and desperate for some hot food.

The change in time zones meant it was 7:45 a.m., just twenty minutes after they'd set off from England. As they stepped off the plane, the sun was breaking and the air felt dry, on what looked like becoming a typical sunny day in the Arizona desert.

An Air Force man in a jumpsuit, mirrored sunglasses and ear protectors brusquely ordered them to follow the yellow line painted on the tarmac to the terminal – though terminal was a grand description for a metal hut with a chipboard floor, five seats and a coffee machine. The only person inside was a stocky black man wearing a powder-blue suit and cowboy hat. He stood up and shook John's hand.

'Marvin Teller, FBI special ops.'

'Good finally to meet you in the flesh,' John replied.

'And these three must be the undercover team.'

Marvin crushed Dave and James' hands as he shook them. James realised it was a test of character and didn't wince. When Marvin got to Lauren, he pulled his hand away and broke into a smile.

'How old is this little lady?' Marvin asked. 'Doesn't look like she's been out of diapers more than a couple of months.'

'I'm ten,' Lauren said defensively. 'What's a diaper?'

James smirked. 'It's what the Yanks call nappies.'

'So, you all hungry?' Marvin asked. 'I know a diner a few miles down the way that'll fill you up with a gut-busting breakfast at four bucks a head.'

*

After stuffing themselves with steaks, hash brown, eggs and toast, Marvin took John and the kids on a sixty-mile journey along the interstate in a black saloon car. Everyone craned their necks around when they passed the exit marked *Arizona Maximum Security Penitentiary*, but the prison was set in a desert basin two miles from the turnoff, so there was nothing to see except the Arizona state flag and a few hundred metres of sand-swept tarmac.

They finished up at a lonely wooden house, at the end of a secluded dirt track, twenty miles from the prison. The sun had cracked the paint off the wooden slats covering the outside, while the inside suggested that the previous inhabitants had been elderly. There were extra handrails on the stairs and two high-backed chairs in the living-room, pointing towards an ancient TV that made you get off your butt and twiddle a knob to change the channel.

'We've found ourselves a friendly judge who'll hear James and Dave's guilty plea early on Thursday morning,' Marvin explained. 'That gives you the rest of today and all of tomorrow to settle in and rest up. There's food in the fridge and two cars in the garage, both with blacked-out windows like you asked for.'

'Was that a problem?' John asked.

Marvin shook his head. 'A lot of people have the windows darkened out here in the desert. It keeps the sun off.'

'I want to get these kids some driving experience on American roads,' John explained. 'They'll need it during the escape and we don't want anyone seeing James or Lauren behind the wheel.'

'I've got errands to run at my office over in Phoenix,' Marvin said. 'I'll be coming back to drive you to the courthouse Thursday morning. I'll also be sending our undercover officer inside Arizona Max up here to give the boys some pointers on keeping out of trouble on the inside.'

*

By noon, the temperature was up in the thirties and the antiquated air conditioning in the house seemed to be expending all its effort on making noise, rather than actually cooling anything down.

John was permanently on the phone, either to CHERUB campus or the FBI office in Phoenix, so James and Dave took it upon themselves to sweep out the bottom of the small outdoor swimming pool and try filling it up. They found pool chemicals in the garage, but the filter was blocked and all they got for their efforts was a little brown puddle and mucky fingers.

Lauren sat beside the pool on a plastic lounger, reading background material for the mission and watching the sweat patches on the boys' shirts growing bigger. She'd have liked a swim herself, but the campus doctor had told her to keep her foot dry until the wound on her sole healed up.

The boys eventually gave up and went inside to shower and change clothes. When they re-emerged, they stood on either side of Lauren's sun lounger with mischievous expressions on their faces.

'What?' Lauren asked suspiciously.

'Nothing,' James grinned. 'It's just, the escape plan recommends that you get some elementary driving experience, in case you end up behind the wheel when we're on the run from the cops. John wants us to give you your first driving lesson.'

Dave jangled a set of car keys. It wasn't true that John had wanted the boys to take her driving. They'd begged John and he'd reluctantly agreed, because he was having trouble concentrating on the mission preparations with three bored, jet-lagged kids lurking around the house.

They got into a beat-up Toyota station wagon with blacked-out windows. Dave took it out of the garage, before switching seats with Lauren. She had to prop herself on a cushion, and even then the only way she could see over the dashboard and put her feet on the pedals at the same time was by sitting at the edge of the seat and practically hugging the steering wheel.

James adopted a crash position in the back and started giggling. 'We're all gonna die.'

Once Dave had explained the controls, he let Lauren take

off the handbrake and slide the automatic gearbox into drive. She rolled forward a few metres before stamping clumsily on the brake and sending James sprawling out of his seat in the back.

Dave looked around at him. 'Put your seatbelt on, dummy.'

Driving an automatic car when there's no other traffic around is pretty easy. Once Lauren had mastered the driveway and made some easy three-point turns to get used to steering and reversing, Dave let her out on the dirt road leading up to the interstate.

Half an hour in, Lauren started complaining that her foot was hurting. James hadn't driven a car in three months and after sitting in the back watching Lauren, he was busting to give the car a thrashing on the dirt road. After he switched places with Lauren and belted up, he turned around to Dave.

'You got any American dollars on you?'

Dave nodded. 'Why?'

'Remember that donut place we passed on the interstate? How about I drive out there and pick a box up?'

Dave checked out the money in his shorts. 'I've got enough. Have you driven in America before?'

'Heaps,' James lied. 'I was on a mission in Miami last year.'

James had only managed one brief high-speed getaway in Miami, but the CHERUB intermediate driving course he'd been on a few months earlier covered skills for fast roads as well as a few high-speed manoeuvres, so he was a reasonably competent driver.

He floored the gas pedal, setting the rear wheels into a

spin. As he got faster, the car started rocking and pebbles were clattering against the bottom of the car.

'Slow down,' Dave said firmly.

James ignored him and kept his foot on the gas as the car approached the crest of a small hill. Dave put his hand on James' shoulder and spoke louder.

'Cut it out *now*, James. You're going way too fast.'

James broke into a smile. 'Who stuck a rod up your arse, Dave? I thought you were cool.'

The front wheels lifted up as the car skimmed the top of the hillock. James spotted a pickup coming through the glare in the opposite direction, less than a hundred metres away. The road was wide enough for the vehicles to pass, but James hadn't anticipated any other traffic and was driving near the middle.

He felt a shot of adrenalin as he swung hard to the right and stamped the brake pedal. He avoided the pickup, which had swerved the other way, but now James was heading for the drainage ditch at the roadside. He desperately twirled the steering back to the left. The nose turned in, but the violent manoeuvre made the back end swing out and the rear wheels dropped into the ditch.

The steering wheel juddered violently as airbags exploded in James and Dave's faces. The car lurched on crabwise, with two wheels up off the ground and half a mind to roll over.

When it stopped moving and crashed down on to the baked ground, James was too stunned to move. All he could do was breathe petrol fumes and grit, while staring dumbly at the half inflated airbag. His hands were shaking out of control.

Dave stumbled out of the passenger door, before opening up the rear and helping Lauren step out over the ditch. She was breathing hard, but didn't seem hurt.

James finally got his head together enough to realise there was a risk of leaking fuel causing a fire. He undid his seatbelt and stepped out into a cloud of dust. A figure emerged from the glaring sunlight and bundled him against the car.

'I *told* you,' Dave shouted furiously. 'You could have got us *killed*, you stupid little prick.'

James realised that Dave was about to slap him, but he got pulled off by the driver of the pickup.

'Calm it down there,' the driver shouted.

James' legs felt like jelly as he staggered away from the car. Lauren was standing a few metres away, but the thunderbolts coming out of her eyes made it clear she was in no mood to help out.

When the pickup driver had calmed Dave down, he stepped back and let out a wry laugh. The blond-haired man was wearing black trousers and a shirt with a crest and the initials ADOP embroidered on the sleeve. James realised it stood for *Arizona Department Of Prisons*.

'Name's Scott Warren,' the man said. 'I just finished my shift and I headed down here to see three British kids and a man named John Jones. It's not exactly what I had in mind, but I guess I've found them . . .'

11. REGRET

James knew he was an idiot. He felt like running off into the desert and never coming back as he sulked in a stiff-backed armchair. The skin was peeling off the back of his neck where Dave had shoved him against the baking hot roof of the car.

John had dished out a twenty-minute lecture: how totally irresponsible he was, how he could have ruined the mission before it had started, how a two-hundred-horsepower car is not a toy, and how he was going to spend all the time between now and his court appearance grounded at the house studying the background materials for the mission.

James kept seeing the crash in his head; imagining what might have happened if the car had rolled, or Lauren hadn't put her seatbelt on. He'd never have been able to live with himself if she'd been hurt.

While James sat with the curtains drawn feeling seriously sorry for himself, the others were cleaning up his mess. Dave found a tow rope and Scott Warren used his undamaged pickup to pull the back end of the Toyota out of the ditch and tow it back to the house.

The sideways slide had torn off the exhaust, buckled the front suspension and damaged the chassis on the driver's side. The car didn't look a wreck, but Scott said it wouldn't be economical to do much repair work on an elderly car that was only worth a few thousand dollars.

Meanwhile, John drove out to a restaurant on the interstate and picked up fried chicken. When he got back, he told James to wash his face and come to the dining table.

James dragged his chair up to the big Formica table in the kitchen. Lauren and Dave both looked pissed at him. He considered saying sorry, but an apology didn't seem to properly reflect the gravity of what he'd done. He avoided eye contact as he grabbed a box of fries and a couple of drumsticks.

John put a bottle of Coke on the table and handed Scott a cold beer, before sitting down.

'I've spoken to James and he's been punished,' John said firmly, addressing everyone at the table. 'We're all aware of how lucky it was that nobody got hurt. Now, whatever your personal feelings are, we have to draw a line under what happened and get on with preparing for our mission as a team. This mission is too dangerous for us to have people holding grudges and not speaking to one another. Is that understood?'

Dave and Lauren nodded unenthusiastically.

'Good,' John said. 'James, shake Dave and Lauren's hands.'

James reached across the table. Shaking hands seemed like the kind of thing you'd ask a couple of six-year-olds to do, but he understood the point John was trying to get across.

'I'm really sorry,' James said, as he let go of Lauren.

'You should be,' she replied tersely.

'I shouldn't have shoved you,' Dave said, as James grasped his chicken-grease-smeared hand. 'I just freaked out after the crash.'

James smiled uneasily. 'Maybe you scared a bit of sense into me.'

'Anyway,' John said, 'as you know, Scott is an FBI special agent. He's spent the last three months working undercover as a correctional officer inside the boys' wing at Arizona Max. He's just finished a twelve-hour shift and I expect he's tired, so I want you to listen carefully and we'll try not to waste any more of his time.'

Scott had to chew up a mouthful of fries before he began speaking.

'Nothing I say or do can totally prepare you boys for what you're gonna face inside Arizona Max, but I'll give it my best shot. I guess the best way to start is by trying to give you an impression of the kind of kids who end up there.

'Pick up any newspaper, or switch on the TV news, and you'll see items about crimes that turn your stomach. You're going to be sharing that cell with the kind of people who committed those crimes. I'm talking about the meanest, nastiest kids on the face of the earth. Don't underestimate what they're capable of. Most of them have already killed someone and in a prison environment, violence and ruthless bullying only enhances their status.'

'Don't they get punished?' Dave interrupted.

'Like how?' Scott said, shaking his head. 'These guys have zero chance of *ever* being released from prison and there's no threat of the death sentence because the Supreme Court says you can't execute anyone under the age of eighteen. So, even if one of them kills you, the most we can do is move them into solitary confinement for a few months.

'This hard-core of thugs makes up about a quarter of the population, and they make life thoroughly miserable for the remainder. The weaker inmates are mostly kids who went off the rails one time and got themselves in deep trouble: guys who stuck up convenience stores so they had money to splash out on their girlfriend, middle-class kids who thought they could make some easy cash dealing drugs, or who snapped and murdered relatives who beat them up. A lot of these guys didn't get many breaks in life and they're usually a bit underpowered in the brains department. To be honest, I feel sorry for them.'

'So what's the prison itself like?' James asked.

'Inexpensive,' Scott answered abruptly.

The three kids all looked baffled, until Scott began to explain:

'Twenty or thirty years ago, a maximum-security prison was made up of cells, with bars along the front and a sliding door, exactly like you see in the movies. Most of the time you'd be locked up alone, perhaps with one other cellmate. But the prison population in America is exploding and cells are expensive: everyone needs their own walls and doors; their own locks, and washbasins and toilets, etcetera, etcetera. Once you've built all those expensive cells, you need lots of guards to make sure there's nothing naughty going on inside them.

'To get around this, modern facilities like Arizona Max

have dormitory cells. The cell you'll be living in has two rows of eighteen single beds along the walls. Between each bed there's a waist-height partition, a small locker and just about enough room to swing out your legs. At one end of the cell there's a bathroom, with two toilets, three urinals and two shower stalls. A few metres above your heads is a metal gantry, from where hacks like me can look down and keep an eye on you.

'The good thing about this arrangement is that it gives you twenty-four-hour access to Curtis Oxford. The bad news is that if one of your cellmates takes a dislike to you, he'll have twenty-four-hour access to *you*.'

'How much violence is there?' Dave asked.

'In the three months I've been on that cellblock, I've only seen two stabbings, but there are regular fistfights and the weaker inmates get badly bullied. Young offenders' units are often nicknamed *gladiator schools*, because you've got no option but to learn to fight. Teenage boys are the most impulsive and dangerous section of the prison population.'

John interrupted. 'This is why we want you guys in and out of Arizona Max within two weeks.'

'Don't the guards do anything to stop the violence?' Lauren asked.

Scott shook his head. 'The guards – or hacks as everyone on the inside calls them – aren't going to do you any favours. The prison is twenty per cent understaffed and pay isn't far above minimum wage, so don't expect them to risk their necks on your behalf.

'In the daytime there's about one hack for every forty inmates, at night it drops to one for every hundred. Those kind of staffing levels mean you're on your own. If things get brutal, we might fire a couple of baton rounds down from the gantry to break up a fight and we'll drag someone off to the prison hospital if there's a lot of blood sloshing around. Apart from that, you've got to fend for yourself.'

'So what's the best way to deal with the violence?' James asked.

'You can't show any weakness,' Scott said. 'The second you walk into that cell, there are gonna be thirty guys sizing you up. The bad guys will want to know if they can get their hands on your money and belongings. The weaker inmates need to know if you're going to be trying to get your hands on their stuff, or if you're one of the real psychopaths who'll beat them up just for the fun of it.

'Statistics show that you have a seventy-per cent chance of being in a physical confrontation within your first two days inside an American prison. Where you're going inside Arizona Max, I'd put the chances at closer to ninety-nine per cent. Dave is going to be a physical match for anyone in there, but James is going to be one of the smallest. Dave will have to protect him.'

'I've done self-defence training,' James said. 'I'm a second-dan Karate black belt.'

'It's good that you can handle yourself,' Scott said. 'But nobody knows that when you walk through the cell door. All they'll see is that you're young and small, which makes you a target for the bullies. If someone starts on you, go in hard and try to make a good account of yourself. That way you'll earn respect and find that other inmates want you on their side.'

'What about Curtis?' Dave asked. 'Who looks after him?'

'Curtis has a couple of seventeen-year-old skinheads called Elwood and Kirch who make sure he doesn't get damaged. There's also word out that anyone who touches Curtis will be stabbed to death by a biker.'

'Are there any bikers in that cell?' James asked.

Scott shook his head. 'No, bikers are mostly men in their twenties and thirties, but all the kids in your cell are doing long sentences. They'll get transferred to the adult section of the prison when they turn eighteen and there will be a whole bunch of bikers ready to stab someone for Jane Oxford.'

'How come?' James asked.

John answered the question. 'One of the ways Jane has kept her organisation strong is by looking after anyone who gets sent to prison. That means quality legal representation, financial support for families and physical protection inside prison. She's very loyal to people who stay on her side. That's also one of the reasons we're optimistic that Jane will be happy to help you guys out if you successfully bust Curtis out of prison.'

'Of course, it's a double-edged sword,' Scott added. 'People have tried to cut deals with the FBI and give information on Jane Oxford in return for immunity, or a shorter prison sentence. Most of them either met a nasty end inside prison, or withdrew their evidence when members of their family were threatened. One guy even got taken out by a sniper when he was supposed to be under protective custody.'

James threw down a chicken bone and pushed away the last of his fries. Kyle, Gabrielle and the others had probably started their recruitment missions by now. Scott's description of the brutality inside Arizona Max made him wonder if he wasn't really the one who'd drawn the short straw.

12. SENTENCE

James kept his head down on Wednesday morning, staying in his bedroom reading background documents for the mission and feeling bad about the accident he'd caused the day before.

His reading material included the inmate rulebook for Arizona Max, the personnel files of the officers who worked in the young offender block and criminal records of the twenty-nine inmates who currently shared the dormitory cell with Curtis Oxford.

John managed to clean the gunge out of the pool filter and fill it up. They ate lunch in the sunshine at the poolside, while John re-tested the kids on their background stories and ran through the details of the escape plan. When he was satisfied that everyone understood their job, he went inside to make phonecalls.

James and Dave sat next to each other in the shallow end of the pool. Lauren was a few metres behind, on a sun lounger. She resented the dressing over her foot, as she stared at the cool water and lazily fanned herself with a frond she'd snapped off one of the poolside palms.

Dave looked at James. 'You don't seem like yourself. Are you scared?'

'A bit,' James admitted. 'Gladiator school sounds brutal.'

Dave smiled. 'I always get the jitters the day before a mission. You ever been on a rollercoaster?'

'A few.'

'Missions are like rollercoasters. You know the bit when you first get on and you're going clunk-clunk-clunk up the lift hill? And you're thinking to yourself, *Why the hell am I putting myself through this?* Then after the ride, you get off and you're buzzing. You want to run straight around to the back of the queue to have another go.'

James nodded. 'When I got back from my last mission, they told me I had to spend a few months catching up with schoolwork. I was *so* gutted.'

'I couldn't imagine leaving CHERUB and going back to being normal,' Dave said. 'It must be so boring having nothing in your life except school, homework and a few mates.'

'Sorry I didn't slow the car down when you told me to. I was being a tit.'

Dave shrugged. 'I guess we all make mistakes. I've certainly made my share.'

'What's the dumbest thing you've ever done on a mission?'

'*Good* question,' Dave laughed. 'There's been a few. You know I nearly got kicked out of CHERUB after that mission with Janet Byrne?'

'Why's that?'

Dave made a bulge over his stomach using his hand. James kicked his feet out of the water and burst out laughing.

'Oh *that*,' James giggled. 'Janet's totally hot. I can't *believe* you got her pregnant.'

The idea of Dave having a kid was funny, but James mostly laughed out of relief that Dave didn't seem to be holding a grudge over the car wreck.

'It's not a joke, you know,' Lauren said bitterly, suddenly looming over the side of the pool. 'Janet's my Spanish tutor. She cried in her room for days worrying about what to do.'

James couldn't control his giggling, so Lauren whipped him across the back with the dried-out palm stalk.

'That hurt,' James whined, as he scrambled out of range towards the deep end of the pool.

'*Good*,' Lauren yelled, as she hurled the palm away and stormed towards the house. 'You're both sexist pigs.'

James made sure Lauren wasn't coming back out before settling down beside Dave again.

'In a few years' time, some poor guy is gonna get a crush on your little sister and you can't help but feel sorry for him.'

'Yeah,' James nodded, as he rubbed the red mark across his back. 'All girls are nuts.'

*

Lauren came into James' room at 5 a.m. on Thursday morning. Already dressed, she flicked her brother's ear to wake him up.

'John says you'd better get your worthless butt moving.'

James scratched his head as he sat up. Lauren had barely spoken to him since the crash, so he was pleased when she leaned in and wrapped her arms around his sweaty back.

'What's that in aid of?' James grinned.

'Try not to do anything too stupid on the mission, eh? You might be an idiot, but you're the only brother I've got.'

James laughed. Lauren felt a twinge of guilt as her index finger ran over the scratch where she'd whacked him the afternoon before. 'I'm making a nice cooked breakfast for everyone,' she said softly.

James was shocked when he got out of the shower and walked through to the kitchen. Lauren looked composed as she slid a trio of perfectly browned pancakes on to a plate, while bacon and scrambled eggs sizzled over the gas hob.

'I remember you cooking when Mum was alive,' James gasped. 'Burned bits stuck to the pan and mess over the cabinets. When did you get so good at it?'

'I did a few cookery classes on campus.'

'You're getting so mature,' James said. 'You're always surprising me and you never seem to ask me for help and advice like you used to.'

Lauren started to laugh.

'What?' James asked.

'Nothing,' Lauren sniggered. 'It's just . . .' She paused to let out a snorting noise. 'The thought of asking *you* for advice. You're not exactly Mr Maturity, are you?'

James was wounded. 'I'm mature,' he said defensively.

'If you say so, bro',' Lauren snickered.

James didn't get a chance to push the argument, because there was a white car pulling up on the driveway.

The Arizona police car sprang up like it was letting out a sigh, as Marvin Teller hoisted himself out of the driver's door and sited his cowboy hat on his head. Today's suit was custard yellow, with white leather boots.

Marvin walked around to the trunk and reached inside. James felt a nasty pang of reality when Marvin lifted out two sets of bright orange overalls and swung a body chain over each shoulder.

Everyone gathered around the table to eat breakfast. Dave, John and Marvin raved about Lauren's cooking and tucked away seconds; but James could only manage a few bites.

His stomach was turning somersaults. He ran upstairs to the toilet and retched a couple of times, but didn't bring anything up. All the stuff James had learned about the dangers inside prison was really getting to him. He splashed cold water on his face and took slow, deep breaths to try and get hold of himself.

When he got back down to the kitchen, John looked concerned. 'What's up?'

'Nervous,' James confessed.

'You know the rules,' John said. 'You can pull out of this mission at any time and you won't be punished.'

It was true that James wouldn't be punished. It was also true that if he bailed on a critical mission at this stage and ruined it, nobody would ever offer him a spot on another one. He'd spend the rest of his time at CHERUB doing routine surveillance, break-ins and security checks. James wasn't prepared to throw away all the effort he'd put into training and missions, because he'd woken up with a touch of nerves.

'Don't sweat it,' James said, trying to sound cool. 'Once the mission starts, I won't have time to worry.'

Marvin took the boys through to the living-room, while John and Lauren stacked the dishwasher. Marvin told them to strip everything off, including watches and jewellery. They replaced their socks, T-shirts and underpants with prison issue. The underwear smelled of disinfectant, but the stains and rips were an uncomfortable reminder of previous occupants.

The baggy orange overalls they wore on the outside were designed for high visibility, so that a prisoner who escaped in transit could be easily seen. Two suits with *Omaha State Prison* printed on them had been shipped in especially for the occasion. In addition, James and Dave had to pull on fluorescent yellow bibs, like the ones kids wear in football training. They had *DANGER: ESCAPE RISK* printed on them in huge letters. The only normal clothes the boys were allowed were their trainers.

'You won't get any toilet breaks once these are on,' Marvin explained, jangling the chains.

James and Dave both dashed upstairs and took a piss. When they got down, Marvin had the two sets of shackles laid out on the carpet.

He put James' on first. James winced as Marvin clamped the bracelets around his ankles.

'Does it have to be so tight?'

'It's supposed to bite the skin so the bracelet can't move,' Marvin explained. 'Someone would ask questions if I fitted them on loose . . . Hands front.'

Marvin squeezed cold metal cuffs on to James' wrists. A length of chain linked the ankle bracelets to the handcuffs, preventing James from raising his hands any higher than his waist.

'Take a stroll around the room while I fix up Dave,'

Marvin said. 'Moving around in those things takes some getting used to.'

*

The individual holding cells at the Phoenix courthouse were barely one pace wide by three long. The only facilities were a drinking fountain and a filthy steel toilet bowl. James had passed more than a dozen of these sweltering little cages on the way to his own and, judging by the shouts and screams passing in all directions, there were hundreds more.

James and Dave were supposed to have gone into court first thing that morning, but something caused a hold-up and James had lost track of time. Inmates weren't allowed watches and there were no windows. James guessed it was between twelve and one when a clingfilm-wrapped sandwich and bottle of no-brand cola got passed through the bars, but that had been several hours ago.

'Rose, James,' a woman's voice shouted.

The stocky female guard stood by the bars outside the tiny cell holding a clipboard. She had a red face and a torrent of sweat drizzling out of her hair. James scrambled up from the floor. He still had the ankle bracelets on, but his handcuffs had been released on arrival.

'Cuffs,' the hack said sharply.

James picked the handcuffs attached to his ankle chains off the floor and put them on a small metal shelf in the barred door.

'Come on,' she said crossly, 'wrists.'

James realised he was supposed to post his hands through the slot so the hack could fix the cuffs on. She squeezed them a notch further than Marvin Teller had done: tight enough that the tendons in his wrist hurt every time he moved his fingers.

'What's the dirty look in aid of, kid?'

They walked past two rows of the tiny cells and up six flights of stairs to the second floor of the courthouse. This level was air-conditioned and James was pleased to catch sight of Dave waiting outside the courtroom.

'What was the hold-up?' James asked.

Dave shrugged. 'Like they'd tell us.'

The hack knocked on the courtroom door and waited a few seconds, before the boys were ushered in. James had expected a grand setting, with loads of people in the room and wood panelling, like you see in the movies. He got a windowless office with frayed carpet, barely bigger than his room on campus.

The grey-haired judge sat behind a cluttered desk in her stockinged feet, sipping out of a Starbucks cup. Her shoes and handbag rested on the floor, beneath an American flag mounted on a pole. There was a stenographer sitting at a smaller desk off to one side, a guard armed with a shotgun and two lawyers, one of whom James and Dave had met briefly that morning before being taken down to the cells.

The lawyer had explained that when an Arizona defendant pleads guilty, the case is dealt with using a system called *plea-bargaining*. The charges and prison sentence are haggled over in advance between the judge and the two opposing lawyers. The court hearing was a formality.

James and Dave stood in the back third of the room behind a red line. A sign on the wall guaranteed a ninety-day sentence to any prisoner who dared step over it.

'OK,' the judge said, taking a quick glance at her watch. 'It's late, let's roll this along. James and David Rose versus the state of Arizona, case number six-zero-one-nine-nine. Minors charged as adults, with one count of robbery and one count of murder. The defence council has offered to plead guilty to charges of robbery and second-degree murder, with an attached term of eighteen years. Does the prosecution formally accept this bargain?'

'Yes, ma'am,' the prosecution lawyer nodded.

The judge looked up at James and Dave. 'Has your lawyer explained to you that by pleading guilty to these charges and accepting the bargain, you lose any right of appeal?'

James and Dave both nodded. 'Yes, ma'am.'

'Very well,' the judge said solemnly. 'Let the record show that sentence of eighteen years has been passed on James and David Rose.'

The two lawyers leaned forward and took turns shaking the judge's hand. James looked at the clock on the wall and realised that he'd spent the whole day sweltering in a cell, waiting for a hearing that had lasted less than three minutes.

13. INDUCTION

The bus to Arizona Max had a metal cage blocking off the exits and bars over the windows. Two hacks with pump-action shotguns sat up front, facing towards a dozen prisoners riding a bus with room for more than fifty.

James and Dave sat near the back. A couple of women had been placed in the middle, and the men were at the front. Pride of place went to a giant with a long red beard, who'd been put on board last and clamped into his seat with a tubular metal bar.

James looked back to Dave in the row behind. 'What the hell did he do?'

The only other kid on the bus leaned across the aisle and answered. He was a skinny fellow called Abe, who was no taller than James. The tuft of bristles on Abe's chin was the only hint that he was nearly seventeen.

'That's Chaz Wallerstein,' Abe said, as if this should mean something.

James and Dave both looked blank.

'You know,' Abe said. 'Bank robber, turned into a hostage deal. He shot up fifteen people, killed eleven of them.

It was all over the TV news. Where have you two been, Mars?'

James straightened up his overalls so you could read the word *Omaha*. 'They had us in solitary up there.'

Abe smiled. 'Mars, Nebraska, same kind of thing I guess . . . You know you're gonna cop trouble when the hacks see those escape-risk bibs?'

*

Arizona Max was opened in 2002 to deal with the state's rapidly expanding prison population. It was a multi-role prison, capable of holding 6,500 inmates, inside fourteen H-shaped cellblocks. Nine blocks held maximum-security adult male prisoners, two held female prisoners, and two were super-maximum-security (supermax) units containing Death Row, along with the most dangerous inmates in the state. The final unit held close to 300 boys under the age of eighteen.

The vast prison compound stretched over thousands of acres and was surrounded by three electrified fences and two stacks of barbed wire coils more than ten metres high. All vehicles or persons entering the prison had to pass through a single entry point.

The bus carrying James and Dave drove through the first set of gates and into a small holding pen, surrounded by twenty-metre-high walls. These outer gates were operated from a control building beyond the prison perimeter, while the inner set operated from the main control room inside the prison. This dual-control security system, known as a *sally port*, means that inmates can't escape, even if they manage to overpower every guard inside the prison.

Only when the gates behind the bus were locked could the second set of gates leading into the prison be opened. Once they'd passed into the compound, James pressed his face to the window and looked out at the concrete cellblocks radiating across the desert.

He watched the inmates in the wire-fenced exercise yards around each unit. There were armed guards on the roof of the buildings, ready to take a shot if trouble broke out, and tiny specks of men standing inside the air-conditioned watch towers dotted along the perimeter, several hundred metres away in every direction.

Hacks received the prisoners as the bus drew up outside each cellblock. The men got dropped off first, then the women, then Chaz Wallerstein was left outside the supermax block and his single cell on Death Row. The young offender unit was the final stop, a quarter mile further along the road, past a stretch of bare ground set aside for building more cellblocks.

The ankle chain was kept short to stop a prisoner from moving fast. It also meant the only way off the bus was a two-footed jump off the step. Abe, who didn't seem the most athletic type, managed to lose his balance. One of the hacks grabbed him out of the dust and bounced him furiously against the wire fence.

'Better keep upright if you don't want your ass kicked.'

The two hacks shoved the kids through a wire gate and towards the cellblock. The twin-level building was made out of prefabricated concrete sections, with a flat metal roof and every window deliberately narrower than a human body. They passed through a steel door, into a spartan reception area, with a long plywood counter down the middle and showers off to the side. A black inmate, who looked about fifteen, stood behind the counter.

One hack removed James' chains and told him to strip off and run to the shower stall at the end of the room. The other one shook green disinfectant powder over James' head and handed him a chewed-up bar of soap.

James felt sorry for Abe as he twirled in the shower next to him. There was no muscle anywhere on Abe's body and his arms and legs were like sticks. James reckoned Lauren could have taken him in a fight. He wouldn't even make a light snack for the prison bullies.

'Ain't got all day,' the guard shouted, as he dragged James from under the water and handed him a towel. James put the towel to his face and realised it was damp and musty, like it had been used plenty of times before.

By the time James threw his towel down, the guard had pulled a thin flashlight out of his shirt pocket and stretched a set of disposable gloves over his fingers.

'Face the wall.'

The hack began his search at the bottom, making James lift each foot in turn, to inspect his soles and in-between his toes. Next he made James bend forward and pull apart his butt cheeks, before shining the torch under James' armpits, in and behind his ears and vigorously rubbing his fingers against James' scalp to make sure nothing was hidden in his hair.

'Face front.'

The hack shone the light in James' eyes, up his nose and inside of his mouth, including under his tongue and around his gums, assisted by a finger that tasted of rubber. He crouched down and flashed the light into James' belly button, before making him lift up his penis and balls and finally roll back his foreskin in case he'd stashed anything naughty up there. When the hack was done, he gently smacked James on the arse.

'OK, get dressed.'

The black kid behind the counter had laid out three sets of prison kit. The clothes they'd arrived in were gone. The other guard was holding the two yellow ESCAPE RISK bibs in the air and James instantly knew there was going to be trouble.

'Do you know how many people have ever escaped from this prison, James Rose?' asked the tubby little superintendent, whose name was Frey.

James didn't want to act smart, so he lied. 'No, sir.'

'Nobody has *ever* escaped from Arizona Max,' Frey said, stepping forward and grinding the heel of his boot against James' foot. 'Got that?'

'Yes sir,' James said, determined not to let the pain show on his face.

Frey took his boot away, leaving James with a red horseshoe across the top of his foot.

James pulled on grimy prison boxers and T-shirt. The outer clothing was grey cotton shorts and a baggy orange polo shirt with *escape risk* printed on it.

'If you're classified as an escape risk, you've got to wear the orange shirt whenever you're out of the cell,' the inmate explained. 'If they catch you without it, they'll stick you in the hole and just as likely stomp on you as well.'

After pulling on the shirt, James looked under the counter and saw that his Nikes had been replaced by a pair of flimsy cotton slippers.

'Prison issue only,' the inmate explained. 'No possessions from the outside, except your legal paperwork and two family photographs. Anything else you want *must* be purchased from the prison commissary.'

The commissary was a kind of prison shop. James had read about it in the rulebook the day before.

He picked his meagre possessions off the bench: identity card with his picture and inmate number, a prison rule book, a threadbare towel, bedding, one spare pair of boxers, one T-shirt, a plastic cup, toothbrush, toothpaste, a bar of soap and a roll of toilet paper.

14. CELL

The thirty-strong population of Cell T4 stopped what they were doing and stared at the three new inmates in the doorway. There were murmurs about James and Dave's orange *escape risk* T-shirts, including a shout:

'When you going over the wall, man?'

Dave smiled. 'A week next Tuesday. Wanna tag along?'

The noise inside the cell was intense. Prisoners were allowed to buy radios and tiny black and white TVs. Each one was tuned to a different station, with the volume up high.

The smell was even more in your face. There were fans near the ceiling at either end of the cell, but the sun had been cooking the metal roof all day, pushing the temperature into the forties. It was like living under the armpit of someone who never washed.

There were six empty beds in the middle of the room. James and Dave knew the names of their cellmates, what crimes they'd committed and how long they had to serve, but a few seconds looking around gave them more essential knowledge than all the background reading.

Curtis Oxford had a bed next to the entrance, surrounded by the beds of the toughest white inmates, who were all skinheads. The areas around these guys' lockers were overflowing with personal possessions. Their prison-issue clothes looked pristine and were accessorised with brand-name trainers and tracksuit tops, in clear breach of the prison rules. As you got to the middle of the cell, the inmates looked steadily weaker until you got down to fragile looking kids who possessed nothing, except nervous dispositions and the prison-issue clothes they stood up in.

The empty beds at the centre of the cell marked a racial divide. The radio stations and chatter beyond this point was mostly Spanish. The inmates were all Latino, and the beds at the bottom of the cell were an olive-skinned mirror of the beds near the door, with the biggest and meanest of the Latinos strutting in crisp underclothes and designer accessories.

Short of turfing someone off their bunk, James and Dave's only immediate option was to take two beds next to each other in the centre of the room, while Abe grabbed one across the aisle. James spread his sheet and blanket over his skimpy plastic mattress, then crouched down and put everything else in his locker before crashing out on the bed.

*

It took a couple of hours for the loud conversations and competing radios and TVs to really start drilling into James' skull. It was seven at night and the closest thing to excitement came when an inmate passed through the cell with a food trolley. Everyone got a paper bag containing sandwiches, a quart of government-surplus milk and two chocolate cookies.

According to Mark – a kid with a black eye who had the bed next to James – lunch was the only hot meal of the day. To save the expense of a large canteen and seating area, inmates got served in twenty-minute shifts between 11 a.m. and 4 p.m., in a small building on the exercise yard.

Like most teenage boys, James was always hungry. He now wished he'd had the stomach for Lauren's pancakes at breakfast. He'd flushed most of the revolting sandwich at the courthouse and the Arizona Max offering was worse: perspiring cheese, brown lettuce and mayonnaise that had soaked through the bread.

'Not eating that?' Dave asked, as he snatched James' clingfilm package off the partition between the beds.

'Mayo makes me spew.'

As Dave crammed the sandwich down his neck, James stared miserably into his paper bag and bit the corner off his last cookie.

'Can I have one of your cookies, for the sandwich?' James asked.

'Can't,' Dave said, as the tip of his tongue lapped up an oily streak dribbling down his chin.

'Come *on*,' James begged. 'That's a good trade, one cookie for a whole sandwich.'

'Already eaten them, though,' Dave said.

James fumed as he slumped down on his mattress. The only things he'd eaten all day were two cookies and a few forced mouthfuls of sandwich. He was getting serious hunger pangs and knew they'd get worse through the night.

'Did you get your commissary form?' Dave asked. 'It's in the food bag.'

James found his folded sheet of paper and a stubby – too short to stab someone with – pencil. His inmate number was scrawled at the top of the form and he started reading the commissary rules printed on the back.

To discourage bullying, gambling and drug dealing, inmates weren't allowed cash. Every prisoner got a commissary account and up to $50 per week could be paid in by a friend or relative on the outside. Prisoners got a commissary form every week and you put a tick next to whatever items you wanted to order, up to your spending limit. The hundreds of items ranged from miniature TVs at $99, down to phone-cards, Marlboro cigarettes, hair mousse, strawberry pop tarts and Reese's peanut butter cups.

According to James' form, the balance of his account was $103.17, which included $20 given to all young inmates by a prisoners' welfare charity and $83.17 that had supposedly been transferred from a commissary account in Nebraska.

Abe came over to the foot of James' bed, holding a cookie and his commissary form.

'I'm not hungry,' Abe said, smiling like he wanted a favour.

'Cheers,' James said, snapping the cookie in half and downing it in two bites.

'I don't get this,' Abe said, waving the form.

James took the form and started explaining how the commissary worked. All Abe had in his account was $20 from the charity.

'You'll need to speak with your mum, or whoever, and try to get them to pay money in every week,' James explained. 'You should buy a ten-dollar phone-card first, so you can call her.'

'And these?' Abe asked, running his finger down the list of items.

'You tick the box for whatever you want, hand in the form and collect your parcel a few days later.'

'Can you help me choose? I don't read so good.'

James grabbed Abe's form and ticked the box next to where it said phone-card. He looked up and realised there were two guys closing in. The absence of cash was supposed to discourage extortion and bullying amongst the inmates, but all it really did was turn the commissary forms themselves into a kind of currency.

To Raymond and Stanley Duff, the sight of two new prisoners with commissary forms had the same effect as a shark sniffing blood in the water. The red-headed brothers weren't quite among the cell's elite, but they were hard enough to hold a place near the top of the pecking order. They were fifteen and sixteen, heavy-set, with flabby stomachs sagging over the waistbands of their shorts.

The Duff brothers were serving life without parole for kidnapping and murdering an eight-year-old girl. Nearly all of James' cellmates were killers, but this was the crime that got under his skin when he read about it. The dimple-cheeked victim pictured in the newspaper clipping had been born two days after Lauren and even looked a little like her.

'We'll help Skinny with his commissary,' Raymond, the younger of the brothers, grinned as he reached out to snatch the form off James.

'Rob him blind, more like,' James said, scurrying backwards across his bed to keep the form out of reach.

'You don't want to give *us* trouble,' Raymond said, tutting and shaking his head.

Dave stood up and faced off the two redheads.

'Lay one finger on my brother, I dare you.'

Anyone could have worked out that Dave packed muscle where Stanley had flab, but brainpower didn't seem to be the Duff brothers' forte.

Stanley swung his thick arm. The punch might have hurt, but Dave could have sat on his bed and clipped his toenails in the time it would have taken to connect. After easily intercepting the fist, Dave plunged an elbow into Stanley's guts, before sweeping his feet from under him as he doubled over in pain.

James remembered what Scott said about going in hard. He sprung up and charged at Raymond. His chunky opponent stumbled backwards across the aisle under a blitz of well-aimed punches, ending up spread-eagled on Abe's bed with a bloody nose and split lip.

James jumped on top and pinned Raymond's arms to his side. James could see the dimple-cheeked face of the little girl Raymond had killed. Bristling with rage, he used one hand to clamp Raymond's neck to the mattress and pulled back his arm, intending to smash Raymond's jaw.

'That's enough,' Dave shouted.

James realised he'd overdone it and let Dave pull him away. They had to step over Stanley, who was sprawled out on the floor in a daze.

'Sorry,' James gasped.

One of the Latinos shouted a warning. 'On the rail.'

James looked up to see a hack stepping on to the metal

gantry that ran the length of the cell above the beds on Abe's side of the room.

'Stan*ding* count,' the guard shouted.

James and Dave didn't know what this meant, but the others all scrambled. They switched off their TVs and radios and stood at the foot of their beds, ready to be counted. Once they twigged, James and Dave did the same.

Stanley Duff managed to drag himself into position, but Raymond remained on Abe's bed, holding his hands over his face and sobbing in pain. The hack leaned over the balcony, inspecting Raymond's face.

'All *keep* still,' the hack shouted. 'Anyone who moves or opens their smart mouth gets two nights in the hole.'

The hack moved briskly to the end of the rail and grabbed a telephone. If the threat of the tiny pitch-black cell known as the hole wasn't enough to keep the inmates in line, there was a rack at the end of the metal gantry, containing stun grenades and guns that could fire tear-gas cartridges, or plastic baton rounds.

The boys stood to attention for a quarter of an hour, waiting for two trustee inmates from the prison hospital. When they'd rolled Raymond on to a stretcher and taken him away, the hack gave the order to stand down.

People started moving around and the radios and TVs got switched back on. James looked at the smears of blood on his hands, then at Dave, expecting some kind of rebuke.

'Well,' Dave said, as he raised a single eyebrow. 'I guess everyone knows we've arrived.'

15. TACTICS

Going to the bathroom meant taking a trip into Latino territory. James and Dave walked down the aisle between the beds, stepping over a dice game and respectfully asking people to move aside.

A scrawny fourteen-year-old Latino boy kept the bathroom spotless. Everyone called him BAM, which was short for *bucket and mop*. In return for his cleaning duties, BAM got looked after by the toughest Latinos, who slept close to the bathroom entrance and didn't want to be troubled by nasty smells.

After James had used the urinal and washed his hands, face and arms, he realised he ought to clean the blood off his T-shirt as well. He tugged it over his head, while BAM fussed over a few splashes on the floor around the urinals. James didn't have his bar of soap, so all he could do was give the shirt a soaking and rub out as much blood out as he could, before quickly wringing out the water and heading for the exit.

'We like our toilet clean,' one of the Latinos said.

Cesar was a big shot, dressed in a black Fila tracksuit with a gold chain around his neck. He had his hairy palm against the wall, blocking the exit of the bathroom.

'You respect our toilet, yeah?' Cesar said. 'Then we'll respect *you*.'

Dave nodded. 'We've got no problem with that.'

'And you,' Cesar said, putting his hand on James' bare shoulder and giving it a friendly squeeze, 'you messed up that baby killer. Good for you. Give your shirt to BAM and he'll wash it properly. We have soap powder. He puts it up near the fans and makes it dry for you by morning.'

James handed his soggy T-shirt to BAM and nodded his appreciation to Cesar, who took his hand off the wall to allow them out of the bathroom.

Cesar looked at one of his lieutenants. 'Have we still got the lemon soft?'

The lieutenant reached under his bed and produced two plump yellow rolls of toilet tissue for James and Dave.

'Thank you, Cesar,' Dave said.

'The prison issue is *brutal*,' Cesar grinned. 'You need anything else?'

Dave shook his head. 'We're cool.'

'You're two tough guys,' Cesar said. 'As long as you leave my people alone, you and I have no problems.'

'You haven't got any food going, have you?' James interrupted. 'I'll replace it when I get my commissary order.'

Dave gave James a stern look, as if to say *don't push your luck*; but Cesar laughed noisily and grabbed a melted Snickers bar and a small can of sour-cream Pringles out of his locker.

'Beauty,' James grinned.

James ripped the lid off the Pringles can as he led Dave back to their beds.

'Seems a cool guy,' James said, crashing on to his bed with a mouthful of chips.

'Don't you believe it,' Dave smiled. 'Cesar just wants to needle the skinheads.'

'What do you mean?' James asked.

'Sit here.'

James stepped over the partition and sat up close to Dave, so they could talk in confidence.

'There's a pissing contest going on between the Latinos at that end and the whites at this end.'

'Obviously,' James nodded. 'It's not exactly an advert for racial harmony in here, is it?'

Dave grinned. 'Elwood and Kirch are the top dogs on the white side, and we pose a threat to them. They'll see BAM washing your T-shirt, they'll see our baby-soft toilet tissue and you filling your chops with Latino munchies. If Elwood and Kirch think we're getting support from Cesar, they're going to start worrying about us undermining their whole power base in this cell.'

'Couldn't we just go up to Elwood and Kirch, shake hands and say hello?'

'If we go over there now, we might look scared,' Dave explained, shaking his head sharply. 'Before we can convince Curtis to escape with us, we've got to earn his respect. We'll only manage that if Elwood and Kirch respect us too.'

'So, what then?' James asked.

'Well,' Dave said slyly, 'it doesn't take a tactical genius to work that out. Does it?'

James looked irritated. 'So I'm not a tactical genius; just *tell* me.'

'You put Stanley Duff's little brother in the prison hospital. You can guarantee that a meathead like Stanley will try to get us back. I doubt Elwood and Kirch will show their hand until they see how well we deal with that.'

'Got you,' James grinned. 'So we've got to take out Stanley Duff.'

'No. Elwood and Kirch might get worried if we're too aggressive. We'll wait for Stanley to come after us. He knows we can do him, so he'll try a surprise attack, probably with a knife.'

'You reckon he can get hold of a knife?'

Dave nodded. 'I don't think he'll find it hard. You've seen how much contraband there is floating around in here.'

'When do you think he'll move on us?' James asked.

'Tonight most likely, when he thinks we're both asleep. We'll have to take turns staying awake. If we take out Stanley tonight, then tomorrow we can straighten things out with Elwood and Kirch in the exercise yard. We'll make it clear that we're not in bed with the Latinos and we just want a fair share of the action. Once that's sorted, you can start chumming up with Curtis.'

'Always assuming Stanley doesn't stick a knife in our guts before we get a chance,' James said, smiling uneasily as he held the Pringles can up in the air and drained the crumbs into his mouth.

'Just in case,' Dave said, 'rub the end of your toothbrush against the concrete floor to sharpen the end. Then sleep with it in your hand.'

16. SLEEPERS

A standing count at 10:30 p.m. was followed by lights-out. The guards needed to be sure that the inmates weren't digging a tunnel or killing each other, so a line of tubes down the middle of the cell stayed on. It was enough light to read by and most of the TVs and radios kept going too, along with the bragging matches and rowdy dice games.

The noise died back after midnight, but James still felt like he was in hell. He sat on his bed with his back to the wall, studying the beads of sweat rolling down his chest. There always seemed to be at least one winged black speck wandering over his skin, while hundreds of larger insects had decided to spend the night clanking their heads against the fluorescent lights near the ceiling.

James wrestled with his sheet, but it was soggy and hopelessly tangled around his legs, so he threw it away in frustration. He studied the white marks covering the shiny plastic over his mattress. He hadn't been able to work them out earlier, but now he disgusted himself by solving the riddle: it was crusted salt from the previous occupant's dried-out sweat.

James looked over the partition. Dave had put a towel over his eyes to shield the light and been asleep by 10:45. James remembered how his mum used to call people like Dave sleepers. Lauren was another sleeper: stick her in the back of a car, or on a couch in some strange house and she'd be out in no time. Unless he was exhausted, or sick, James could never do it. He needed a decent bed, with pillows and the duvet tucked under his chin exactly how he liked it.

'Dave,' James said, nudging him awake.

Dave sat up drearily, with a string of drool stretched between his face and his pillow.

'Keep lookout a minute. I need a slash.'

James tucked the sharpened toothbrush handle into the waistband of his shorts, grabbed his empty cup and wandered towards the bathroom, while Dave rubbed his eyes. It was a clear walk up the aisle, though a few kids were still lying awake, with their tiny TV screens flickering in the half-light. They either ran on headphones or were turned down to a whisper.

It took James' eyes a while to adjust to the brightly lit bathroom. One of the younger Latinos stood by the middle sink, pushing down the tap head and splashing water over his chest. James thought he heard the kid sob while he stood at the urinal. When he moved to wash his hands, the kid sobbed again.

'You OK?' James asked.

James reeled when the kid turned to face him. He had a burn on his chest, surrounded by a black scorch mark in the exact shape of the plastic mug in James' hand. The skin was all blistered and weeping pus.

'My baby brother got toothache,' the kid explained tearfully. 'Grandma paid the dentist instead of my commissary, which meant Cesar didn't get what I owed him.'

James felt scared when he realised this horror had happened tonight, while he'd been only a few metres away. With all the noise, you could be screaming in agony and nobody would notice.

'How?' James asked.

'Cesar's trademark: he makes a hole in the bottom of a cup and fills it up with matches. Then he press it against your skin and sets them alight.'

'*Jesus.*'

James remembered that he was deep in Latino territory. If one of Cesar's guys came in, he'd want to know why James was sticking his nose where it didn't belong. James pressed on the tap, splashed water all over his body to cool off and then gulped some down, before refilling his mug to take back to bed.

'I'm sorry,' James said uneasily, as he backed away.

The kid edged a smile. 'Not as sorry as me.'

James shuddered, thinking how excruciating the burn must feel, as he walked back to his bed. Something thumped into him. Thick arms wrapped around his stomach as he hit the concrete floor between two empty beds, with Stanley Duff on top of him.

'For my brother,' Stanley announced theatrically, as he reached into the waistband of his shorts and pulled out a twenty-centimetre blade made from a strip of sharpened metal.

'Help,' James yelled desperately, realising that Dave must have dropped his guard and fallen back to sleep.

The blade would have plunged through James' neck if he hadn't found the strength to move at the last second. He got hold of Stanley's wrist and started trying to twist the weapon out of his grip.

'*Dave*. For god's sake, help me . . .'

James spotted Abe's skinny legs cutting across the aisle to Dave's bed. Stanley was far heavier than James and he was gradually winning the battle to free his wrist and take a second stab. The blade nicked James' palm as Stanley snatched it free.

Stanley broke into a big grin. James reached to pull out his toothbrush handle, but as Stanley raised the blade into the air, James spotted the kind of opening you dreamed about every time you got thrown to the mat in combat class. He thrust his hand forward, smashing his palm into the base of Stanley's chin. Stanley's head whipped back and made a sharp crack as the vertebrae in his neck impacted.

Dave was out of bed and committed to a charging movement. He crashed into Stanley, knocking him off James, as the rows of lights over the beds started flickering. This was followed by a popping noise, like the loudest cork bursting out of the biggest champagne bottle you've ever seen. It echoed around the cell, as Dave somersaulted on to the bed beside him and screamed out in pain.

A shout came from one of the two guards who'd run on to the gantry. 'Break it up.'

James caught a glance of the hack holding the huge baton-round gun, as it recoiled from the second plastic shot. It hit

Stanley in the arse, making him buck forward and smack head-first into the cell wall. The plastic round deflected off the bed frame and tore into James' thigh.

'Stand apart, *now*.'

Scared that he was going to be the next target, James dragged himself up and stumbled out into the aisle, fighting a dead thigh muscle.

'Standing count,' a female guard shouted. 'Standing count.'

The whole cell had been woken by the shots and everyone started moving to the end of their beds; except Dave and Stanley, who'd each taken a baton round and were in no state to go anywhere. James looked up at the gantry, unsure if he was supposed to move.

The hack with the gun rocked his head and tracked James the four paces back to his bed. James knew a third, excruciatingly painful plastic round would come his way if he stepped a millimetre out of line.

James was expecting the medical team, like earlier, but the guards had pressed the emergency alarm, which brought out the Prison Emergency Response Team, commonly known as PERT. The six-strong team rolled back the cell door and burst through at a run. They looked fearsome, dressed head to toe in black body armour, with gloves, crash helmets and their leader yelling his lungs out:

'Beds and *heads*.'

James copied his cellmates, as they jumped on to their beds and sat with backs to the wall and hands on heads. Kirch, who was nearest the door, didn't have time to move. He was smacked into the aisle with a riot shield and got his ankle crunched under a running boot.

The first to reach Dave and Stanley threw down his shield and ripped a can of incapacitating pepper spray off his belt. Dave screamed out and rolled in a ball, as the PERT leader blasted him with the gooey liquid.

James breathed a hint of the concentrated pepper that had drifted into the air and immediately felt tears in his eyes. It must have been a million times worse for Dave.

Each member of the PERT team had a specific role. While the leader moved in on Stanley with the pepper spray, the second through fifth members dragged Dave into the aisle and grabbed one limb each. When Dave was spread out in an X-position, the final member of the team laid a plastic harness over his back. Strings of pepper spray dangled out of Dave's long hair as he panicked for breath.

The two men holding Dave's arms bent them into the harness and pulled them tight under a heavy nylon strap. Once they were secure, Dave's legs were twisted until his heels almost touched his bum, then strapped into this excruciating position.

The PERT team moved their attention to Stanley, dragging him out into the aisle by his ankles. But the leader screamed out.

'Break it *off* . . . Look at the head.'

Stanley was now unconscious and you only had to look at the way his head was twisted unnaturally backwards to see that something was badly wrong. The smallest on the PERT team, who James now realised was a woman, took off her gloves and helmet and crouched down over Stanley. She flinched as she got a whiff of the pepper spray, then looked up at her team leader.

'It might be a broken neck. He's definitely a hospital job.'

The leader looked up at the two guards on the rail. 'Get us a medical team.' Then he pointed at Dave. 'Take *that* to the hole.'

Two of the PERT team put their hands under Dave's armpits and picked him up. His eyes and nose were streaming and he had a huge red welt on his ribs where he'd been hit by the plastic bullet.

James trembled as he watched Dave get dragged out of the cell, with his bare knees grazing along the concrete floor. James knew it could as easily have been him who'd ended up being hauled away in agony. Or even worse: what if Stanley had got the knife in?

17. YARD

With Dave locked in the hole, James felt vulnerable. His need for sleep finally overcame his fear at around 4 a.m., an hour after Stanley Duff had been stretchered off to the prison hospital.

The cell door and the gates on to the exercise yard opened at nine, but most kids were still asleep as James limped towards the bathroom, with his bar of soap and toilet roll. He had the sharpened toothbrush handle tucked into his waistband, just in case.

BAM hovered with his mop, while James took a dump. The steel bowls were mounted on the wall, without doors or partitions, so you got zero privacy. The shower was even worse. The water only ran while you held the button down and the lukewarm dribble meant you couldn't get soap out of your hair.

James dried off quickly, desperate to get out of the rank cell and breathe fresh air. A corridor led past three other cells and up a short ramp. To get to the exercise yard, you stood in line to get padded down by a hack, before passing through a metal detector.

As James' canvas slipper took its first step into the sand, another inmate passed him a white paper bag containing his breakfast. James got called back before he had a chance to see what he'd got.

'Rose.'

Superintendent Bob Frey was the pot-bellied, yellow-toothed man who'd crushed James' foot in the reception room the previous afternoon. Frey took James under a veranda and made him stand with his back pinned to the cellblock wall.

'Been in *my* cellblock less than fifteen hours, haven't you?'

'About that, sir.'

'I got two brothers in the hospital. One of 'em's just a busted nose and concussion, but the other fella's got neck damage that's gonna cost this prison tens of thousands in medical bills.'

James shifted awkwardly, not knowing how to answer.

'Then I got your brother in the hole,' Frey grinned. 'You ever been in the hole, boy?'

'No sir.'

'You got no light, no ventilation, not a strip of clothes and no toilet. We hose it out once a day, like an animal cage. Any more trouble and that's where I'll have you. Understood?'

'Yes sir,' James nodded. 'How long's Dave in there for?'

'Long enough,' Frey grinned. 'Now get out of my sight.'

James opened up his breakfast bag as he walked on to the sun-bleached yard. The milk was warm, the three pieces of fruit were past their best and the muffin was on the dry side, but it was edible and James was starving. His last decent meal had been the fried chicken two nights earlier.

The yard was oval-shaped and the size of three football pitches. It was scooped out of the desert basin around the back half of the cellblock. The facilities were basic: shelters to keep off the sun, a few basketball hoops and chin-up bars and the small prefabricated building where lunches were served. Beside the perimeter fence was a five-metre stretch of concrete behind a red line, which was known as the shooting gallery. No inmate was allowed on the shooting gallery and to make it clear, the notices dotted along the fence had a little stick man standing inside a gun sight with *Lethal Force Authorised* written beneath him.

'Hey,' Abe said, jogging up behind James with a banana in his hand.

James smiled. 'You did me a big favour last night. Dave was *supposed* to be watching my back . . . I just gotta hope Stanley doesn't have any pals popping out of the woodwork.'

'The two big white guys were in the shower when I went for a piss. They asked if I'd seen you.'

'Which guys?' James asked anxiously.

'Elwood, and the one with the German name.'

'Kirch. What did they want?'

'They just asked where you were.'

'Did they sound angry?'

Abe shrugged. 'All they said was one sentence. *Have you seen the little psychopath?* I told them I thought you were already out on the yard.'

'They called me a psychopath?' James said, unsure if this was a bad sign or a mark of respect.

'I think you broke that guy's neck.'

'It was me or him: he *was* about to slit my throat.'

James threw away the core of his apple and took a slug from his bottle of milk. He was frightened. If Dave had been around, Elwood and Kirch would have been manageable. But with Dave in the hole, he'd be outgunned if things turned heavy.

'I'll wait for them to come on the yard,' James said. 'At least there's space to run away out here.'

James and Abe found a spot under a shelter with a view over the whole yard and sat together in the dirt.

Kirch came through the metal detector first. He was a seventeen-year-old skinhead, two metres tall, with massive pectoral muscles inside a sweat-stained vest. Elwood was taller and thinner, shaved bald. A swastika with MOM written underneath it was tattooed on his neck. Curtis came next. He was an average build and the same height as James, but he looked undernourished standing between his massive bodyguards.

The three boys joined up with a bunch of similarly fierce looking skinheads from another cell, who were standing around a set of chin-up bars taking it in turns to do sets. The gang was bigger and meaner than James had expected. He realised they were going to have no problem hurting him if they wanted to.

A couple of minutes later, while Kirch was on the chin-up bar, Elwood spotted a little guy passing by. He tucked the kid's head under his arm and squeezed until it turned red. After a while, he let go and knocked him down with a savage right hook. The kid was fighting tears and holding on to his face as he walked off.

'I gotta split,' Abe said, shocked by what he'd just witnessed.

James knew Abe wasn't going to be any help in a fight against the Elwoods and Kirches of the world, but he appreciated having a friendly face to talk to.

'What's your problem?' James asked.

'They already asked me where you are. If they find me with you, they're not gonna like it.'

'I guess I'll have to face them some time today,' James said pensively. 'So go and earn yourself some merit points by telling them I'm right here.'

After what had happened to the last passer-by, Abe didn't sound keen. 'Why don't *you* go over to them?'

James pointed a finger at the armed hack standing on the roof of the cellblock less than ten metres away. 'I feel safer here.'

Abe reluctantly set off across the dirt towards Elwood and the others. His steps seemed to slow down as he got closer. At one point Abe changed direction so much, James thought he was going to chicken out and walk straight by.

Abe got off with a nod of thanks for his trouble. Elwood immediately set off towards James, backed up by an entourage that included Kirch and three younger skinheads, with Curtis dragging up the rear.

James looked up for comfort, only to discover that the hack on the roof had disappeared.

'You look pale, Rose,' Elwood said, when he got up close.

'I figure six against one is never good,' James said, trying to keep the fear out of his voice.

'True,' Elwood grinned, looking back at his crew.

'What is it you want?'

'I liked the way you dealt with Stanley Duff.'

'Those two started it,' James said. 'I didn't go looking for trouble.'

'I've got no beef over that pair of walnut brains,' Elwood said. 'But you gotta understand my concern, when guys like you and your brother arrive in my cell and start turning people over.'

James nodded.

'I've either got to cut you to pieces, or cut you a deal; unless you've already got one with the Latinos.'

'My brother said Cesar was trying to stir up trouble between us,' James said, feeling a glimmer of confidence, as he sensed that he might get through the meeting unscathed. 'But Cesar only cares about the other Latinos.'

Elwood nodded. 'Your bro' sounds smart.'

'When he stays awake,' James said bitterly.

'So why'd you accept gifts from Cesar?'

'Because I was hungry.'

Elwood roared out with a false laugh, which set off all his cronies. 'I guess free food is free food, wherever it comes from . . . So what about your bro'? You got word?'

James shook his head. 'That hack, Frey, pulled me over. He wouldn't tell me when they're letting him out of the hole.'

Elwood laughed again. 'I've been in that hole *enough* times, but the max is forty-eight hours if you're under eighteen. After that they either put you in a single cell, or back in the dorm.'

'Right,' James said, relieved that Dave would probably be back soon.

'So, to business,' Elwood said. 'Me and Kirch run our cell. That means *everyone* kicks up to us, including you.'

James nodded; not that he was in any position to negotiate.

'I want you and your brother to give me ten bucks of commissary each, every week. In return, I'll give you Abe.'

'Abe?' James said, confused.

'Abe's your personal property. Rip off his commissary, beat his brains in; do what you like. I don't want you touching any of the others, they belong to Kirch and me. I'll also set you up with decent prison-issue clothes and blankets, and I'll make it known that I'm on your side when the Duff brothers come back.'

'Sounds fair,' James nodded, as they shook on the deal.

'Did you lose anything good when you came in through reception?' Elwood asked.

'Only my trainers.'

'For ten dollars of commissary, I can get them back if you want them.'

'Course,' James said, looking at his canvas slip-ons. 'These things are rubbish.'

'You better stick with us until your brother comes back,' Elwood said, scratching at the swastika on his neck. 'Not everyone around here is a sweetie-pie like me.'

18. BEASTS

James loved animals when he was tiny: the furry toys on his bed, the singing characters in animated movies and the overweight cat that wandered into his nan's garden, knowing it would get a saucer of milk just for bothering to turn up.

Aged seven, James did his first school project on lions. His mum taped a show off the Discovery channel that was on after bedtime. He watched the female lions licking their cubs and lazing under a tree in the sun. Then the animals went hunting.

The lionesses chased into a herd of antelope. They dragged down a straggler and began tearing it apart. Ripping off its legs, clawing open the stomach and then dipping their snouts inside the twitching carcass; tearing out hunks of flesh and running their long tongues through the blood on their faces. Until that moment, James had no idea nature could be so brutal.

He got as far as the living-room door, intending to find his mum and start bawling, but something changed his mind. He went back to the couch, tentatively rewound the video and watched it again. He watched it over and over, appalled, but utterly fascinated by what the lions were doing.

The in-your-face nastiness of the young skinheads in the Arizona Max exercise yard reminded James of the video for the first time in years. They brought out the same mixture of feelings: power and viciousness, combining into a perverse kind of glamour.

James showed off, working up a sweat on the chin-up bar, before lying back in the dirt next to Elwood and listening to him talk about things the gang of skinheads had done. Elwood pointed out scared kids who handed their commissary form to him each week, in return for not getting beaten up too badly. He revelled in stories about people he'd tortured, stabbed, poured boiling water over and bullied to the point where they'd tried to kill themselves.

The history of violence wasn't all one way. Elwood proudly showed off scars on his leg, chest and back from three different knife attacks. He said you could never judge who would snap and come at you with a knife. It was as likely to be the puny little bookworm as the brooding psychopath with arms like joists.

James was appalled, but he listened intently and laughed when he was expected to. It was mostly out of relief. The last forty-eight hours had been amongst the most traumatic of his life, but with the skinheads offering some protection, the tight ball in his stomach had eased off. He finally felt he was getting to grips with the mission. The next step was to chum up with Curtis.

*

Lauren didn't have much to do back at the house; her part of the mission would only begin once James and Dave escaped. She welcomed the chance to catch up on sleep and relax after basic training, though it would have been more fun if there'd been someone like Bethany to hang out with.

John took her to a shopping mall and even let her drive part of the way, so she could get used to handling the car in traffic. Unfortunately, the pair had radically different ideas on shopping.

Lauren would have happily cruised the mall all day: nosing around, maybe buying clothes and some things for her new room on campus, before stopping off at the food court for lunch. John's idea of shopping was to write a list and take the place by storm: finding the quickest route between shops you had to visit on the map by the entrance and then charging from one to the next. When Lauren suggested that they *have a look around* before leaving, John scowled at her like she was a three-headed alien and steamed towards the car park.

The latex swimming sock was the one good thing to come out of the trip. Lauren could pull it over the small dressing on her foot and it would keep dry while she was in the pool. It was the hottest part of the day when they got back to the house and she put it to immediate use. She swam a few gentle lengths, but mostly just floated on a blow-up lounger and laughed at the rude bits in a teen magazine she'd got at the mall.

John had threatened lunch, but after an hour Lauren dripped into the kitchen, only to find him yelling at a telephone.

'As far as I'm concerned . . . Well . . . I don't know if he can do it . . . Sure James has his head screwed on. But we *are* talking about a thirteen-year-old boy . . . So what does Scott Warren say? . . . OK, OK . . . If he can get me in I'll drive up there straight away.'

'Was that Marvin?' Lauren asked. 'Are the boys OK?'

John had been so involved in the call he hadn't noticed Lauren standing behind him.

'James is fine,' John said. 'But there was a fight and Dave ended up in the hole. He's had a bad night in there and . . . Listen, everything's up in the air and I don't know all the details myself. Can I leave you here on your own for a couple of hours? Don't spend any more time in the pool, you've got fair skin and it's not used to that kind of sun.'

'What if anyone calls?'

'I'm on my mobile,' John said, snatching his keys and a false FBI badge off the kitchen cabinet. 'Don't wander off from the house. I'll pick up something for dinner on the way back.'

*

James' hot lunch was watery mash, peas and a rectangular slab of mincemeat that everyone, including the servers, referred to as baked turd. Desert was a comparatively edible fruit sponge, washed down with the inevitable government-surplus milk.

'Not bad, compared to the filth you get in Omaha,' James said. 'Practically gourmet.'

'You want another dessert?' Kirch asked.

'Mmm, sure,' James said. 'Can I go up to the counter and get one?'

The five skinheads around the table laughed.

'Just tax one,' Curtis said.

James looked over his shoulder at the table behind him. He realised he'd look weak in front of his new friends if he didn't rip off someone's pudding, but fate had twisted the knife: out of the four kids at the next table, Abe was the only one who hadn't started eating his sponge.

James stood up. 'Abe man,' he said awkwardly. 'You eating that pudding? Only . . .'

'I'm eating it,' Abe said guardedly.

The skinheads roared with outrage.

'You cannot say that, man,' Elwood gasped, shaking his head and pounding on the table. '*Serious* disrespect.'

Abe realised the error of his ways and pushed the plastic bowl towards James. But it wasn't fast enough for Kirch, who reached over and dragged Abe off his chair by the scruff of his shirt.

'You got no manners, boy,' Kirch shouted.

He banged his fist against Abe's mouth, then dropped him to the floor, before spitting a mouthful of milk and chewed-up food in his hair. James looked anxiously at the hack standing behind the serving counter, but it was exactly like Scott Warren said: hacks didn't interfere as long as nobody was getting killed.

'You'd better start learning,' Kirch growled.

Elwood and the others were laughing as Abe crawled back to his seat with milk streaking down his face. James joined the laughter as he took Abe's pudding and sat back down, but he really felt terrible. Abe had saved his life by waking Dave up a few hours earlier. Now he had to sacrifice their friendship for the good of the mission.

It was the middle of the day when they trawled back out on to the exercise yard. With the temperature touching the forties, Kirch led the gang to the cell. With no air conditioning, it was no cooler indoors than out, but at least you were shielded from the blinding sunlight.

James' status as an associate of Elwood and Kirch meant a bed nearer the door. Kirch took five seconds to bust open the combination locker on the bed opposite his own. He threw out Stanley Duff's belongings, while James collected his things from his old bed in the middle.

Stanley had some decent stuff. James grabbed his deodorant and shampoo, as well as a bunch of snack foods and a radio. What James didn't want got thrown out for the weaker guys to fight over. Abe grudgingly accepted first pick of an electric razor, some rice crackers and a half used toilet roll.

'That was messed up in the canteen,' James whispered guiltily.

Abe had a fat lip from the punch. 'A guy like you and a guy like me were never gonna move with the same crew for long,' he said casually.

James found Abe's acceptance of his low status depressing. Abe was doing twenty years, and looked like spending most of it getting slapped around and bullied. James wanted to think up some desperately clever scheme that would make everything fair, but he knew the world didn't work that way; least of all inside a place like Arizona Max.

James' new bunk was comfortable. The bed had three thin mattresses laid on top of one another. Extras were only supposed to be issued to inmates with bad backs, but inevitably it was the bullies who gained the extra comfort.

Elwood's connection in the prison laundry had already delivered James a spare set of sheets and an extra pillow, plus a towel and some underwear. It looked years newer than the rags he'd received in reception and his black Nikes were supposed to be on their way.

James laid back on his bed reading a book about the Mafia that had belonged to Raymond Duff. It wasn't as exciting as the cover suggested, but it was all James had to take his mind off the heat, until a hack leaned over the gantry above his head and shouted his name.

'Rose, you got an EA.'

'A what?'

'Educational Assessment,' Curtis explained, shouting over the bed between them. 'They must have sharpened their act up, it usually takes weeks to sort out the new inmates. I'll show you the way if you like. I can ask if my books have arrived.'

19. CURTIS

The education area was built above the cells, but to get there you had to go outside on to the yard and walk around the edge of the building, along a path enclosed in a wire cage. It was James' first chance to get to know Curtis, who kept to himself in the presence of the more powerful skinheads.

'What courses do you do?' James asked, as they walked side by side.

'Everyone's supposed to get three hours' education a day,' Curtis explained. 'But there's not enough teachers for normal classes, so they just give you textbooks to read. I only go because you're allowed to buy extra books. It's supposed to be related to what you're learning, but the censor only stops a book if it tells you how to make explosives, or if it's porno or something.'

'Do they force us to go to class?'

Curtis laughed. 'It's compulsory; but imagine you're a teacher and you've got twenty guys like Elwood in your class. How hard would you try to make them turn up?'

'See your point,' James grinned.

'I'd like to do an art course,' Curtis said. 'All I ever did when I was a kid was paint or draw, but all they'll let you have here are the stubby pencils like you get with your commissary forms. I did get a box of colouring pencils smuggled in, but the hacks wouldn't stand for any big stuff.'

James tried to gently move the conversation towards the idea of escaping as they rounded a corner.

'So, you ever getting out?' James asked.

'Doesn't look like it,' Curtis said. 'You?'

'Eighteen years,' James said.

'Not bad,' Curtis said. 'You'll be in your thirties. You've got a shot at living some kind of life.'

'I'm getting out *way* before eighteen years,' James grinned.

'Nobody escapes from here, James. This place is new-built; state of the art.'

'Me and Dave worked out a plan when we were in Nebraska. If they'd ever let us out of solitary, we'd have pulled it too. But here's the *weirdest* coincidence: Omaha State and this joint are exactly alike. They must have been built by the same people.'

James knew that Omaha State and Arizona Max were twins: designed by the same architect, built by the same construction company and opened within six months of each other. It was an essential detail in the background story that explained how James and Dave could know how to escape from Arizona Max within days of arriving.

'The *exact* same?' Curtis said.

'More or less. Same security systems, same kind of cellblocks, even the same fixtures and fittings. When me and Dave were in solitary, we had this hack on our landing who used to talk to us all the time. He'd come over to my cell door for a chat. I think he felt sorry for me because I was young, but he was one of those guys who loved his own voice. He moaned non-stop. I mean, I'm the one locked in solitary twenty-three hours a day, but he'd be whinging about *his* life. His wife, his kids, his house and about the superintendent busting his balls and keeping him on night shift.

'Whenever he moaned about work, I started asking subtle questions. Like, how many staff there were on duty at night and what kind of security passes they used. Dave's cell wasn't far away and he started doing the same. By the time we'd been in solitary for a few weeks, this big-mouth had told us *way* more than he should have.'

'You really believe you could escape?'

'I reckon I'd make it out the gate. The tricky part is what to do after that. You need money, and connections to pay for a false identity and set up a new life. There's no point going on the run for a few weeks, getting caught and ending up buried in solitary with ten years added to your sentence. You've got to find a way of avoiding the cops for the whole rest of your life.'

'How would you break out?' Curtis asked. 'You've got to get out of a locked cell for starters.'

'No offence,' James said, 'but the only people who'll ever know that are the ones going out with me.'

Curtis seemed to understand the need for secrecy and they were nearly at the metal door of the education unit anyway. A hack padded the boys down, before they passed through another metal detector. It was two flights of stairs up, then past three small classrooms to a door with *Education Officer* written on it.

'You mind if I go in quickly first?' Curtis asked. 'I want to ask Mr Haines if my books have arrived.'

Curtis knocked on the door and got hailed in by a voice James recognised as Scott Warren.

'Isn't Haines here?' Curtis asked, looking surprised as he pushed the door open.

Scott, who was sitting at a desk, shook his head. 'I'm covering for him today.'

James spotted John Jones standing behind the desk.

Curtis pointed at James. 'I came to show him the way and see if my books were in.'

'Yeah ... Umm, sorry,' Scott stuttered. 'What's your name, son?'

'Curtis Oxford.'

'Curtis ... It's probably best if you wait until the education officer is back ... Tomorrow. I'm not familiar with the procedure for handing out books.'

Curtis backed out of the office, looking at James. 'Do you know the way back on your own?'

James nodded. 'I'll see you out there.'

He stepped into the office and shut the door behind Curtis. John and Scott were both in a state of shock. They stared at a black and white CCTV monitor, until it showed Curtis reaching the end of the corridor and starting down the stairs.

'Sheesh!' Scott said, putting both hands over his heart. 'That gave me a fright ... I never expected our target to come wandering into the room with you.'

'You might have guessed what was going on,' John said tersely.

'You only said we might have to meet in the *visitors'* room,' James snapped back.

'Well, whatever . . .' John huffed.

James felt his temper rise up as he ran his hand through his sweaty hair. 'You know what?' he said angrily. 'I'm boiling hot, I've not slept or had a decent shower, I've eaten nothing but crap food, I've seen people get beaten up, pepper-sprayed and have their skin burned off . . . I've even had some psycho come at me with a knife and try to kill me. If you don't like the job I'm doing here, you can take this mission and shove it *right* up your arse.'

John looked startled by the outburst.

'We appreciate that you're working under a lot of stress,' Scott said gently, trying to calm James down.

'James,' John said, sounding extra sincere. 'I apologise. I didn't mean to have a go at you. It was just a shock when Curtis came in here and saw all of us together . . . We called this emergency meeting because there's a serious situation with Dave.'

'Why don't you sit down?' Scott said, as he reached over to a water dispenser. 'How about a cold drink?'

James sat down, as Scott filled a paper cup from the water cooler.

'They pulled Dave out of the hole for a doctor's examination earlier this morning,' John explained. 'The baton round fractured three of his ribs. One of them broke badly. A bone fragment has snapped off and punctured the surrounding tissue, causing internal bleeding.'

'How serious is that?' James asked.

'If Dave had been x-rayed and treated immediately, it

wouldn't have been bad,' John said. 'But by the time they dragged him out of the hole this morning, a blood clot had formed on his chest wall. He's having difficulty breathing and he'll be hospitalised for at least two weeks. After that, he'll be on medication to break up the clot. He won't be back to full fitness for a couple of months, at least.'

'So that's it,' James sighed. 'You're gonna pull me out of here?'

'As soon as practicable,' John nodded. 'We're as sorry as you are that this didn't work out, James. I've been in the intelligence game for twenty years and I'm afraid complicated plans like this have a habit of going awry.'

James drained his paper cup and nodded when Scott offered a refill. Part of James was relieved at the prospect of getting back to campus unscathed, but a much bigger part was bitter at having gone through so much stress for nothing.

'Is there no way I could carry on without Dave?' James asked.

'I can't see how,' John said. 'You need protection.'

'Not any more I don't. You saw me come in with Curtis, and Elwood spent half the morning telling me his life story. Nobody's gonna give me hassle when we're best buds.'

This was news to Scott and John, who exchanged a long glance.

'Hmm,' Scott said, drumming his finger thoughtfully against his cheek. 'Sounds like you've put in some valuable work there. It might put a different complexion on things . . .'

'But how would James handle the escape without Dave?' John asked. 'Dave was the advanced driver and the only one big enough to wear your uniform during the escape.'

'I'm a good driver,' James said. 'Lauren can navigate and the roads over here are nice and straight.'

'Your driving didn't seem so great to me the other afternoon,' Scott said bluntly.

'I've been able to drive for nearly a year and that's the only accident I've ever had. Well . . . Except, right at the beginning when I nearly killed some woman's dog.'

'Actually,' John nodded, 'despite James' idiotic little adventure the other afternoon, he did score top marks on his intermediate driving course. But there's *still* no way he can get out of here disguised as a hack.'

Scott rested an elbow on the desk and waggled his finger at James. 'Stand up a minute, James. How tall are you?'

'A hundred and sixty-two centimetres,' James said, as he climbed out of his chair.

Scott looked baffled. 'What's that in American money?'

John smiled. 'About five feet two inches. Have you got any men that small?'

'Not men, I haven't. But we're an equal opportunity employer and there's a young lady on our cellblock who's about James' size.'

John broke into a smile. 'Could you alter the staff rota so that she's on duty the night of the escape?'

Scott nodded. 'That shouldn't be too tough. We might have to make a few adjustments to the plan, but this is definitely doable.'

'So we're back in business?' John asked.

'I can't see why not,' Scott said. 'As long as James is sure he's up to it.'

20. TIME

Of course I'm up to it. The words glided out easily enough. The mission was saved, and James felt like a hero as Scott grasped his hand and shook it robustly.

Reality dawned as James passed down the stairs and out of the education block. The sun was brutal and the mountains of barbed wire lining the prison compound shimmered in the heat. The same light caught the powerful torsos of the predators scouring the yard and the guns cradled by the hacks on the cellblock roof.

James felt smaller than one of the grains of sand under his canvas shoe, as he looked around and realised what he'd got himself into: a thirteen-year-old boy, alone against a black-hearted machine built to contain the nastiest people on the planet. For an instant, he considered running back to the office and telling John he'd changed his mind. He stopped walking, took a deep breath and ran his tongue around his dry mouth.

James thought about the moment he'd pulled the trigger on the guy in Miami, scared out of his mind. It had been a terrible experience, but he could draw strength from it now.

He thought back to his training, all the seemingly impossible things he'd achieved when the instructors pushed him through the pain barrier. Whenever a trainee was on the point of giving up, Mr Speaks used to scream in their ear: *This is tough, but cherubs are tougher*. James had got so sick of the phrase he thought he'd never want to hear it again, but now the words felt like a comfort.

He whispered it under his breath as he started walking again. 'This is tough, but cherubs are tougher.'

*

The exercise yard was at its most comfortable in the hour before the inmates were locked down for the night. The sun was low and a gentle breeze made the heat almost tolerable. James sat with Curtis near the chin-up bars, while Elwood and the others prowled for some unfortunate who'd failed to deliver his commissary package to Kirch's bunk earlier in the day.

The two boys had been talking for an hour, sitting in the sand, trading stories and getting friendly with each other.

'So, you shot three people dead and tried to blow your own brains out,' James said, giving Curtis a shocked look, as if this was news to him. 'If I'd met you in the street, I'd never have booked you for anything other than a totally straight kid.'

Curtis smiled, clearly pleased to have somebody brighter than Elwood and Kirch to talk to. 'We were always moving around when I was growing up. Canada, Mexico, even South Africa for a while. It was cool, just me and my mom together, but we had some close scrapes with the law. I started getting stressed out, worrying about what would happen if Mom got busted. Sometimes I got so depressed. The blackest feeling, like the whole world was closing in on me.'

'Did you see a doctor, or anything?' James asked.

Curtis nodded. 'I've had every kind of pill going. In a lot of the places we lived, my mom would take me to see a psychiatrist. Every one of them acted like they knew what they were talking about, but they all came up with different answers. If you ask me, psychiatrists are a bunch of phoneys.

'Two years ago, it started getting real bad. I'd go to bed and stay under the covers all day. My mom took me to this shrink in Philadelphia – some hotshot she'd read about in a magazine article. He reckoned my problems were down to a lack of structure in my life: moving from place to place and not having proper schooling or relationships with other kids my own age. So he puts this bright idea in my mom's head to send me to a military school. I begged her not to send me, but I was a mess and Mom had tried everything else, so she went along with it.

'The place was a toilet. They had me up every morning running laps. Making beds, polishing boots and that whole playing at being soldiers gig. One night, the commandant ripped into me for not knotting my tie properly. He gives me this little nailbrush and tells me to start scrubbing out this whole massive shower room. I did it for about ten minutes, then I ran off, busted into the weapons locker and stole the commandant's car keys. Two hours later, there's three dead bodies and I've got half the Arizona police department pointing guns at me.'

'That's what you call chucking a wobbler,' James grinned,

making a mental note to mention Curtis' visit to the famous child psychiatrist in Philadelphia to John or Scott as soon as he saw them. 'Do you still get depressed?'

'Not so much,' Curtis said. 'Though it gets really boring in here sometimes.'

*

James spent the evening watching Curtis' miniature TV and eating Stanley Duff's snacks. Stanley's battered brother was back from the hospital. Raymond looked like he was going to cry when he saw that Kirch had stripped everything he owned from his locker. He didn't even have a change of underwear or a pillow.

When James woke up, with his neck clamped to his bed and a cut-throat razor glinting in front of his eyes, he guessed it was Raymond Duff, but he was wrong.

'You one of us?'

James got a whiff of BO, a flash of grinning teeth and the rush of sheer terror that you get when you think you're about to feel serious pain.

'Are you one of us?' Elwood growled again.

Curtis and the other skinheads were standing around James' bed, laughing.

'I am,' James said, though the hand crushing his windpipe made it come out as a croak.

Kirch's arm reached over from the next bed and dabbed James' cheek with a wet brush.

'You look too hairy to me, Rose.'

Elwood pressed the razor against James' skin, close to the point of making a cut.

'What is this?' James gasped. 'Come on guys . . .'

'If you're one of us,' Elwood grinned, 'you gotta get rid of that faggot haircut.'

Kirch waggled a wet shaving brush in his face.

'Cut my hair,' James nodded, as Elwood let go and allowed him to sit up. 'But can't you use the battery razor I gave to Abe?'

Kirch, Curtis and the three others who'd got out of bed for the occasion laughed.

'Where's the fun in an electric razor?' Elwood giggled. 'You're not scared, are you?'

'Why would I be scared of you?' James asked, trying to act as though being woken at 3 a.m. with a psycho waving a razor under his nose was the kind of thing that didn't bother him in the slightest.

Kirch moved in with the shaving brush and sploshed warm, soapy water into James' hair. After a couple of strokes, he got fed up and drained the whole mug of sloppy mixture over James' head. James screwed up his face in pain as it streamed into his eyes.

'Better keep still,' Elwood giggled.

He placed the razor against James' forehead and swept it upwards. A soapy blond clump dropped into James' lap. Elwood hacked off hair from here and there, until James' head was a shocking mixture of bald spots, crazy tufts and the occasional bloody nick from the blade.

'Perfecto,' Elwood said, backing away like an artist admiring a painting.

The skinheads were cracking up as they sauntered back to their beds. When the others were lying down, Curtis came back with a set of battery-powered clippers.

'You want me to sort that mess out?'

James and Curtis walked to the bathroom. After James had wetted a towel and mopped the soap and blood off his head, he knelt on the tiled floor, while Curtis leaned over and finished shaving him bald.

'So your brother's definitely not coming back?' Curtis asked, as he rinsed the clipper attachment under a tap.

'With his escape record and Stanley getting his neck broken, that hack Warren told me he's put in a request for Dave to be re-categorised as a high-risk inmate. He'll be put in a single cell over on the supermax block.'

'So the escape is off?'

'It's hard without Dave,' James whispered, 'but my uncle beats the shit out of my little sister and I really want to get her out of there. The thing is, Dave could have got a job or something, but I don't see how someone our age can survive on the outside without help.'

'You know what I said about my mom? Hiding out, living under false names and stuff?'

James nodded.

'I don't know where she is right now,' Curtis said. 'But I know people who can contact her. If we busted out together, she'd be able to set you up with a new life.'

'So now *you* want to escape,' James said, trying to sound cynical, while containing the ten-metre-wide smile that wanted to break out across his face.

'I got nothing to lose,' Curtis said. 'They can't add one day to life without parole. And so what if they shoot my ass? What's worth living for in Arizona Max?'

'If I *did* let you break out with me, it's just you, me and my kid sister,' James said firmly. 'It's my show and I don't want Elwood, or any of those other lunatics muscling in.'

Curtis nodded. 'But if I can keep my mouth shut, you'll take me?'

'You can't get out of here without me and I can't make it on the outside without you,' James smiled. 'Funny how life works. It must be fate . . . or something.'

21. WEDNESDAY

FIVE DAYS LATER

James got hold of a spare bed sheet. When everyone at his end of the cell seemed to be asleep, he began cutting it into metre-long strips, using the sharpened end of his toothbrush. He ripped the cloth quietly, stopping now and then to make sure there wasn't a hack spying down from the metal gantry above his head. After he'd turned the sheet into strips, he took three pieces at a time and plaited them together for strength.

When James had finished, he put the lengths of rope in his locker and noticed that sunlight was flickering behind the blades of the ventilation fans in the cell wall. He was dreading another sweat-soaked day inside Arizona Max. But if things went to plan, this would be the last one.

*

James asked Curtis to hang back when the rest of the skinheads went on to the yard. The cell never emptied out entirely, but no one was paying attention as James pulled a strip of cardboard out of his shorts.

'It's my visit today,' James explained. 'If I can get Lauren on her own for a few seconds, without my uncle, I'll tell her to pack a bag and expect us at the house at three tomorrow morning.'

Curtis nodded. 'What's with the cardboard?'

'That's how we're getting out of here.'

'*Cardboard*,' Curtis said, looking at James like he was insane.

James stepped across to the emergency door in the middle of the cell. There were two of these sliding doors along the cell wall in between beds. They were designed to allow the PERT team to enter if the prisoners rioted and barricaded the main door, or as emergency exits in a fire.

'How *exactly* do you plan to get a solid steel door open with a piece from a Kleenex box?'

James grinned confidently. 'Watch and learn.'

He checked the gantry to make sure there wasn't a hack around, then walked to the door and went up on tiptoes. He slotted the card through the gap between the top of the door and its frame and jiggled it in and out, before tucking it back into his pocket.

'Now we wait,' James said, as he moved away and sat on the end of a bed.

'This is your great plan?' Curtis asked indignantly.

Thirty seconds later, a hack walked purposefully on to the rail. He disappeared down a flight of spiral stairs behind the door. The door slid open thirty centimetres and the hack pushed his head through the gap. He inspected the inside for signs of tampering before shutting it again.

'*What . . . ?*' Curtis gasped, as the guard walked back up the steps. 'What happened?'

'Remember I told you about that big-mouthed hack in Omaha?'

'Yeah.'

'He always moaned about the faulty doors. Every door inside Omaha State had an anti-tamper device. If someone starts fiddling, an alarm goes off on the console in the cellblock control room. They have to send a hack out to check both sides of the door and reset the alarm, but they're very sensitive. All it takes is a gust of wind, or someone hitting the door to set it off. The hack said he spent half his life wandering around cancelling false alarms.'

'And the doors here are the same?'

James nodded. '*Exactly* the same. And the thing is, the guards get so sick of the alarms, they assume every one is false.'

Curtis nodded. 'That hack didn't even look over the rail to see if someone was waiting on the other side.'

'Within a minute of taking out the guard, we can be up on the rail and tooled up with stun grenades and pepper spray.'

'And from there?'

'You've seen how few staff there are on duty at night,' James said. 'If we rip off the hacks' security passes and put on their uniform, I reckon we can bluff our way out of the front gate before the alarm goes off.'

'Definitely tonight?'

James nodded. 'As long as I get a chance to speak with my sister. Let's hit the yard.'

There'd been a knife fight between two rival gangs the previous morning. Everyone had been sent back to their cells and locked down for the rest of the day. As James and

Curtis lined up to pass through the metal detector, all the other inmates seemed tense, like something bad could flare up at any second.

As they closed on their regular spot by the chin-up bars, James spotted a kid balled up on the ground sniffling. Elwood had just slapped him around in front of a dozen laughing skinheads.

'James,' Elwood said, pointing down at the ball. 'Wanna finish him off?'

'I'm good,' James said, waving his hand in front of his face.

The victim was Mark, the friendly kid with the black eye who'd slept next to James on the first night. Mark had no relatives on the outside to pay in commissary money. This ruled out extortion, but didn't stop Elwood beating him up for fun.

'Boot him,' Elwood snarled. 'You're such a pussy, James.'

James spun quickly and kicked Mark up the arse. He knew this would amuse the crowd, without hurting his victim too badly. The skinheads roared as Mark rolled over in the dirt. James pulled down the front of his shorts.

'Now get out of here before I piss over you,' he snarled.

Mark scowled back at James, as he scrambled to his feet and limped off.

'Why'd you let him go?' Elwood asked angrily.

James shrugged. He kept trying to find ways to minimise the daily violence without appearing soft, but he knew that the more time he spent with psychos like Elwood, the more chance there was he'd end up involved in an incident where someone got badly beaten, or stabbed.

'So,' James said, desperate to change the subject. 'Is there a riot going down, or not?'

The prospect had been hotly debated in the cell overnight. Whenever there was serious violence, the hacks closed the yard and locked everyone in the cells. But locking inmates down for long stretches only fermented the anger.

'I *love* riots,' Kirch said, making a rare excursion into the world of speech.

'Yeah,' Elwood said. 'You should have seen the last one, James. There were baton rounds whizzing across this yard from every direction. *Poom, poom, poom.* I was one of the last to make it back to the cell and dudes were laid up everywhere: either stabbed, or shot up.'

Kirch looked at the sky with a smile across his face. 'Happy days,' he nodded. 'Easily worth a month of lockdown.'

James sat down in the dirt. After a week of Kirch and Elwood's bullying and bragging, he could happily have laid them out in return for five minutes' peace.

'The riot was the scariest hour of my life,' Curtis whispered, leaning into James' ear. 'I thought I was gonna die. Elwood hid under one of the shelters. He was as scared as I was.'

James smiled. 'What about Kirch?'

'Kirch really *is* a psycho. I think he loved every minute.'

'We've gotta get out of here,' James said, shaking his head. 'This place is doing my brain in.'

*

If the cellblock was put back in lockdown, visitation would be cancelled. James wouldn't get to see Lauren and the escape would be off. As the morning wore on, James got increasingly nervous. There was a fight inside the canteen when the first batch of lunches was being served. It was shut down while the mess was cleared up inside and a rumour flashed around the yard that it wouldn't reopen. A sullen crowd, most of whom had missed their main meal because of the lockdown the day before, gathered around the prefabricated building looking for trouble.

Superintendent Frey prowled on the roof, watching the commotion through binoculars. James anxiously studied his body language for any sign that the cellblock was going back into lockdown, but the canteen re-opened and the backlog of prisoners gradually got served.

When it was time, James enthusiastically walked to the reception room at the front of the cellblock. Before entering the visitors' area, he had to strip naked and put his clothes in a cardboard box. After a body search, he buttoned on a pocketless yellow overall that nobody had ever thought to wash.

The visiting room had tables for six inmates, but Lauren and a wiry FBI agent James had never seen before were the only ones in the room. James walked barefoot across the tacky floor and sat opposite them. Lauren leaned forward and gave her brother a hug.

'What happened to your head?' Lauren gasped, looking at the five-day growth of stubble.

'You hang with skinheads, you gotta look like one,' James grinned. 'If I don't get out of here soon, I might end up with a tattoo.'

'Prison tattoos are very dangerous,' the FBI man said

stiffly, in the poshest American accent James had ever heard. 'The needle penetrating the skin is unlikely to be sterile. You'd risk being contaminated with any number of infectious diseases including hepatitis and AIDS.'

'I read my briefings,' James whispered. 'I take it you're my new uncle John.'

'Theodore Monroe,' the stick man nodded as he shook James' hand, 'but everyone calls me Theo. I'm afraid John Jones was compromised when Curtis saw him in the education block. Scott Warren already works here and Marvin . . . Well, it would obviously be inappropriate to send an African American undercover pretending to be your uncle.'

James smiled. 'So are we expecting company in here?'

'Scott organised the visiting roster so that it only contained inmates who never get visitors,' Theo explained.

'Are we being bugged?'

Theo shook his head. 'There is recording equipment in this room, but they need permission from a judge to switch it on. We have to get it every time Curtis' supposed uncles turn up.'

'You know that note you passed to Scott Warren about the psychiatrist in Philadelphia?' Lauren asked excitedly. 'The FBI followed up your lead and found a picture of Jane Oxford.'

'At least we think it's her,' Theo interrupted, reaching inside his impeccably tailored suit and pulling out a blurry colour photo.

James stared at the face of an ordinary looking middle-aged woman, wearing large rectangular glasses. The boy standing at her side was clearly Curtis.

'It's a video surveillance picture from the first class check-in counter at Philadelphia International Airport, a couple of weeks before Curtis was sent to the military school. Interestingly enough, the psychiatrist Curtis visited turned out to be on the board of directors at the military school.'

James laughed. 'Curtis *said* psychiatrists are a bunch of crooks. I bet he earned a nice bonus for every poor kid he sent there.'

'The FBI have also traced multiple transactions on the credit cards Jane Oxford used to book the flights. All in all, it's a commendable piece of intelligence work. John Jones and Marvin Teller told me to pass on their heartiest congratulations.'

James couldn't imagine the phrase *heartiest congratulations* ever passing the lips of John Jones or Marvin Teller, but he got the point.

'So, does any of this actually get us anywhere?' James asked.

'Perhaps,' the FBI man said, as he swept invisible crumbs from his jacket with his spindly fingers. 'Even if your escape attempt fails, this photograph represents a significant breakthrough.'

'What about the escape?' James asked. 'We'd better still be on for tonight. I can't handle it here much longer. I was scared about what might happen to me at first. Now I'm more worried about what I might be forced into doing to someone else. Things are on a short fuse out on the yard right now.'

'There's no hold-up at our end,' Theo nodded. 'There will

be three staff on duty in your cellblock tonight. Scott Warren, of course, the female guard Amanda Voss and lastly a man named Golding, who will be working at the cellblock control console. You have to be exceedingly cautious around the control room. Golding will be within reach of an emergency alarm that can instantly deactivate every door in the prison, even for those with swipe cards.

'When you get out of the cellblock and reach the staff lounge, you're unlikely to bump into a member of staff. I'm led to believe that the conditions are rather insalubrious. It's not the kind of place where you'd want to spend time hanging around after your shift.

'Apart from Warren, the only other person who will be on duty inside the prison and who knows about the escape attempt is a man named Shorter. He works inside the central prison control room and operates the staff exit door. As you know, Dave has certain physical similarities to Scott Warren and the original plan was for him to show his face to the security camera when you passed through the main gate. Unfortunately, neither yourself nor Curtis are big enough to easily pass as an adult male, so we've brought in Shorter as an insurance policy. He's been an employee of the Arizona Prison Department for nearly forty years, and we expect the inquiry into your escape to make him the scapegoat. Shorter understands this, but the FBI has agreed to offer to pay for his early retirement, in return for cooperation.'

'So that should get us out of the front door,' James said. 'What next?'

'You meet up with Lauren, as per the plan. It is of

considerable importance that you move quickly. Arizona is sparsely populated and there are not many roads in and out of the state. You can expect police roadblocks to be set up on all the major roads near to the prison within half an hour of the escape being detected.'

'I've already tuned the car radio to a local news station,' Lauren said. 'So we'll know as soon as the alert goes out.'

'Assuming you make it away from the prison, we're then relying on Curtis to find the way back to his mother,' Theo explained. 'We recorded the conversation during Curtis' visit on Saturday and he made no mention of the escape. Do you have any idea where you'll be going?'

'I told Curtis we should go into a heavily populated area to minimise our chances of being recaptured,' James said. 'Curtis says he knows people who used to work for his mum in Los Angeles, so that's where we're heading. He didn't mention the escape to his visitors because he knows this room is bugged. Don't forget, Curtis has spent his whole life on the run. He might only be fourteen, but he probably knows more about police and FBI operations than most major criminals.'

'That's a valid point,' Theo nodded. 'So is his plan clear? Has Curtis mentioned where any of these connections live, or how they came to do business with his mother?'

'I get the impression they're bikers,' James said. 'Or ex-bikers. The idea is that we get out of Arizona as fast as we can. When we reach LA, we find a phone booth and start making calls.'

They spoke for a few more minutes about the finer points of the escape plan, before the FBI man wished

James luck and headed for the door. James gave Lauren another hug.

'Play it safe,' Lauren said. 'Don't go getting yourself killed tonight.'

22. DOORS

Scott Warren took the 2:30 a.m. count. Unlike a standing count, when inmates stood to attention at the end of their beds, this one only required Scott to lean over the gantry and count heads. He'd only wake the inmates up if he couldn't see someone.

When he was done, Scott clanked along the metal gantry to the control room. If things went as planned, the escape wouldn't be noticed until the next count was due in four hours.

Scott reached the control room at the centre of the H-shaped cellblock and tore a form off his clipboard. He handed it to the chunky figure of Golding, who sat at a three-metre-long console covered in switches, surveillance monitors and lights.

Golding stared at the sheet as Amanda Voss came towards him and handed him another.

'No escapes, boss,' the petite twenty-three-year-old grinned.

Golding picked up a telephone and called the central control room. 'Hey Keith, this is cellblock T for trouble. I'm calling in a count of two-fifty-seven inmates at two-thirty-seven in the a.m. Situation here is all normal.'

Warren rolled his chair back so he could put his feet up on the console and picked up a newspaper. As he did this, a buzzer sounded, accompanied by a flashing red light.

Golding angrily flung down his newspaper. 'Those *freakin'* doors . . . Cell T4, side entrance B. One of you go and shut that thing up.'

'I gotta take a dump,' Scott said guiltily, looking towards the toilet. 'Can you deal with it, Amanda?'

*

Good people sometimes get hurt when you're trying to catch bad ones. When the door began to slide, James' conscience tripped over the idea of laying out a girl; but the mission depended on him holding his nerve.

His fist smacked Amanda in the temple, with enough force to knock the opposite side of her head against the edge of the metal door. There's no such thing as a good head injury, but a clean shot to the thinnest part of the skull was unlikely to leave Amanda with anything more than a mild concussion and a two-day headache.

James dragged Amanda's unconscious body backwards and lowered her to the floor at the bottom of the spiral staircase.

'Come on,' James whispered anxiously to Curtis. He wanted the door closed before any other inmates spotted the opening and decided to come with them.

Curtis stepped through and slid the door shut, as James put on Amanda's ADOP baseball cap, then unbuttoned her black shirt and pulled it on. Combined with his black trainers and a pair of Curtis' black tracksuit bottoms, James could pass as a prison officer provided nobody looked too hard.

'Tie her up before she comes to,' James ordered. 'Ankles and mouth gag, then tie her hands around the stair rail. Use the constrictor knot, like I showed you.'

Curtis had a couple of James' plaited ropes slung over his shoulder. While he tied up Amanda, James swiftly ran up the spiral stairs and crept across the rail to the weapons rack. He grabbed a can of pepper spray and tucked a stun grenade into his pocket as Scott came through the door. James looked behind to make sure Curtis was still out of earshot.

'You OK?' James asked.

Scott nodded. 'Go for my nose and make it look real bloody. Be careful around Golding, he was a football player at high school. Use the handcuffs in the blue storage cupboard behind the console.'

James stepped back into a fighting stance and thrust his palm at the base of Scott's nose. Blood trickled over Scott's lips as he laid himself down on the metal floor. James ripped the safety pin from a can of pepper spray. He shot a quick blast into Scott's hair and face, then quickly crammed a piece of balled-up rag into his mouth.

'Sorry, mate,' James whispered, as he rolled Scott on to his chest and began tying his wrists.

Curtis was coming up the spiral stairs a little too noisily for James' taste. Scott went limp, as though James had knocked him out.

'Ssssshh,' James said. 'Is she well tied?'

Curtis nodded. 'Just how you showed me.'

'Did you get her ID badge and swipe card?'

'Course,' Curtis whispered, grinning as he looked down over the rail. 'I never thought I'd see the view from up here.'

James unhooked an electric shock device from Scott's belt and stripped everything out of his pockets, including his keys and wallet, before shuffling down to tie his ankles. He threw Curtis the bunch of keys.

'One of those works the gun locker,' James explained.

Curtis opened the clear plastic front of the cabinet, while James bent Scott's legs up and began tying the bindings on his wrists to the bindings on his ankles.

Curtis took one of the large baton-round guns. 'Looks complicated,' he said.

'Help me move him, then I'll show you.'

They pushed Scott's body to the inside of the gantry, so that the inmates below couldn't see him. James grabbed a small cylinder of compressed gas from the locker and snatched the gun from Curtis.

'I watched the hacks do this the other day,' James explained. 'Screw the gas cylinder on the top of the gun, like so. Turn the valve, then you break her open and . . . Give us a baton round.'

Curtis handed James one of the fat plastic slugs. James slid it into the barrel, closed the gun and handed it to Curtis.

'Only fire if we have to,' James said. 'You know how noisy they are.'

Curtis shoved more pepper spray, stun grenades and rounds for the baton guns into his pockets while James armed another gun for himself.

James opened the door at the end of the gantry. The short

corridor led to the control room. James kept his back to the wall as they crept forward with their guns poised.

When James reached the end, he poked his head into the control room and eyeballed Golding; who sat with his feet on the console reading the sports page. It was eerily silent, apart from the hum of the air conditioning.

'We've got to distract him from the console or he'll hit the alarm,' James whispered.

Curtis nodded, as James crouched down and pulled out one of Scott's coins. He rolled the coin out into the room. Golding heard it drop in the middle of the floor and looked over the top of his newspaper.

'You've dropped a quarter down here, Scott,' Golding said. He stared for a few seconds, before shrugging and going back to his newspaper.

James looked at Curtis, shaking his head with frustration. He rolled another coin. This time Golding looked put out. Too lazy to stand up, he slapped his newspaper down and wheeled his chair backwards towards the coins.

'What's going on there, Scottie? You got a hole in your pocket or something?'

As Golding spun his chair around to look down the corridor, James and Curtis both fired. The rounds hit Golding in the chest and stomach. His chair shot backwards, before tipping over. The fat man roared as he blasted the chair out of his way with a powerful kick and rolled over, struggling to stand up.

James' ears were whistling from the gun blast as he ran towards Golding and drenched his face in pepper spray.

'See what we do when we catch you,' Golding gasped, as

he slumped blindly back to the floor, trying to rub the spray out of his eyes. 'Scott . . . Amanda . . . Where the hell are you?'

'They won't be along any time soon,' Curtis gloated.

'When we get you two in the hole, I'm gonna come in after you and bust every bone in your bodies.'

Golding had plenty of fight in him and James didn't fancy a tussle with somebody so heavy. He pushed another plastic round into the gun and held it menacingly in Golding's face. Although classed as a non-lethal weapon, the baton round was deadly if fired into a vulnerable area from close range.

'Hands in the air, fat boy,' James shouted ferociously.

When the muzzle touched his face, Golding put his arms up and allowed Curtis to knot them together. After this, he let Curtis stuff a piece of cloth in his mouth and tie a gag over it. Meanwhile, James located the rack of handcuffs Scott had told him about.

It took both boys to drag Golding a few metres across the polished floor towards the staircase leading down to the reception room. James cuffed Golding's hands around the top stair rail. Curtis cruelly stepped on the bracelet, so it closed down a couple of extra notches.

'Remember when you put them on me?' Curtis snarled. 'You like them nice and tight, don't you, Golding?'

Golding screamed curses into his gag as the boys ran back to grab their guns. James noticed Golding's backpack under the console. He tossed out a baseball magazine and sandwich box and stuffed the pack with baton rounds, pepper spray and stun grenades before slinging it over his back.

Curtis found a lightweight black jacket with the Arizona

Prisons Department logo on, which had belonged to Amanda Voss. He zipped it over his black T-shirt and found that it fitted OK.

The boys sprinted downstairs, emerging through an unsecured door into the reception room on the ground floor. James jogged towards the exit door and swiped Amanda's card through the lock. He smiled with relief when it clicked.

'Keep calm,' James said, as they stepped out into fresh air. 'Remember, it looks suspicious if we run.'

James swiped the card again and they passed through a wire gate into the main prison compound. The tarmac road went arrow-straight, all the way down to the exit. The only light came from a few lamps around the wire fences of the cellblocks and the glowing watchtowers around the distant perimeter.

A passing refuse cart and a wave from a hack taking a cigarette break was the only excitement during the eight-minute walk towards the sally port, but James tortured himself with images of sirens, gunfire and the savage beating he'd undoubtedly take if the hacks recaptured him.

A hundred metres shy of the vehicle gates, there was a giant signpost ordering everyone to follow a colour-coded line painted on the asphalt: red for inmates under transportation, yellow for visitors and green for staff. The area beyond the sign was floodlit and CCTV cameras were perched every place you looked.

Curtis' voice was quaking. 'We're never gonna pass through this.'

'Act normal,' James whispered. 'We're dressed like staff,

we have swipe cards. Unless the emergency siren goes off, there's no reason for anyone to look at us too hard.'

The green line ended at the door of a small metal shed marked *Staff Only*. James peeked through a window into a small room with a line of vending machines. A miserable looking hack sat on a plastic chair drinking from a tiny cup. James swiped his card in the entrance door, went up two steps and cautiously poked his head into a narrow corridor that smelled of floor polish.

'Looks sweet,' James said.

They stepped inside, passing by the frosted glass entrance of the room with the vending machines, then dashing along the corridor towards the staff exit.

James swiped Amanda's card through the lock on the door. A man's voice came out of a loudspeaker. James hoped it was the friendly Mr Shorter in the central control room, but he had no way of telling.

'Look up at the camera, state your name and staff ID.'

'Voss, Amanda, Y465,' James said, trying his best to sound like a girl.

'Who's your buddy?' the loudspeaker asked.

Curtis looked uncertainly up at the camera. 'Warren, Scott, KT318.'

'Hey Scottie, you don't sound so good tonight. You got flu or something?'

'Yeah,' Curtis said uncertainly.

'Sorry to hear that, man. You go home and catch yourself a good rest.'

The door buzzed to indicate that it had been unlocked. James and Curtis passed through and walked along a wire-enclosed path. They stood behind a red *Wait* sign, while a chunky door built into the armour-plated wall of the sally port rumbled backwards. Once it was fully open, the boys stepped into a tunnel.

When the door at their backs closed fully, a green bulb began pulsing above the door at the opposite end. James realised there was a slot for a swipe card. He couldn't remember if he was supposed to get interviewed a second time and was relieved when the metal door began rumbling.

As they stepped out of the secure compound, James spotted the sign pointing towards the staff car park and headed off briskly. Curtis was so shocked that he could barely open his mouth.

'Unbelievable,' Curtis mumbled. 'Unbeeeeelievable. You're a genius, James.'

'Don't count your chickens,' James said, as they strode along a paved path through the night air. 'This is only the beginning.'

23. CARS

James couldn't risk hanging out in the car park too long, but there were more than fifty parked vehicles and he couldn't walk straight up to Scott's without Curtis wondering how he knew which one it was. James aimed the plipper at every car, until he got a blip and a set of flashing lights from a Honda Civic in the next row across.

As they cut between two cars, a battered pickup rolled over a speed bump into the car park. The boys instinctively ducked as the truck pulled in a few spaces along from the Civic. The driver swung out his legs and paused on the edge of his seat to light a cigarette. James recognised the face as it glimmered in the match light.

'Frey,' Curtis whispered anxiously.

James had read Superintendent Frey's personnel file. It said he was a hard worker who thought of cellblock T as his personal property, but nobody had expected him to turn up three hours before a shift. This was bad news. James had to think fast.

Frey was wearing a football shirt and jeans, but even allowing time for him to change into uniform, maybe drink a coffee in the staff lounge and walk up to block T, he'd still be discovering the tied-up hacks and raising the alarm within half an hour.

Taking Frey out was the obvious option, but the boys were on open ground and there were CCTV cameras everywhere. James decided to let Frey go unmolested. He was far from certain it was the right decision, but he remembered how the PERT team had treated Dave and he didn't want Golding's prediction of them ending up in a dark cell getting a beating to come true. The further away from the prison they were if they got caught, the greater the chance that John Jones and the FBI team would be able to pull James out before the hacks got hold of him.

Once Frey had locked his truck and headed off down the cactus-lined path towards the staff entrance, they ran across to the little Civic and jumped inside. It was a flash model: racing seats, ten-spoke alloys and a beefy engine. James pulled a red seatbelt across his waist and hit the start button. He remembered what had happened the last time he'd driven a car, but there was too much adrenalin flowing for him get hung up over it. He had to get on with the job.

James kept the speed down on the road leading out of the prison, but once he hit the interstate he couldn't hang about. The sporty little car had a firm suspension and the steering felt sharp. James got a sense of invincibility as he dodged between the three lanes of traffic.

The twelve-mile ride to the dirt road turnoff took less than ten minutes. A Ford Explorer with bull bars on the front was parked up, with its headlamps switched on, a few hundred metres past the junction.

'Grab the weapons,' James said to Curtis, as he pulled the Honda up alongside the Ford and flung open his door.

Lauren had left the engine of the four-wheel-drive Ford running and was already belted into the front passenger seat. James climbed into the driver's seat and hit the gas as soon as Curtis slammed the door behind him.

'You got the car up here OK?' James asked Lauren, as he pulled on to the dirt road.

'Uncle John didn't wake up,' Lauren nodded. 'I got his road maps and worked out the route to Los Angeles.' She looked behind. 'And you must be Curtis.'

'Hey,' Curtis smiled. 'Good to meet you Lauren. Where'd you learn how to drive?'

'Me and Dave taught her,' James explained. 'We took her with us a couple of times when we were out on the rampage.'

'I'm a bit short to reach the pedals,' Lauren added. 'But there's hardly any traffic on the road up from our house.'

'What you got in the backpack over there?' Curtis asked.

'Clothes, money, toiletries,' Lauren explained. 'I even managed to sneak into the bedroom and get John's forty-four.'

'We've got a proper gun?' Curtis asked. 'Where is it?'

Curtis didn't need an answer; he spotted the huge revolver on the armrest between the two front seats.

The 4×4 seemed like it was on sleeping pills after driving the nippy little Honda. James pressed the gas pedal as they hit the interstate and it felt like nothing happened at all.

'Forty-four magnum,' Curtis grinned as he picked up the gun. 'Dirty Harry special. You can blow a guy in half with one of these.'

Lauren looked out the window as the donut place whizzed by. 'James you *tit*, we're going the wrong way.'

'What?' James gasped.

'You turned the wrong way when we pulled on to the interstate.'

'Arse.'

There was a metal barrier between the lanes. James started looking for a junction where he could pull off and turn around.

'Didn't you tune that radio?' James asked.

'Oh, yeah,' Lauren said, reaching forward and flicking it on.

'We saw the superintendent of our cellblock in the prison car park,' James explained. 'We're not going to get anything like the four hours we'd hoped for. We'll be lucky if we get another twenty minutes before the police are on our tail.'

James spotted a break in the barrier and swung the tall car into a wide arc, across a strip of scrub in the middle of the road and into the opposite lane. A sedan car blasted its horn, as the driver slammed her brakes to avoid shunting them up the back.

'Whoops,' James said, as he floored the gas pedal and began slowly picking up speed. 'So how far is it to the border with California?'

'Just under sixty miles,' Lauren said. 'Los Angeles is two hundred miles further than that. It's a five-hour journey if we don't stop.'

'We'll have to stop at least once, for gas.'

Traffic was light and the unlit road almost straight. When James checked the speedometer he was doing eighty miles an hour, which was over the limit, but in line with what most of the other traffic was doing at this time of night. If he drove any faster, he'd look conspicuous.

The radio station was holding a phone-in and the topics were *Are there alien beings walking among us?* and *Who is the greatest popular musician of all time?* As far as James could work out, most of the people who rang in believed that the answer to both questions was Elvis Presley.

The digital clock on the dashboard said 03:43 when the DJ cut off a caller and got seriously excited.

'. . . *We're picking up breaking news of an escape from Arizona Max. Two male escapees, both aged fourteen. That's one four, folks, not four zero . . . One prison officer is believed to have died during the escape. Arizona police are setting up roadblocks at strategic locations. The escapees are described as white skinheads, going by the names of James Rose and Curtis Oxford. Both are convicted murderers and police say that you should treat the boys with the same degree of caution as you would if you spotted a dangerous adult offender . . . That's red-hot news, listeners, stay tuned, because were gonna be keeping you up to date on this all night long . . .*'

'You *killed* someone,' Lauren gasped.

Scott Warren's faked death had always been part of the plan, but they had to act surprised in front of Curtis.

'We didn't kill nobody,' Curtis said.

'One of the hacks must have had a heart attack or something,' James said.

'This is *so* bad,' Curtis said. 'If you kill a hack, you're done for. They stick you in solitary and the hacks make your life hell: spitting in your food, playing loud music right outside your cell until it drives you nuts . . .'

'Then we'd better not get caught,' James said.

'Oh god,' Curtis said, shaking his head and sobbing.

'What do you want me to do,' James shouted bitterly. 'Go back and kiss him better?'

'What if there's a roadblock?' Curtis asked. 'We've only got one proper gun and they'll shoot us to pieces if we try to ram through.'

'Just stay cool and give me a chance to think,' James said. 'Lauren, how far are we from the California border?'

Lauren looked at the map spread out across her legs. 'Thirty-five miles or so.'

'They can have roadblocks in California too, you know,' Curtis said.

'Of course,' James said. 'But there can't be many cops out here in the desert and they don't know what way we're going. The further out you get, the more roads they'd need to block, so if we hit a roadblock I'd bet on it being sooner rather than later.'

James watched the lines of cat's eyes whiz by for a few more minutes. A woman called the radio phone-in and said that the escapees should get the death penalty, even though they were only fourteen. The follow-up callers all agreed.

'. . . OK folks. A little more news on the jailbreak. Police are now looking for a silver Honda Civic IS. Apparently that's a distinctive Jap box with fancy wheels and a little wing over the back window . . .'

James smiled. 'We're one step ahead of 'em.'

'The cops will check out your uncle's house pretty soon,' Curtis said. 'They'll find this car is missing.'

'But it buys us some time,' James said.

'Up ahead,' Lauren squealed.

Sitting on the right gave Lauren half a second's advantage in spotting the flashing blue lights blocking the road.

Roadblocks are usually positioned after bends, so that approaching traffic doesn't get a chance to pull off, although they have to leave stopping room or cars would smash into them. There was a queue of about a dozen cars, passing through a single lane that had been created by parking two cop cars with their lights flashing across the other two lanes of the interstate. Every car was being stopped while an officer inspected the passengers inside with a flashlight.

James pulled into the side of the road and slammed to a halt. He looked back over his shoulder. All four tyres screeched as he did a backwards U-turn through the traffic. If the cops hadn't seen this manoeuvre, they certainly heard the horns of two approaching cars blasting as they swung out of his way. One car sideswiped the metal barrier in the centre of the road, making a shower of orange sparks as it juddered to a halt.

'Dammit,' James shouted, as he pushed the stick back into drive and rammed the gas pedal, heading into the oncoming traffic.

The police cars in the roadblock sounded their sirens and began moving towards them, as James noticed a break in the metal barrier and ploughed across the central reservation on to the correct side of the road.

'Lauren,' James said anxiously. 'Where's that backpack I brought with me?'

'Down by my feet,' Lauren said.

'Take it, it's full of weapons. They're not looking for you, so soon as we stop I want you to jump out.'

Lauren nodded. 'I'll see what I can do.'

'You can't *stop*,' Curtis screamed. 'We've gotta get out of here. If they catch us now that hack's dead, our lives won't be worth shit.'

'I got you this far,' James shouted back angrily. 'Just *calm* down.'

'Screw you,' Curtis hissed, furiously grabbing the magnum off the armrest as the car pulled up in the sand at the side of the road.

Lauren dived out with the backpack and rolled down a modest slope into some scrub. Both cop cars pulled up, one in front and one behind the 4×4. A cop jumped out of each car with their gun pulled: one male, one female.

'There's no way I'm going back to prison,' Curtis yelled.

The man stood behind in a covering position, while the lady cop jogged through the headlight beams towards the big Ford with her handgun pointing.

'Turn off the engine and put your hands on the steering wheel,' the lady cop shouted.

James did as he was told, but he heard Curtis cocking the gun. The cop didn't see Curtis until she got in close because of the tinted windows.

'There's no need for that,' the cop said.

James assumed Curtis had the magnum pointing at the cop, but he glanced in the driver's mirror and realised Curtis was pointing it at himself.

'Curtis, *don't*,' James shouted.

James heard the gun click.

A white light and a deafening blast flashed as a stun grenade exploded in the wheel hub of the front police car, ripping apart the tyre. Four more grenades exploded along the roadside, followed by a final blast that took out a tyre on the cop car at the rear.

James, Curtis and the two cops were temporarily deafened and blinded by the pulses. A few passing drivers had wobbly moments, but the traffic was mercifully light and the only harm done was a couple of tyre squeals and a car almost swerving off into the desert.

Lauren had buried her face in the sand after laying the last grenade. She counted the explosions with her fingers plugged tightly in her ears. After the sixth blast, she jumped up and ran towards the male cop. Before he regained his sight, Lauren gave him a 90,000-volt nip with Scott's electric stun gun.

He collapsed in a shuddering heap, where he would remain paralysed for the next couple of minutes. Lauren snatched the gun from the cop's limp hand and fired it harmlessly into the air above the Ford. The lady cop had regained enough hearing to duck, as Lauren closed her down and zapped her with the stun gun.

Lauren dropped the ammunition clips out of the police pistols and hurled the guns into the desert, then opened the driver's door next to her brother.

'James,' Lauren shouted.

James could barely hear Lauren's voice over the high-pitched whistling in his ears, but the white smears in front of his eyes were starting to clear.

'How many stun grenades was that?' James asked.

'All of them,' Lauren grinned, as she clambered over her brother's legs and back into the passenger seat. 'Can you see to drive?'

'It's getting better,' James said, as he reached forward and turned the key in the steering column to restart the engine.

James rubbed his eyes, while Lauren looked back at Curtis. He was lying across the back seat with a tear running down his face.

'What the hell just happened?' Curtis asked, staring at the end of the gun.

'I'm not keen on guns,' Lauren explained. 'I didn't load the magnum because I didn't want anyone getting shot. It's for fright value only.'

'You're nuts,' Curtis screamed. 'The cops keep bullets in *their* guns you know, little girl.'

'Only so idiots like you can shoot themselves,' Lauren screamed back.

'I wish I was *dead*,' Curtis whined.

'Will you two *shut* up,' James said anxiously. 'I'm trying to concentrate.'

He waited for a gap in the traffic, before manoeuvring out between the two disabled police cars and pulling through the gap in the metal barrier, on to the side of the road that headed towards California.

As James put his foot on the gas, the steering wheel shuddered violently out of his hands. He nudged the pedal more gently and the car picked up a little speed.

'What's wrong?' Lauren asked.

'No idea,' James said, as he fought to keep the car going

straight. 'But I did hear something go crunch the last time we passed over the barrier.'

They were doing less than thirty miles an hour and a truck was closing up behind at double that speed. The driver blasted his horn as he swung into the middle lane to overtake. James tried giving the accelerator another dab. The steering wheel almost ripped his arm off as the car veered dangerously towards the side of the passing truck.

'It's OK when it's slow, but I can't put any power down.'

'What are we gonna do?' Lauren asked.

'God knows,' James said, shaking his head. 'We're certainly not gonna get anywhere near Los Angeles in this box of bolts.'

24. TRUNK

The interstate ran through open desert where their abandoned car would rapidly be spotted, but every few miles there was a cluster of outlets: drug stores, diners, fast-food joints; and at this time of the morning they were all closed. James pulled off at the first batch he came to, arms aching from his battle with the steering wheel.

He flipped off the headlamps, put the car in neutral and coasted into the empty parking lot of an ice-cream store, navigating by the light from a giant pink sundae dangling over the highway. He pulled around to the back of the store, stopped beside a row of dumpsters and flipped on the vanity light above his head.

James glanced back at Curtis. He kept pulling the trigger of the empty revolver and laughing, but at the same time he had tears pouring down his face.

'You think one day I might get a gun that works when I try and blow my brains out?'

James was shocked by the way Curtis had turned into an emotional wreck. It looked pathetic, but was actually scary. For the first time, James truly felt the presence of a personality that could murder three complete strangers after a minor bust-up with a teacher.

'So where are we exactly?' James asked, leaning over Lauren's lap.

'If I've followed the map right, the interstate goes on for a couple more miles before it passes by a small town called Nix.'

'So, that's where we'll go,' James said. 'The cops don't know we've had car trouble. As long as nobody discovers this car, we should have an hour or two before anybody comes looking.'

'What's the plan when we get there?' Lauren asked.

James shrugged. 'Either we find some place where we can hole up until they take down the roadblocks, or we steal a car and try to make it through. We'll have to play it by ear based on what we find.'

Lauren folded the map, while James walked around to the trunk and took out the backpack containing their money and essentials. Curtis was still slumped over the rear seat. James opened up the door beside him.

'Come on,' James said stiffly.

'What's the point?' Curtis sobbed. 'I never should have listened to you. I was being looked after inside.'

James had to get Curtis in shape and there wasn't time for persuasion. He reached in and grabbed Curtis out of the car by the scruff of his jacket. Although the two boys were about the same size, James was fitter and much stronger.

'You listen,' James snarled, as he thumped Curtis' back against the outside of a car. 'You *asked* to come with me and you knew it would be dangerous. It's too late to change your mind now.'

Curtis stared into space as though James wasn't even there.

'We're gonna walk into town and get our hands on another car. Then we're gonna get to LA and you're going to contact your mum, exactly like we planned.'

Curtis didn't reply until James bunched a fist. 'OK,' Curtis sniffed reluctantly.

'We got this far,' James said, changing his voice from mean to friendly. 'We all need each other and we can still pull this off if we keep our heads.'

Curtis looked like he wanted to believe James but didn't. It was the look you get off a scared kid when you're trying to convince them that there aren't monsters under the bed.

Lauren had the pack with the weapons over her back, ready to move off. She caught a glimpse of herself in the window of the car and was surprised by the tangled hair and sandy clothes looking back. She could hardly believe she'd just taken out two cops. It had been the wildest night of her life, but she felt oddly calm, as though her brain couldn't believe that all this was for real.

She got a shock as she snapped back to reality and looked up at the boys. 'You better lose the clothes,' she said sharply.

James realised he was still wearing Amanda Voss' black prison-issue shirt. As he unbuttoned it, he was relieved to see Curtis removing his jacket without any prompting. Hopefully he was settling down.

James hooked the backpack of clothes and stuff over his shoulder and started walking briskly towards the interstate, with Lauren at his side.

'Do you think we've still got a chance?' Lauren whispered quickly, before Curtis overheard.

James shrugged. 'The plan was based on us being in California before the alert went up. We're probably screwed, but I'm not giving up until we're forced to . . . Whatever you do, don't let suicide boy get his hands on another gun.'

Curtis jogged up beside them. 'What are you two whispering about?'

'You,' James said bluntly. 'Are you back in the human race now?'

'I'm really sorry,' Curtis said. 'But there's no way I'm going back to prison.'

'Think positive,' James said. 'This time tomorrow, you could be back with your mum.'

A police car flashed by as they walked. A minute later they dived into the scrub when a whole row sped past. The three kids had done less than a third of the walk to Nix when they reached a line of broken wire and wooden posts that might have been considered a fence about a decade earlier.

'Trailer trash,' Curtis spat, as they stared into a gloomy field of the outsized aluminium caravans Americans call trailer homes.

Lauren looked at James. 'Reckon we can pinch a car from here?'

'Do you know how to steal cars?' Curtis asked.

'I can hotwire the old ones,' James explained. 'But every recent car has a security chip in the ignition key. You need special tools to get those going.'

'You don't find many rich people in trailer homes,' Curtis

said. 'So this is where it's at if you're looking for scrap metal.'

'We want something that'll make it to Los Angles, though,' Lauren reminded them.

They cut along the wire fence, heading away from the interstate, and ducked through one of the gaps. There were a few trailers in a cluster near the entrance, but there was too much risk of being spotted around there. Lauren took the lead, crunching her way towards a lonely trailer at the rear of the park, with only a burned-out shell a couple of berths along for company.

There was a lamp on inside the trailer and a hum from the air conditioning unit on the roof. James crept up to a Dodge sedan parked alongside and peered through the driver's side window. Although the car was shabby, it had an airbag in the steering wheel and a CD player: both indications that it was too modern to be started by short-circuiting the ignition.

'No chance,' James whispered, as he looked back over his shoulder. 'They're probably asleep in there. I suppose I could try sneaking inside and grabbing the key.'

As James said this, he heard the aluminium door of the trailer crash open, followed by the unmistakable sound of a double-barrelled shotgun being pumped. He spun around in time to find the end waving under his nose.

'So *you're* the brats that keep messing with my car,' the woman shouted. 'Where you from? I've never seen you round here.'

She only looked about twenty, with long brown hair, wearing mules and a nightshirt.

'I don't want trouble,' James shouted, raising his hands in the air. 'We're out of here, don't worry.'

'Oh, you think you're just walking away, do you?' the woman asked. 'It cost me two hundred bucks when you slashed my tyres. You're coming inside and I'm callin' the cops.'

'We've never been here before,' James said. 'We're—'

The woman tutted. 'Don't feed me your lies, kid . . . You're lucky it's me that caught you. Some of the guys in the trailers down the front are so sick of you kids busting up our cars, they'd have busted *you* up rather than calling the law.'

Lauren crept forward and sobbed theatrically. 'Please don't shoot my brother.'

The woman looked confused as Lauren moved another step closer. She backed up to the door of the trailer.

'Don't you come no closer, girl.'

'Pleeeeeease,' Lauren sobbed.

'*Listen*,' the woman said, anxiously shifting her gun towards Lauren.

James could tell from the woman's expression that she didn't have the heart to shoot anyone, least of all a ten-year-old girl. He ducked under the gun and grabbed the muzzle, while Lauren scrambled to safety behind the car. James forced the gun around so that it was parallel with the woman's chest and used it to pin her back against the side of the trailer.

'Let it go,' James said, grabbing the woman's skinny wrist and peeling her hand off the stock.

The woman sobbed as James took control of the gun. 'Please don't hurt my baby.'

'Get inside,' James snarled.

The woman walked up two metal steps and into the trailer.

'Is there anyone else in here?' James asked, as he flipped a light switch.

'Just my daughter.'

Lauren and Curtis followed them inside and quickly pulled up the door.

'Lauren,' James said. 'Find a radio and tune it to that station: we need to know what the cops are doing.'

The inside of the trailer was well worn, but clean, with little kids' toys scattered everywhere. There was a sofa on one side, a row of kitchen cabinets opposite and a three-year-old asleep on a small mattress by the window.

'Sit on the sofa,' James ordered.

Lauren found a radio and switched it on. James realised that the gun was terrifying the poor woman. He broke the barrel open and tipped the cartridges out on to the carpet.

'I'm not gonna hurt you, but we do need your help,' James said. 'What's your name?'

'Paula.'

'Paula,' James said, 'the three of us are in a spot. We're on the run and our car died on us.'

'On the run?'

'From the cops. Me and Curtis here just busted out of Arizona Max.'

Paula buried her head in her hands and took a deep breath as the radio confirmed James' story:

'. . . *Two police officers were seriously assaulted at a roadblock six miles outside the town of Nix. Police say the two teenage killers are now heading for California along Route Sixty-three. They are* believed to be travelling in a blue Ford Explorer SUV and armed with guns and explosives.

'One of the escapees, James Rose, has at least one previous escape attempt under his belt and the police are warning everyone to be ultra-cautious around these individuals . . . I sure hope we don't lose any more law-enforcement officers out there tonight, folks. Remember to keep them in your prayers and stay tuned to Western Arizona's number one station for news and talk . . .'

Lauren went to the fridge and passed out cans of soft drinks.

'Are we staying or going?' Curtis asked, as he sat on a kitchen chair drinking from his can.

'Give me a minute to think,' James said.

He was feeling the pressure. On James' previous missions, he'd always had mission controllers or older agents close by. This time it was down to him to outsmart the entire Arizona police department.

James had an idea. He looked at Paula. 'How big's the trunk of your car?'

'I don't know,' Paula said. 'It's a normal trunk . . .'

'Could you fit someone in it?'

'I guess. It's pretty roomy when you take all my junk out.'

'What are you thinking?' Lauren asked.

'I don't think we can stick around here,' James said.

Lauren nodded. 'When the cops find that car, this trailer park is the first place they'll come knocking, but there are bound to be roadblocks in our way somewhere between here and California.'

'That's why either me or Curtis has to go in the trunk,'

James said. 'Paula can drive, with one of us in the front and one in the back next to the baby.'

'That's not a bad plan, bro',' Lauren nodded, as she realised it made sense. 'We'd look like a family outing. The cops might just fall for it.'

'Or they might look in the trunk and bust us,' Curtis said.

Paula looked completely stressed out. 'You want *me* to drive you past the police roadblocks?'

'And on to Los Angeles.'

Paula rubbed her eye. 'Assisting an escape, you know that's serious jail time?'

'Please, Paula,' Lauren grovelled. 'If my brother gets caught, he'll go back to prison for the rest of his life.'

'And what if the cops start shooting at us? What if my daughter gets hurt?'

'Why are we asking her permission?' Curtis said. 'Stick the bloody shotgun in her back and make her do what she's told.'

'Because . . .' James said, wrestling with the uncomfortable fact that Curtis had suggested the course of action that most desperate fugitives really would have taken.

'What else *can* we do?' Curtis asked. 'If we leave her here we've got to tie her and the brat up so they don't snitch.'

James hadn't planned for any strangers to get tangled up in the escape, especially not taken hostage. He had three options and none of them were nice: tie Paula up and steal her car, make Paula drive them, or restrain Curtis and call John Jones to say that he'd decided to abandon the mission.

'Listen,' James said, looking at Paula. 'I don't want to go sticking a gun in your back, but if the cops get hold of Curtis and me, we're dead meat. Once we get to LA, you can go to the cops and say we forced you to drive us. You won't get punished . . . Hell, you'll probably make few bucks selling your story to the newspapers.'

'Either that or you tie us up?' Paula said, nervously rocking her legs up and down.

James noticed a gaudy pink and white dress hanging on the door by the toilet.

'You work in that ice-cream place down the road?' James asked, deliberately ignoring Paula's question. 'How much does that pay?'

'Six bucks an hour.'

'Lauren,' James said. 'You grabbed John's savings, didn't you? What have we got?'

Lauren nodded. 'There's about four thousand bucks in the large backpack.'

'I'll give you half our money if you drive us,' James said. 'Think of all the ice cream you'd have to shovel to earn two thousand buckaroos. A thousand stays here in the trailer. You'll get the other half in LA.'

Curtis was shaking his head. 'Why are we doing this?' he sneered. 'Elwood kept saying you were a pussy.'

James angrily stepped up to Curtis and faced him off. 'What use is Paula if she freaks out the second a cop shines a flashlight in her face? If I'd listened to you, we'd have already ended up getting shot to pieces after some stupid car chase.'

Lauren sat beside Paula on the couch and did a big sniffle. 'Could you please help us?' she begged. 'My uncle beats me up so bad . . . *Please* don't make me go back to him.'

Paula's expression altered completely when she heard this. She looked towards Lauren and smiled gently. 'My step-dad knocked me into the hospital when I was about your age.'

'You know how it feels then,' Lauren sniffed, trowelling on the waterworks and feeling guilty about the way she was manipulating Paula.

Paula reluctantly looked up at James, who was standing over her. 'I got problems, and two thousand bucks can fix most of 'em.'

25. LUCK

Curtis volunteered to ride in the trunk. James couldn't predict his mood: one minute Curtis was bright and cooperative, the next he was suicidal. Kids who haven't been through CHERUB-style training usually have difficulty handling dangerous situations, but Curtis didn't seem up to any kind of stress and James was getting worried. If they made it to Los Angeles, they'd be relying on him to keep his head together and make contact with associates of his mother.

It was 4:30 a.m. when they hit a big roadblock, a mile shy of the border with California. Five police cars blocked the left-hand lanes and a long snake of rear lights merged slowly into the single remaining lane. More police cars were parked on the opposite side of the road, with pursuit drivers ready to give chase and a helicopter circling overhead. James knew the chopper would pack a heat-sensitive camera, able to detect anyone who tried to bail out of a car and cut through the desert.

Considering what they were putting her through, Paula was keeping her head together. Lauren sat next to her in the front, pretending to sleep. James was in the back with a hoodie pulled over his skinhead and Paula's three-year-old daughter, Holly, was dead to the world in the child seat next to him.

It took a quarter of an hour to crawl to the front of the queue. Every car got a cursory glance, as cops shone a torch inside and fired a couple of quick questions at the driver. Most cars were waved on, but any that looked suspicious were told to pull into a second line for a detailed inspection. This roadside check involved everyone getting out of the car and having their ID run through the police computer, while the inside of the car was thoroughly searched.

James knew it would all be over if they got picked for inspection. With Paula behind the wheel and thirty well-armed cops in the vicinity, any attempt to escape would be short and bloody.

Paula opened her window as she rolled up alongside a cop.

'Licence, registration, ma'am.'

The cop glanced at the documents, while another walked around the car shining a flashlight inside.

'Are these your children?'

'The little girl in the back is my daughter. These two are my brother and sister.'

The other cop knocked on the window beside James' head. 'Let's have a look at you, son.'

James rolled down the window and got a blast of the flashlight in his face.

'How old are you?' the cop asked.

'Thirteen,' James said.

'Would you pull that hood down for me?'

James' heart banged as he slid the hoodie down, revealing the half centimetre of bristles on his head.

The cop looked at his colleague. 'Got a blond skinhead here; about the right age too.'

The other cop leaned in beside Paula. 'I'm sorry, Miss, but I'm gonna have to ask you to join that queue over to your left for an inspection.'

James silently mouthed a string of curses. He just hoped John found a way to pull him out before he got hauled back to Arizona Max. Paula rolled forward a single car-length to join the tail of the inspection line. Lauren glanced over her shoulder at James with a resigned look.

'We gave it our best shot,' James shrugged. 'I'm sorry we put you through this for nothing, Paula. Tell the cops we threatened to hurt Holly if you didn't help us.'

'How much extra time will they give you for escaping?' Paula asked, sounding as if she genuinely cared.

'Enough,' James said. 'Five, ten years, maybe.'

'You don't seem like no criminal,' Paula said sympathetically. 'At least, I've known a few and you seem far too nice a guy to have gotten yourself in so much trouble.'

All their heads snapped around as a cop thumped on the metal roof above them. The next car in line had been ordered to pull over, but the inspection queue hadn't moved up and there wasn't room for it to join without blocking the traffic that was being waved through.

Paula reopened her window as the cop crouched down beside the car. 'We got too many cars backed up here,' he explained. 'I'm gonna let you guys pass through. You seem pretty harmless to me.'

'I've never been called harmless before,' Paula grinned sweetly, 'but I'll settle for it if it gets me to LA before the little lady in the back wakes up.'

'You have a safe journey, now,' the cop smiled, as Paula backed up, making enough space to pull out of the queue.

With the traffic being filtered through one car at a time, the three lanes heading towards California were deserted.

Lauren looked back at James and gasped. 'That was *too* close.'

James grinned. '*Way* too close.'

*

They pulled up at a McDonalds fifty miles into California. Lauren went inside and bought some breakfast. James checked no one was around, before letting Curtis out of the trunk. Once he'd walked the cramp out of his legs, Curtis faced the sunrise over the desert and stretched out his arms.

'Beautiful,' he said, turning around and slapping James on the back as he pulled him into a hug. 'You were *so* cool, man. I'm sorry I messed up last night . . . When my head goes dark like that, I act like a total dick.'

'Glad Lauren didn't put bullets in the magnum now?'

Curtis smirked. 'Your sister must be my guardian angel, or something.'

Lauren came around the side of the restaurant holding a cardboard tray of drinks and two brown paper bags stuffed with food. Curtis snatched one of the bags and took out a muffin.

'Double sausage and egg,' Curtis said, tearing out a massive bite. 'I love these, man. It's been a year since I had one of these. *Mmm* . . . This is *sooooooo* good.'

James left Curtis to eulogise over his McMuffin and leaned in the back of the car to speak with Paula. Holly had woken up grumpy and Paula sat next to her daughter, trying to persuade her to eat something.

'You did us a big favour back there,' James said. 'I owe you one.'

'You *owe* me a thousand,' Paula said, only half joking.

James nodded. 'As soon as we get to LA; you've got my word on that.'

'I don't think I've ever had a thousand dollars in one go,' Paula said. 'When I was a little girl, I always wanted to go to Disneyland and stay in a real hotel, but we were as poor as dirt. When I drop you guys off, I'm gonna drive Holly up there. It's only thirty miles.'

'Sounds fun,' James smiled, 'but it's better if you call the cops first. You don't want to get in trouble for helping us and they'll hardly believe your story if you head off to Disneyland.'

Paula looked a little crushed. 'I guess you're right.'

'You don't have to tell the cops about the money, though,' James said. 'Drive out there in a week's time, or something.'

With Paula and Curtis both happy, James felt more at ease than he'd done for ages. He was miffed when Lauren broke the mood.

'We better get moving,' she said. 'We might have got past one roadblock, but that doesn't mean the cops have stopped searching for us.'

*

They caught the morning rush hour when they reached the outskirts of Los Angeles, ending up in fourteen lanes of solid traffic, crawling along at walking pace. When they hit a downward slope, there was a vista of tens of thousands of cars packed in close formation, with sunlight reflecting off the windscreens. After fighting their way out of the sparsely populated desert, it was a relief to be sitting in one anonymous car amidst thousands.

They had to find a place to split from Paula. Lauren picked out a route to Hollywood on the map, because it was the only place in town that she'd heard of. They wound up at a grey mall on Hollywood Boulevard called Showbiz Stores. It was 10 a.m. and James couldn't help getting a little buzz when he spotted the famous Hollywood sign on a hill in the distance.

They parked in an underground lot beneath the mall. James walked around to the back of the car and counted a thousand dollars out of the backpack, before slinging it over his shoulder. Paula grabbed Holly and they took an elevator up to the food court on the top level. James got everyone drinks and an ice cream for Holly.

He passed the thousand dollars under the table to Paula as he spoke. 'We passed a taxi rank on the way inside. You sit here and finish your drink. Give us twenty minutes or so to get away, then cover yourself by calling the cops before you do anything else. OK?'

Paula nodded as she took the money.

'Can I trust you?' James asked.

Paula smiled. 'If it works out, you can send me a postcard.'

'Remember,' James said, 'if the cops hear about the money, they'll take it off you. But they're trained to sniff out lies, so you've got to tell the truth about everything else.'

'OK.'

James drained his mug of hot chocolate and tousled Holly's hair as he pushed back his chair.

Curtis smiled at Paula. 'Sorry about last night.'

Lauren, Curtis and James scrambled quickly down two escalators to the ground floor. They strode through a corridor of upmarket shops and stepped outdoors near the head of the taxi rank.

James looked at Curtis. 'You've lived in LA: where's a good place to go? Somewhere three kids won't stand out and you can make your phonecalls?'

'Santa Monica beach,' Curtis said, without a millisecond's thought.

The cab journey was a fifteen-mile ride down Sunset Boulevard, passing through Beverly Hills on the way to the beachfront. James and Lauren stepped out to a scene that reminded them of their mum taking them on a daytrip to Brighton five years earlier: there was an old-fashioned pier with a funfair at the end and wooden decking along the seafront. The palm trees, restaurants and lavish beachfront hotels gave off a glimmer of serious money.

'This is the kind of place where I'll live when I'm a millionaire,' Lauren said.

James smiled. 'How are you planning on becoming a millionaire?'

'Pop star, successful businesswoman . . . Possibly both.'

Once the cab pulled away, they stood in a line looking out at the waves crashing in the distance.

'My mom had a beachfront house down the road in Venice,' Curtis explained. 'My first elementary school was a few miles up that hill over there. Even after we left, we'd come back here for a few weeks most summers.'

'It looks nice,' James said. 'But we can't hang around; you've got calls to make.'

'Call,' Curtis said. 'Just one.'

James looked surprised. 'You said you had to find some numbers. I thought it was going to take a while.'

'No offence, James,' Curtis said, 'but I had to feed you a line. I couldn't totally trust you until I knew this escape was for real. When I was living with my mom, there was always a chance something would go wrong while I was out at school or something. Wherever we stayed, there was always a backup plan.'

'So who are you planning to call?' James asked.

'When Paula goes to the police, they'll track that cab down and ask the driver where he took us, so I couldn't go direct to my dad over in Pasadena. This little diversion to Santa Monica should throw the pigs off the scent.'

'Your *dad*,' James gasped.

According to the background information James and Lauren had read before the mission, Curtis claimed to have no idea who his father was and neither did the FBI.

Curtis nodded. 'I've only met him a few times, but he's the one guy in town who'll definitely know how to get in touch with my mom.'

26. TECHNOLOGY

The FBI team were following the kids' movements by tracking the signal from a cellphone in Lauren's shorts. While Curtis made his call, Lauren pretended that she needed to use one of the beachfront toilets. She locked herself in a stall, grabbed the tiny flip-phone and speed-dialled the FBI office in Phoenix. She told Theo their exact location and about Curtis' revelation that his father lived somewhere nearby.

John Jones and Marvin Teller had landed in LA a couple of hours earlier and were at the airport awaiting developments. A second FBI team was using the cellphone signal to shadow James and Lauren's movements, at a distance of around half a mile.

While Curtis and Lauren were making their phonecalls, James popped fifty cents into a newspaper rack and took out an *LA Gazette*. The pictures of Curtis on the front page looked fine, but someone on Marvin Teller's team must have got inside James' criminal file and doctored the picture taken at Phoenix courthouse, because it barely looked like him.

James read the accompanying story:

4 A.M. NEWS – OFFICER KILLED AS BOYS, 14, ESCAPE ARIZONA MAX

(Maricopa county, AZ) A correctional officer, Scott Warren, died after a daring prison breakout by two boys. The fourteen-year-olds, James Rose and Curtis Oxford, are believed to be the first minors ever to escape from a maximum-security institution.

Oxford is the son of internationally renowned arms dealer Jane Oxford, who is currently in the number-two slot on the FBI's Most Wanted list. Rose was recently transferred from Omaha State prison, where he had been held in solitary confinement after the failure of a previous escape attempt.

Following the escape, two police officers were overpowered at a roadblock heading westbound along 163, using grenades and a stun gun stolen from the prison armoury. Despite this setback, a spokesman for the Arizona State Police said that officers were confident of recapturing the two young killers.

The high-tech, 6,500-inmate, Arizona Maximum Security prison has been plagued by operational difficulties since it was opened in 2002. These include critical glitches in the software that controls security systems and low wages that have resulted in up to 30% of job vacancies at the prison remaining unfilled.

Prison staff and friends have paid tribute to Scott Warren, the 32-year-old officer who died during the escape. Warren, a New Yorker with no known family, was attacked with pepper spray and then gagged and bound by the youths. He was known to suffer from respiratory illness and police suspect that the officer died following an asthma attack brought on by the spray. A female officer was also taken to hospital with concussion and required a number of stitches to a cut in her head, while the two police officers attacked at the roadblock were treated for minor cuts and bruises.

The three kids sat on a bench at the edge of the beach reading the newspaper, until a limousine Curtis had ordered on his father's account stopped at the kerb. It took them on an hour-long freeway ride to a business park in Pasadena, on the eastern outskirts of the city.

The black Mercedes pulled up in the parking lot outside a cube-shaped office building clad in reflective black glass. The corporate logo over the automatic door was a fighter plane with *Etienne Defence Consultancy* written above it. The security guard sitting behind his plinth looked rather surprised by the three grubby kids walking towards reception. He was powerfully built, more like a nightclub bouncer than the middle-aged men who usually sit in the entrances of office buildings.

Curtis rested his elbows on the high counter. 'Call extension five-five-three and tell Mr Etienne that Curtis is on his way to see him.'

Curtis stepped towards the elevator, but the guard called him back.

'Don't move *one* more step, boy,' the guard said firmly. He picked up the phone behind his desk and dialled five-five-three.

The guard had a brief conversation.

'Looks like you're wanted,' the guard said, beckoning the kids towards the elevator doors with his beefy hand.

The guard swiped a security pass through the elevator control panel and hopped out of the car before the door closed. They went directly to the fifth floor, exiting into a large reception area, where they were greeted by a middle-aged lady in a grey business suit.

Curtis smiled as the woman swept him into her arms. 'Hey, Margaret.'

'You've grown,' Margaret said. 'You must have been nine or ten the last time I saw you ... I'm afraid your father is away at a conference in Boston, but he saw the reports on the television news and sent a message to say there was a chance you'd end up here.'

James looked around at the fancy halogen lighting and the abstract paintings on the walls. He didn't have a clue what a defence consultancy did, but if its owner was Curtis' dad, it surely had some connection with Jane Oxford.

'It will take me some time to organise your documentation and arrange air transportation to somewhere safe. In the meantime, the three of you can use Mr Etienne's shower and put on clean clothes. I'll arrange for lunch to be delivered if you're hungry.'

Mr Etienne could have lived in his office if he'd wanted to. As well as the workspace, with a massive desk and a row of Bloomberg financial information screens on the wall, there was a bathroom, a lounge area with massive sofas and even a room off to the side containing a bed and a wardrobe full of suits.

After the kids had taken turns showering, Margaret brought in a selection of delivery menus from nearby restaurants. They settled on an upmarket hamburger joint.

James tucked away a steak sandwich with a side of onion rings, followed by a chocolate dessert for two, which he managed by himself after Lauren said she was full. CHERUB kept James on a tight fitness regime so he usually avoided pigging out, but after a week of prison food he reckoned he deserved a treat.

Curtis turned on the TV in the lounge and they switched to a local news channel. There was only a tiny bit about the escape at the end of each half-hourly bulletin. Lauren snuggled up beside James in her clean T-shirt and shorts and was soon fast asleep.

James had been too stressed to feel tired while he'd been on the run, but now his belly was full and he'd calmed down, he realised he'd barely slept in the last fifty hours. He closed his eyes and drifted off.

27. COUNTRY

By the time the kids woke up, Margaret had driven out to a local mall and bought each of them a new set of clothes for their onward journey. It was a sensible precaution, because the cops investigating the escape would have made attempts to identify the clothing that the kids had taken with them.

James and Curtis both got tracksuits and trainers, but Lauren got a white dress, pink canvas deck shoes and a sparkly silver headband. Her scowl could have melted a steel bar. The last time Lauren had worn a dress, she'd been a seven-year-old bridesmaid and she'd deliberately trailed it through mud to get out of wearing it.

'You'll look so *pretty*,' James said, howling with laughter as soon as Margaret and Curtis were out of earshot.

'One more word,' Lauren said angrily, wagging her finger in his face. 'One more word and I'll deck you.'

'*Quite* the little princess.'

'Wait a minute,' Lauren gasped, anxiously looking around at the carpet. 'Where are my dirty shorts?'

James shrugged. 'Looks like Margaret took them away while we were asleep.'

'Crap,' Lauren scowled. 'The phone was in the pocket. I should have stuffed it down the sofa cushion, or something.'

James looked around the floor, in case it had dropped out of the pocket. 'If it's gone it's gone,' James said. 'You can act innocent and ask Margaret for it back, but I get the impression that she's a lot more than Etienne's secretary. She knows it might be used to track us and I bet she won't let you have it.'

*

John Jones and Marvin Teller spent the afternoon sitting around in the FBI station at Los Angeles airport. Theo Monroe and Scott Warren – now going by his real name of Warren Reise and sporting cropped hair – had just arrived on a scheduled flight from Phoenix.

John stood up and shook Warren's hand, as he walked into the drab office. 'Back from the dead, my friend. Your nose looks a mess. Is it broken?'

Warren nodded. 'James might only be thirteen, but that's one of the hardest whacks I ever took.'

'That's how we train 'em,' John grinned. 'When I went to my job interview at CHERUB, I was shown the martial arts training area. You wouldn't believe these eight- and nine-year-olds with their black belts, pulling off the most frightening moves . . . I tell you, I wouldn't want to tangle with *any* of them.'

Marvin nodded. 'It certainly produces impressive results. When I was with Lauren the other day, I had to keep reminding myself that I was talking to a ten-year-old girl.'

'Kids' brains are like sponges,' John explained. 'They're capable of way more than most adults give them credit for. When I worked for MI5, we sent agents on six-month courses to learn foreign languages. CHERUB can train a bright eleven-year-old to the same standard in two ... Did you check in on Dave before you left Arizona?'

Theo nodded, as he hung his jacket over a hook on the wall. 'I purchased books for Dave to read in the hospital. He is fine physically, but still rather depressed about not being involved in the escape. Arizona State Police came in to interview him early this morning. He set them off on a few false lines of inquiry, as we discussed.'

'And that doctor won't declare Dave fit to return to Arizona Max?' John asked.

'Under any circumstances,' Theo nodded. 'The doctor knows the score and the hospital doesn't much care as long as the bed is being paid for.'

'I'd like to send Dave back to Britain,' John said. 'But Oxford has proved so good at sniffing out undercover operations over the years, we can't pull him out of the Arizona prison system in case she finds out and smells a rat.'

'How are the other two getting along?' Warren asked.

'They spent the afternoon at the headquarters of Etienne Defence Consultancy,' Marvin explained. 'We had two local agents outside the building all afternoon. The kids were picked up half an hour ago in a limousine. The limo company uses uncoded radio and according to their signals, the car is taking them to Orange County airport as we speak.'

'Is Etienne on the radar?' Theo asked.

'No,' Marvin said. 'The FBI have no file on either Jean Etienne, or his company. There are hundreds of small, high-tech companies like EDC in Pasadena: the California Institute of Technology acts as a magnet for them. Etienne specialises in developing military hardware. They've done consultancy work for most of the big weapons manufacturers. Cutting edge stuff: unmanned aircraft, reactive body armour, electromagnetic pulse weapons.'

'So is it a front for Jane Oxford?'

'Too early to be sure, Theo. We can't start any kind of investigation into Etienne right now without creating suspicion and endangering James and Lauren. But we will eventually and if I were a betting man, I'd have my dollars on Oxford and Etienne being in cahoots.'

Theo smiled. 'This is the best lead we've had since I joined this team three years ago.'

'EDC is a nice juicy fish,' Marvin nodded. 'But that company won't be going anywhere. Right now, we've got to stay focused on our little cherubs out in the field, trying to reel in the whale herself.'

Warren picked up a ringing phone and took a short call.

'That was FBI Orange County,' he explained. 'She says there are seventeen flights out of Orange this evening. Three are aircraft for hire, which are the ones I think we need to be looking at. One has filed a flight plan for Chicago, one for Philadelphia and one for Twin Elks, Idaho.'

'What about regular passenger flights?' John asked.

Warren shook his head. 'There's a seven o'clock curfew on large jets out of Orange. Check-in closed on the final flight fifteen minutes ago.'

'Has Lauren called in on her mobile?' Theo asked. 'I diverted the Phoenix number through to here.'

John shook his head. 'The last call we got was an adult

female, probably pressing the last number redial to see what she got.'

'Was she suspicious?' Theo asked.

'I don't think so. I pretended I was Lauren's uncle. When the kids left, the cop said Lauren was wearing a white dress. I've lived with her for the last couple of weeks and it's not her style.'

'The change of clothes makes sense,' Theo nodded. 'It looks like they're being looked after by someone who knows how to play the game.'

'OK,' Marvin said, clapping his hands together. 'We can't afford to lose these kids. I'm gonna call downstairs and have an FBI jet fuelled up and put on standby. As soon as we know which airplane the kids are getting on, we'll set off after them.'

'Can we hold them up?' John asked.

Marvin nodded. 'Sure, I'll get air traffic control at Orange to delay their takeoff clearance, so we arrive before them.'

*

The flight to Idaho in the north-west of the United States took three and a half hours. The small turboprop aircraft had seen better days, with the logo of a previous owner clumsily over-painted and the six passenger seats ripped up. The foam inside crumbled to dust when you brushed against it. The three youngsters were alone, apart from the pilot's cigarette smoke creeping through the top of the cockpit door.

It was dark when they landed at Twin Elks aerodrome, a tiny facility used primarily by amateur pilots. James and Curtis ignored the freezing air and sprinted to the side of the runway to pee in the grass. Lauren looked around forlornly, until she spotted a grubby toilet block beside the control tower. Halfway through peeing, she heard a muffled ring from a telephone in the next stall.

It rang three times before stopping. Lauren stood up and poked her head into the next stall, noticing that a flip-phone had been abandoned on the plastic cistern lid. She picked it up and looked at the display:

1 MISSED CALL
RING BACK?

Lauren leaned outside to make sure nobody was around before hitting the redial key.

'Hello?' It was John Jones' voice.

'You got here quick,' Lauren said.

'Our jet was faster than your turboprop. The only trouble was, with so few flight movements out here in the wilderness, we thought it best to go to another airport. We had to hire a car and race over here.'

'How did you know I'd come over to the toilet?'

John laughed. 'Three hours on a plane without facilities, it was a fair guess. I'm in the trees about thirty metres away from you. Now listen up, we've only got a minute. It's too risky tracking you by cellphone. It would be suspicious after they confiscated the other one and I doubt you'll get a reliable cellphone signal out here in the back of beyond anyway. I've taped a packet of short-range tracking devices under the cistern lid. They go on your body, like a sticking plaster. Put one on whenever you're about to move and press down hard for about three seconds to activate it. It'll send a tracking signal every thirty seconds until the battery runs out— Look out, someone's heading towards you.'

Lauren quickly bolted the stall door. A strange man's voice boomed out.

'Lauren honey, we're waitin' in the car. We need to get out of here as fast as we can. The local sheriff likes to come and poke around if someone lands out here at this time of night.'

'Oh, um . . . I'm doing number twos,' Lauren said, turning red with embarrassment. 'Just a minute.'

She waited until she heard the man step back outside, then prised the lid off the toilet cistern. She peeled away a small plastic bag and tucked it into her jacket. After quickly washing her hands, Lauren stepped outside and was greeted by a bearded man dressed in jeans and a plaid shirt.

'Name's Vaughn Little,' the man explained as they jogged towards a black Toyota four-wheel drive that already had James and Curtis sitting in the back.

*

It was an hour's drive through dense forest, winding up hillsides, past huge trees silhouetted against the moonlight. James kept the window beside his head open and found the blast of cool air a thrill, after all the sweat-glazed hours inside Arizona Max.

'You boys are back on CNN,' Vaughn said, in a honeyed voice that gave the impression of a man about to break into a song about his lonesome cattle. 'Seems your cellblock tilted off the edge when they heard you bunked out. Half a million dollars' worth of damage. Took the riot squad six hours to get the inmates back under control.'

'Hope they busted up some hacks,' Curtis grinned.

'Anybody injured?' James asked.

'A few got hurt bad,' Vaughn said. 'But nobody dead.'

James could see how the news of the escape would have played on the minds of the other inmates and turned the already tense situation into a full-scale riot. He hoped that guys like Abe and Mark had come out OK. On the upside, he couldn't help feeling the riot was another detail that would make the escape more believable to Jane Oxford.

'Have you heard from my mom?' Curtis asked.

Vaughn nodded slowly. 'You're gonna be staying up in the mountains with us for a few weeks. She's out of the country and she wants the heat to die down before meeting up with you.'

'What did she say about James and Lauren?'

'Says she'll fix them up with a good family. Get false ID. Cross the border into Canada, maybe.'

'Good,' Curtis smiled. 'You ever been to Canada, James?'

'Nah.'

'It's nice,' Curtis nodded. 'Clean, safe, you'll like it . . . Can I call Mom tonight?'

Vaughn shook his head. 'You know what she's like. Won't even say hello unless she has the call scrambled and bounced off five different satellites.'

The car pulled on to a track and Vaughn sent Curtis out to open a metal gate. Two women emerged in a shaft of light on the doorstep of a large timber-framed house, as the car slipped around on a muddy path, heading towards them. One was Vaughn's wife, Lisa; the other his fourteen-year-old daughter, Becky. When they piled out of the car, Lisa stepped barefoot on to the cold gravel and squeezed Curtis into a hug.

'Good to see *youuuuuu*,' Lisa said, as she pushed a handful of hair away from her face. 'You remember Becky, don't you? When we lived at the old place down the hill, you two used to act so cute together. I've got stacks of pictures of you in the albums.'

'I remember,' Curtis said vaguely, sounding like he wished he didn't.

James stepped up to the house and glanced at the cute teenager standing on the doorstep in her socks. She wore jeans and a plaid shirt, like a clone of her parents.

'Hey,' Becky said sweetly. 'You must be James.'

Becky led James and Lauren to the kitchen, where something smelled good.

'You want hot soup?' Becky asked, reaching into the cupboard and pulling out a stack of bowls. 'It's homemade and we got coffee in the jug if you want a warm-up.'

The smell of vegetable soup made James and Lauren realise they were hungry. They pulled out chairs and sat at the dining table.

28. HOBBIES

TWO WEEKS LATER

Crime wasn't supposed to pay, but Lisa and Vaughn Little seemed to have done well enough out of it. Vaughn had been a heavy-duty weapons smuggler in the 1970s. He'd served six years in a New Mexico prison. When his parole was up, he moved north to Idaho, bought a small ranch and spawned four daughters. Only Becky, the youngest, still lived at home.

Lisa bred Arabian horses and Vaughn earned money customising and restoring motorcycles, but these businesses were more like hobbies. The Little family's comfortable lifestyle was mostly funded by the well-invested proceeds of thirty-year-old weapons deals.

Everyone fell into a daily routine. Lauren hung out with Lisa and learned to ride and groom the horses. She'd never shown any interest in riding before, but took a shine to the animals and a bigger one to Lisa.

Most days, Curtis disappeared off on long walks into the woods with a sketchbook. Sometimes he'd come back with a drawing of a leaf or rusted-up car, others a whole landscape sketched in impossibly tiny pencil strokes. He was more than a kid who was good at drawing; it could easily have passed as the work of a professional artist. When it rained too hard to go out, Curtis lay on a rug in front of the Discovery Channel and sulked.

James hung out with Vaughn each day and it was like the two of them had been missing each other their whole lives. Vaughn had always wanted a son and James would have settled for a dad just like him. Vaughn had a million stories and a way of telling them that always made James smile. Everything from punching out his high school principal, his wild exploits as a member of the Brigands bike gang, shady weapons deals and stories from his time in prison.

Vaughn took James out on little jobs around the ranch, mending broken fences and old guttering. They'd usually spend a couple of hours in the afternoon working on the motorbikes and Vaughn was patient, explaining to James the way a bike worked and how the different parts fitted together.

Usually when adults ask a kid to help, the kid ends up standing around holding a spanner like a gherkin for three hours, but Vaughn kept James busy and actually trusted him to do stuff. He even let James blast around the muddy ranch tracks on a little Kawasaki dirt bike, though his pleas to have a go on one of the Harley Davidsons got short shrift.

*

James and Lauren slept in the guest room, which had a double bed. They acted as if sharing a bed was some kind of hellish punishment, while both secretly quite liking it. Lauren had been asleep for an hour and had managed to wind most of the king-sized duvet around herself.

James undressed quietly and brushed his teeth in the en-suite bathroom, then pulled the cover back and tried to slip under without waking his sister. He enjoyed the first few moments of warmth, looking at Lauren's long hair spread out over the pillow and listening to her breathe.

Before his mum died, James had never given a moment's thought to how much he loved his little sister. But ever since, he had tortured himself with the idea that something unexpected could happen to her as well. Lauren could get run over, or get cancer, or get hurt on a mission, or . . . A couple of times James made himself cry just thinking about it, although he'd never admitted that to anyone, even the counsellor he occasionally saw on campus.

James closed his eyes and started thinking about a cool Japanese bike he'd read about in one of Vaughn's magazines. All the time he'd spent hanging around the workshop listening to Vaughn's biker stories had convinced James that he wanted his own motorcycle more than anything in the world.

James wasn't sure how old you had to be to ride a motorbike in Britain, but if it was seventeen like a car, he realised he'd be able to get one in three and a half years. He could use some of the money his mum left him when she died, maybe get some kind of job to pay for insurance and petrol . . .

James was doing a hundred miles an hour down the motorway, with a fit girl hugging his waist, when Lauren jabbed him in the ribs.

'You awake?' she asked acidly.

'Just about,' James said, opening his eyes and letting out a big yawn.

'How's *Becky?*' Lauren asked.

'Fine. Why?'

'I put my head around her bedroom door to say goodnight.'

'Oh,' James said anxiously. 'We just started talking and one thing led to another . . . you know. Besides, there's no law against snogging. I'm nearly fourteen, I know guys my age who get up to a lot worse.'

'But what's Kerry gonna say when she finds out you cheated on her?'

'She's ten thousand miles away,' James said.

'Was that the first time you snogged her?'

'Yes,' James lied, knowing that eighth or ninth was probably nearer to the truth. 'And one snog is hardly cheating.'

'I doubt Kerry would see it that way,' Lauren snapped. 'Swear you'll break it off with Becky and I won't say anything, but I'm not gonna sit back and let you cheat on Kerry. She's my friend too.'

'OK, I swear,' James said, trying to sound extra sincere.

'On our mum's grave,' Lauren added.

'On our . . . *No*,' James gasped. 'Can't you just stay out of this? You're ten. You're too young to understand.'

'I might not be into boys yet, but I still know Kerry would be really upset.'

'Why don't you keep your voice *down* and your snout out of my business?'

Lauren turned away and buried her face in the duvet. 'You're a total pig, James. *Goodnight.*'

29. OINK

James' conscience kept him awake half the night and Lauren's evil eye across the breakfast table made him feel worse. Lisa asked if something was up, but they both said it was nothing.

James knew cheating on Kerry was shitty, but he hadn't seen her for months and he fancied Becky like mad. He couldn't see what harm a little fling would do, but Lauren finding out made everything more complicated.

James rushed up to Becky's room when she got home from school.

'Lauren knows,' he said. 'She saw us last night.'

Becky shrugged. 'So?'

James could hardly tell Becky he was a secret agent with a girl back home. He'd spent half the day thinking up a way to explain why Lauren shouldn't find out.

'Lauren's been through a lot,' he said. 'First our dad dying. Then my uncle giving her a hard time and me and Dave getting sent to prison. It's not surprising she wants me to herself for a while.'

'So, you're *never* gonna have a girlfriend in case your sister gets jealous?' Becky asked, as she combed ink-stained fingers through her short brown hair. 'She'll just have to grow up a bit.'

'I just think we should stop all this,' James said. 'I'm moving on to Canada, or wherever, in a few days and—'

'James, you're a cute guy. I know this isn't gonna last forever, but it's more fun than sitting downstairs every night.'

James didn't appreciate being regarded as nothing more than an alternative to TV, but Becky healed his wounded look by stepping closer and kissing his cheek.

'You know what your trouble is, James?' Becky grinned. 'You think too much.'

James tried not to imagine the grievous injuries Kerry would inflict on him if she found out about this, as he leaned forward and returned Becky's kiss.

*

Lisa made spaghetti and meatballs for their evening meal. The Littles always ate as a family at the dining table, then moved to the living-room for dessert in front of the TV.

James stacked the dishwasher, while Vaughn and Becky got the wood-burning fire going. They were set for walnut cake and the second part of a mini-series when the phone rang in the hallway.

'Curtis,' Vaughn shouted.

Everyone looked around anxiously, knowing there was only one person who'd be calling for Curtis.

'Mom?' Curtis grinned, as he snatched the receiver. 'What's going on? . . . Can't you tell me where I'm flying to? . . . OK, but we'll meet up at the other end? . . . Great, so I'll see you tomorrow . . . Yeah, James is right here, I'll call him over . . . James, my mom wants to speak to you.'

James could hear his heart thumping, almost as loud as the faint voice in his ear. 'Mrs Oxford, hi.'

'Hey there,' Jane said. 'My son tells me good things about you, James. I expect this is the only time you and me are ever gonna be safe to talk, but I had to thank you in person for what you did.'

James couldn't help smiling. 'That's OK. What's gonna happen to me and Lauren?'

'I got you new identities. There's a hotel in Boise sorted for tonight and you're on an early flight to Canada in the morning. I've got you and your sister set up with a real good family up there. I've sorted it financially, so there's money behind you. You'll be safe, as long as you keep yourself on the right side of the law.'

'Sounds brilliant,' James said. 'Thanks.'

'That's my four minutes up. Tell Vaughn it's the Comfort Lodge.'

The phone clicked abruptly. James hooked the receiver over the wall-mounted phone and wiped a sweaty palm against his leg.

'She's not one for goodbyes,' Vaughn explained. 'The shorter the call, the less chance the FBI have of tracking her down.'

'How far is Boise?' James asked, still startled by his brief conversation with one of the world's most wanted.

'Three hours by road.'

'When are we leaving?'

' 'Bout as soon as you've got your things packed.'

Lauren looked solemnly at Lisa. 'Can I say goodbye to the horses?'

'I can pack her stuff if you want,' James said. 'We've only got a few clothes and bits.'

Lisa tapped Lauren on the back. 'Quickly then,' she said. 'Go and put your coat on.'

James tried to think as he took the stairs two at a time. With him and Lauren flying to Canada, and Curtis off to meet his mother in some unknown destination, it looked like his prospects of a face-to-face meeting with Jane Oxford had shrunk to zero. All he could do was try and find out where Curtis was going, so that the FBI had a team waiting to intercept him when he met his mother.

James stepped inside his room and began stuffing everything into a backpack. Becky came up behind him.

'I guess this is it then,' James said, feeling a mixture of sadness and relief that he couldn't get a handle on.

A pistol and a couple of large ammunition clips bounced on to the bed in front of him.

'You might need those,' Becky said.

James was shocked. 'Is that your dad's gun? You'll get in trouble.'

'Don't trust Jane Oxford. I've heard talk about things she's done over the years and believe me, you might want that by your side.'

'She said she's found me and Lauren a family,' James said, staring indecisively at the gun on the bed.

Becky picked up the lightweight gun and shoved an ammunition clip into the base. 'What was your bargain with Curtis? You break him out, Jane sets you up with a new life.'

James nodded.

'Well, you already broke Curtis out. So what are you to Jane Oxford now, except trouble and expense?'

This thought had occurred to James on a number of occasions, though the mission briefing described Jane as loyal to anyone who helped her out.

Becky held the gun in front of James' face. 'Pull back the stock to load the first bullet, like this . . . The safety is this little lever here. It's a Glock machine pistol. Each magazine holds twenty-five shots and it's fully automatic, like a machine gun. Just flip the switch to auto.'

'You really don't think we can trust her?'

Becky shrugged as she pulled the elastic of James' tracksuit pants and tucked in the gun. 'I don't know. Better safe than sorry's all I'm saying.'

The last time James had got into a bad situation with a gun, he'd ended up killing someone. He didn't want to get into that situation again and it was the only thing on his mind as Becky's parting kiss brushed his cheek.

'I'll leave you to it, James Rose,' Becky said sadly. 'Pull your hoodie on, so no one can see the gun, and look after yourself.'

James smiled a little. 'I'll do my best.'

Lauren looked torn up as she passed Becky in the doorway.

'That didn't take long,' James said.

'I couldn't face them,' Lauren sniffed. 'I ran back to the house.'

James was surprised at how attached Lauren had become to the horses. He gave her a quick squeeze.

'Here, put this on,' James said, handing his sister one of the tracking patches. 'We might get separated.'

Lauren unbuttoned her jeans and stuck the transmitter, which looked exactly like a sticking plaster, to the top of her thigh where nobody would see it. At the same moment, a crashing sound erupted from Curtis' bedroom.

James shot down the hallway and into a sea of torn paper. Curtis had shredded his dozens of sketches and drawings, then ripped his wardrobe door off its hinges, before burrowing into a narrow space between his bed and the wall.

'What's the matter?' James gasped.

'I like it here,' Curtis sobbed. 'My mom's gonna go mad at me for killing them people. Then we'll be on the run again. She likes the danger, but I get scared and it does my head in. I just want to stay in one place and draw my pictures and go to school . . .'

James couldn't think what to say as Vaughn stepped into the room behind him.

'Are you two fighting?' Vaughn asked angrily. 'Look at the state of this room.'

'He's messed up,' James said, uncertainly. 'He needs help.'

James looked at Curtis, sobbing pitifully into the wall and wished there was something he could do.

'I don't want to go back to prison,' Curtis howled. 'I don't want to go back on the run. I wish I was dead, but I'm too useless even to kill myself . . .'

James sat on the end of the bed and touched Curtis' hand.

'You know these moods always pass,' James said. 'Once you're back with your mum, you can have a proper talk with her and sort yourself out. I bet it'll be OK.'

'She never listens,' Curtis sobbed.

'I need the pair of you downstairs and ready to roll in five minutes,' Vaughn said firmly. 'James, get Curtis a cloth to wipe his face. We've got a long drive ahead. He'll have to get a grip on himself.'

30. CALLS

John Jones and the three-man FBI team had been unable to contact James and Lauren during the two weeks they'd spent on the isolated ranch. To compensate for the lack of access, they'd watched any comings and goings from a safe distance and set up laser microphones in the trees. The invisible beams of light detected vibrations in the windows and converted them into muffled speech using a laptop computer.

Theo was starting a six-hour shift, sitting in the trees fifty metres from the front gate of the ranch, when he heard the kids were on the move. He pulled off a skiing glove and grabbed a radio to call Marvin.

John, Warren and Marvin were fifteen miles away, having a meal in a pizza place near their motel. As Marvin was talking to Theo on his walkie-talkie, he extracted a ringing cellphone from his jacket and handed it to Warren. The call was confirmation from the FBI phone-monitoring unit, who had overheard both ends of Jane Oxford's telephone conversation.

'OK,' Marvin said, taking a final bite of pizza as he stood up. 'I'll make some calls to see what kind of manpower we can rustle up around Boise. I'll try and get someone to stake out the Comfort Lodge, then I'll drive on ahead. There's so little traffic around here, they'll spot us in three seconds flat if we tail them. John, I want you and Warren to take the second car and try to follow the tracking signal from the kids, but keep your distance. Theo will have to sit tight until they leave the ranch and catch us up.'

*

Vaughn's big Toyota had three rows of seats. Lauren sprawled out with a row to herself as they drove towards Boise in the darkness. She closed her eyes and tried not to get upset again.

Making and breaking close relationships was the part of CHERUB missions that newly qualified agents often found toughest to deal with. Lauren knew James would tease her about blubbing over a bunch of horses, but she couldn't help feeling sad every time she thought about them. She remembered the first morning at the ranch, when Lisa had lifted her into the saddle and led her around the small paddock on a rein. Lauren had been terrified of falling off, but time had turned it into a fond memory.

Curtis was a wreck, slumped down without his seatbelt on. The wet streaks on his face caught in the headlight beams of the cars going in the other direction. Before the mission, all James knew about Curtis came from reports about the killings and Warren's observations from inside Arizona Max. Now James had got to know him, he couldn't help wondering if such a sensitive soul would have turned into a killer if he'd grown up in a normal home, instead of on the run with his thrill-addicted mother.

James sat up front, alongside Vaughn. The drive was boring, but he felt too edgy to do anything other than stare at the road ahead, with the handle of the Glock digging into his belly. Shortly after a sign reading *Boise 15 miles*, Vaughn handed James a cellphone.

'Dial information and get the number of the Comfort Lodge.'

James held the phone to his ear with his shoulder, as he scrawled the number on the corner of a road map. He dialled and waited to hear ringing before handing the phone back to Vaughn.

'That the Comfort Lodge?' Vaughn said into the handset. 'My name is Hermann. I got a reservation with you for tonight, but I'm supposed to be meeting a pal of mine first. I believe he's left me a message in the lobby to say where I'm supposed to meet him for dinner. Would you be kind enough to read it to me?'

Vaughn held the phone silently, while the woman on the other end retrieved a folded slip of paper from a cubby behind her head and read it out.

'So that's the Star Plaza,' Vaughn nodded. 'You wouldn't happen to know where that is, would you? . . . Don't worry yourself, sweetheart. I'll get my buddy here to look it up on the map.'

Vaughn ended the call and chucked the phone on the dashboard.

'Who are we meeting?' James asked, as he unravelled a map of Boise city centre.

'Nobody. It's a precaution, in case Jane's phone was being bugged. She tells you to go to one hotel, then leaves a message there under a false name. The message gives you the name of some hotel on the other side of town, which is where you'll really be staying.'

James had hoped that the FBI would have the room at the Comfort Lodge staked out by the time they arrived. Now he was relying on the patches stuck to his and Lauren's skin, and these tiny devices were notoriously unreliable.

'You don't really think the FBI could have tracked us all the way up here, do you?' James asked.

Vaughn shrugged. 'I doubt it, but Curtis' ma has to be real careful. The feds pull out the stops once they put you on that most wanted list. See that cellphone?'

James nodded.

'Came to me in a Fed-Ex package two days ago, with instructions not to even switch it on until we were on the move. Maybe Jane is over-cautious, but there are prisons full of people who weren't cautious enough.'

*

The Star Plaza was a bog-standard business hotel a few minutes' drive from Boise airport, with the usual marble and faux-antique furnishings in the lobby. Vaughn looked nervous as he strolled past reception with the three kids in tow. He approached two old-timers, sitting in armchairs around an occasional table. They wore cheap looking suits and their long white beards suggested the men had been bikers in their younger days.

'Bill, Eugene,' Vaughn said, nodding guardedly. 'Didn't expect to find you two in this neck of the woods.'

'Well you did,' Bill said grumpily, furrowing his brow as though he resented the fact Vaughn existed.

Vaughn gestured with his hand. 'This is James, Curtis and Lauren.'

'You don't say?' the old geezer croaked. 'The lady says you'll get your money transfer in a few days. We'll take 'em up to the rooms. No need for *you* to stick around.'

James got a whiff of pomade, as Bill hauled himself out of his chair. He noticed that Eugene, the other old man, wore a hearing aid.

'So, I'd best be going,' Vaughn said, as he looked fondly at James. 'I can see you out there in Canada, cruising on your Harley in a few years' time.'

'Yeah,' James smiled, 'I hope so.'

'But at least my daughter's safe from you now.'

James missed a beat, as Vaughn burst out laughing. 'You think Lisa and me didn't realise you were carrying on?'

'Yeah um . . . Well . . .' James babbled nervously, as he caught an extremely frosty look off Lauren.

'When my eldest got her first boyfriend, I wanted to kill him. By the time you get to the fourth one, you know better than to put up a fight.'

James grinned, as Vaughn gave him a hug and slapped him on the back. Lauren and Curtis got the same treatment.

'For Christ's sake,' Bill grouched, as he took a step towards the elevator. 'We got everyone in the world eyeballing us here.'

James felt a touch of sadness as he snatched a final glance at Vaughn, heading into the darkness through a revolving door. He might have been a gun smuggler, but Vaughn Little was one of the nicest guys James had ever met.

They had two connecting rooms on the fifth floor of the

hotel, each with a pair of double beds. Eugene and Bill already had their old-man stuff spread out in one room: bottles of pills, hip flasks, y-fronts and the most unfashionable trainers known to man with grey socks balled up inside them. The connecting door was wedged open and Eugene turned the TV up loud enough that you could have heard it on Mars.

The kids had checked out the room and were chilling on their beds for a while when Bill wandered through.

'Can we go and use the pool?' James asked, desperate to get out of the room and contact the FBI, in case they hadn't picked up on the change of lodgings.

'Nah,' Bill said, scratching his armpit and revealing a glimpse of the holster under his jacket. 'It's gone ten o'clock. You boys have been all over the news, so you're better off staying out of sight. Order food from room service if you're hungry, then shift yourselves to bed. Eugene's taking a nap. If he wakes up, tell him I'm down at the bar having a nightcap.'

Within thirty seconds of Bill heading out the door, Curtis dived off the bed and grabbed a can of beer and a bunch of miniature spirit bottles from the fridge.

'Mini-bar time,' Curtis grinned, hurling James a little Jack Daniels bottle as he drained his own into his mouth.

James was wary: the last time Curtis got drunk he ended up getting a life sentence. On the other hand, with Eugene asleep, Bill at the bar and Curtis hitting the bottle, he had a golden opportunity to contact Marvin. It was too risky using the phone in the room, because the call would get itemised on the bill, but he'd seen payphones in the lobby downstairs.

'I know,' Lauren said excitedly. 'Why don't we try and find out where we're all going tomorrow?'

'Good idea,' James said, impressed by how smart his sister could be at times. He'd been so focused on making sure the FBI team knew where they were, he'd forgotten that their main objective was to find out where Curtis was going to meet his mother.

'Where are you gonna look?' Curtis asked.

James shrugged, but Lauren dived purposefully into the next room, where Eugene was sleeping soundly, and grabbed a snazzy leather document wallet she'd eyed up earlier.

'Bet it's in here,' Lauren said.

James understood her logic: the smart item was out of style with the elderly men's other possessions. Someone else had clearly handed it to them.

Lauren unzipped the case on the bed. It contained a brown envelope stashed with a mix of US and Canadian dollars and three fake passports. The first was Brazilian, containing a picture of Curtis under the name Eduardo Santos. There was a computer print-out inside, detailing flights from Boise to Dallas and a connecting flight to Rio de Janeiro.

'Eduardo Santos,' Curtis said, in a rubbish attempt at a Spanish accent. 'Sounds good, hombres?'

He gulped a small bottle of gin as Lauren pulled out the two Canadian passports.

'Go easy on the booze eh?' James said, still holding the unopened Jack Daniels in his hand. 'So where are we going?'

Lauren and James looked set to become Scott and Ellen Parks, of Toronto. James was no expert on forged documents, but the passports looked good to him. Fake identification of this quality would have cost thousands of dollars.

'OK,' James said. 'Put the case where you found it, before Bill gets back.'

Curtis crashed on his bed and ripped open a packet of dry-roasted cashews. James and Lauren walked into the other room together. They made sure Eugene was still asleep before exchanging hurried whispers over the noise from the TV.

'Keep Curtis busy,' James said. 'Start a pillow fight or something. I'll run out and try to make a quick call.'

'What if Curtis asks were you are? Or Bill comes back?'

'We're kids,' James shrugged, 'people expect us to muck about. Just say I'm getting ice, or whatever.'

James opened the door, while Lauren wandered back to join Curtis. He peeked along the corridor, finding nothing except a couple of uncollected room-service trolleys. Their room was at the end of a long corridor near a fire escape. James walked through the fire door and down a single flight of concrete steps to the fourth floor, where there would be no chance of bumping into Bill.

James was planning to use the phones in the lobby, but he spotted an old-fashioned phone with a dial hanging on the wall near the entrance to a cleaner's closet. It was designed for internal use by hotel staff, but James knew most switchboards are programmed to allow any phone to dial out to an emergency number. He picked up the receiver and dialled 911.

'Emergency, which service please?'

James smiled with relief. 'FBI, I have a station number. It's three-two-four-six and the application code is T.'

Within a second of the operator patching the call through to the FBI, it diverted via an office in Phoenix and on to Marvin Teller's cellphone.

'*We're sorry, the mobile number you are dialling is currently busy. Please try again later or leave a message after the beep.*'

James cursed under his breath. 'Marvin, it's me. I'm at the Star Plaza, room five-three-four. Curtis is on a zero-nine-thirty flight to Dallas on American Airlines. He's flying on to Rio using a passport in the name of Eduardo Santos . . .'

31. BRAZIL

James got back to the room without Bill, Eugene or Curtis even noticing that he'd gone. He was almost certain Marvin would have listened to the cellphone message, but it played on James' mind as he lay in the dark room, with Lauren and Curtis asleep and Eugene's snores rumbling through the connecting door.

James was half awake at 5:30 a.m. when Bill crept up to Curtis' bed and shook him awake. The teenager seemed to be suffering the after-effects of his attack on the mini bar as he sat up in bed.

'I thought the flight was later,' Curtis moaned, picking at a gluey eye.

'Keep it down,' Bill whispered. 'I just made a scheduled call to your mother. She's nervous about this whole show. There's been another change of plan and we don't want the two brats over there knowing about it.'

'Mom's whole life has been a change of plan,' Curtis sighed. 'Can't I say goodbye to James and Lauren?'

'Let 'em sleep. You know how this works better than anyone: the less they know about when you got out of here and where you went, the better.'

James had a crick in his neck, but didn't dare move in case the old man realised he was awake.

Curtis swung off his bed and dashed to the bathroom. After bolting the door, James heard him pee, followed by a retching sound as he spewed up in the toilet bowl. James stifled a laugh as Bill wandered over and rapped gently on the locked door.

'You OK in there, boy?'

There was an array of noises from the bathroom, as Curtis cleaned himself up and gargled mouthwash.

'Man,' Curtis gasped, as he exited. 'Must have been something I ate. I hope I'm not sick again on the plane.'

'Something you drank, more like,' Bill grumbled. 'I can smell it comin' out your pores.'

Curtis stumbled meekly across the floor and started picking up his belongings.

'Forget that junk,' Bill said. 'Put your pants and sneakers on, then we're shipping out.'

James racked his brain, wondering if he should follow Bill and Curtis. If Marvin hadn't got the message, or if they were expecting Curtis to be getting a later flight and were still in bed, they'd permanently lose the trail to Jane Oxford. On the other hand, James would blow his cover if he was caught sneaking around after them.

'Ready?' Bill asked, as Curtis wriggled his foot into his trainer and stood up.

'I guess,' Curtis said, uncertainly. He stepped across the room towards the other bed and looked at James. 'Have a nice life, buddy,' he whispered softly.

Curtis followed Bill through the connecting door and

they exited via the other room. James sprang up as soon as the door clunked. He leaned in the next room to make sure Eugene was asleep, before scrambling into tracksuit bottoms and trainers and grabbing a room entry card from the table beside his bed.

He poked his head into the corridor, as Bill and Curtis' backs disappeared around a corner, heading for the elevators. James raced down the back stairs, planning to catch up with them in the lobby. Unfortunately, there were no guest rooms on the ground floor. James found himself at the back of a conference suite, staring at a blank grey fire door that only opened from the other side.

Anxious not to lose Curtis for good, James broke open the fire door and found himself standing in the hotel car park. The sun was peeking over the horizon and his T-shirt did nothing to ward off the bitter wind sweeping across the open tarmac.

James quickly glanced around, making sure there was nobody in sight, before jogging between the lanes of parked cars towards the hotel entrance. When he got close, he noticed a queue of people stepping on to a small bus with *Star Plaza – Airport Shuttle* written down the side. Curtis and Bill were in the line.

James ducked between two cars. He was desperate to go into the lobby and call the FBI team to make sure they knew what was going on, but he was pinned to the spot until the bus left.

Finally, the last passenger boarded and the hydraulic door hissed shut. As the bus began rolling away, a man thumped desperately against the side. The driver hit the brake sharply to let on a final passenger. He was huge black man, wearing a cowboy hat and a suit the colour of red wine. James smiled with relief. He needn't have worried: Marvin Teller had got the message.

*

Lauren woke with a fright. She caught half a second's glance inside the old man's toothless mouth before her whole world turned black. Eugene smeared a pillow over her face and squeezed down so hard she could feel the mattress springs digging into the back of her head. Lauren arched her back and tried to wriggle free, but Eugene swung his knee across the bed and used it to pin down her thighs.

There was no air in Lauren's lungs to scream. She tried to pull some in, but the pillow driving into her face made it impossible, like trying to suck wet concrete through a drinking straw. She knew the numbers from when she'd learned to scuba dive: five minutes to suffocate, but only three for the lack of oxygen to cause permanent brain damage.

Where was James?

Lauren wondered if her brother was already dead, as she realised her right arm was free to move. She felt a glimmer of hope as she fumbled blindly over the top of the bedside cabinet, hunting for some kind of weapon. She recalled the Biro with the *Star Plaza* logo on it as soon as she touched it. She gripped it tight and flipped off the lid with her thumb. It wasn't much, but it was all she had.

Lauren's concentration drifted for a second: the first sign of losing consciousness. She bit her tongue to help focus her mind and blindly thrust with the pen. It hit Eugene in the shoulder, causing only mild discomfort and a blue trail down the sleeve of his shirt. Irritated by the prospect of having to wash out a stain, Eugene shifted his weight as he tried to grab the pen with his free hand.

The pressure moved off Lauren's thighs as Eugene leaned forward. She used all her strength to thrust her knees up into the man's behind. Eugene's grip on the pillow loosened as he jerked upwards, enabling Lauren to twist her head to one side and haul in a lungful of air. Eugene immediately shifted his entire bodyweight back on to Lauren, inflicting extra pain by digging his kneecap into her belly.

Lauren refused to let the excruciating pain deter her desperate escape attempt. She glanced a shaft of light between the sheet and pillow, then spotted one of Eugene's fingertips, as he attempted to straighten her head and reposition the pillow over her face.

'Quite the little fighter, ain't you,' Eugene said, clearly not regarding the ten-year-old's struggle as anything more than a minor setback.

Lauren wriggled her head forward a few centimetres. When she felt the base of Eugene's fingernail pressing against her lips, she bit down hard. The knee slipped off her stomach as the bite sent the old man into a spasm.

Temporarily abandoning his murder attempt to concentrate on his finger, Eugene snatched the pillow away. With the finger still clamped between her teeth, Lauren inhaled through her nose and, now she could see what she was doing, aimed the pointed end of the Biro into the soft tissue at the side of Eugene's throat. The pen sounded like a sink plunger, as the metal point speared his wrinkled flesh.

Lauren let the finger out of her mouth as Eugene slumped across the bed, wailing in agony. Lauren pulled her legs from under him and knocked him cold with a two-footed Karate kick to the side of the head.

Shaking with fear and clutching her painful stomach, Lauren rolled off the bed and lifted the corner of the mattress to retrieve the Glock handgun she'd seen James stash there the night before. She flipped the safety off and quickly checked the bathroom and the floor beside the other bed, terrified she was about to discover her brother's suffocated body.

She held the gun two-handed as she crept into the connecting room, again checking between the beds. The bathroom gave Lauren a shock: Eugene had carefully set out knives and polythene sheeting to dispose of her body.

Lauren was still no closer to knowing what had happened to James. Maybe Eugene had knocked him out while he was sleeping and dragged him off to be suffocated in another room, or maybe he'd been invited downstairs for an early breakfast with Bill and Curtis. *You might as well let Lauren sleep in if she's tired. Eugene will look after her . . .*

With Eugene unconscious and James' fate a mystery, Lauren knew she had no option but to call Marvin. As she picked up the receiver, she heard someone enter the next room.

Realising she had surprise on her side, Lauren crept towards the connecting door, but managed to stub her bare toe on the leg of a table. Her tiny gasp was enough to send the figure in the next room diving into the shadows behind one of the beds before she'd got a proper look at him.

'I've got a gun,' Lauren shouted as she leaned into the doorway, squeezing the trigger to fire a warning shot.

Lauren didn't realise the Glock was capable of repeat fire, or that she'd inadvertently flipped it to automatic when she took off the safety. She felt like there was a high-pressure hose in her hands, as the recoil from half a dozen bullets shoved her backwards. The shots plunged into the wall, smashed the mirrored front of a wardrobe and knocked clumps of plaster out of the ceiling. Lauren ended up sprawled backwards over one of the beds.

A stunned shout came out through the dust clouds and broken glass in the next room. 'It's *me*,' James coughed, as he stood up with his hands in the air.

'Where the *hell* did you disappear to without bothering to wake me up? I nearly got killed.'

James stepped through the dust and snatched the gun from his sister. 'Mental gun, eh?' he said. 'It's what the SAS use. You're supposed to stand with one leg behind the other so it doesn't push you backwards.'

'So where's Curtis?'

'On his way to the—'

Before James finished speaking, the locks in both room doors clicked simultaneously. James spun around, ready to spray more bullets.

'FBI,' Warren shouted, aiming a gun into the room.

'All safe,' James and Lauren shouted back frantically.

John and Theo had rushed into the other room and ended up staring at James through the connecting door.

'We heard the gunfire. What happened?' John asked.

'The unconscious guy with the Biro sticking out of his

neck just tried to smother me,' Lauren explained matter-of-factly.

'That doesn't make sense,' James said. 'What about the Canadian passports we saw last night?'

'Look for yourself if you don't believe me,' Lauren said, pointing indignantly towards the bathroom. 'I don't go round sticking people with Biros for the fun of it you know.'

James, John, Warren and Theo peeked at the equipment laid out in the bathroom. James felt queasy when he imagined what had nearly happened.

'Wasn't Jane Oxford supposed to be loyal to people who help her out?' James asked bitterly.

'We clearly overestimated the extent of that loyalty,' Theo said. 'But the passports are a classic Jane Oxford ruse. She always makes three or four different plans and only tells people which one she's going to use at the very last moment. It's possible that Bill was given the passports and believes that you two were going to be sent to Canada, while Eugene was under instructions to kill you.'

'It's a clever tactic,' Warren added. 'We've had it a few times where we've broken down one of Oxford's operations and made arrests, only to find that there's a mass of evidence pointing in different directions. When it gets to court, the defence lawyers use the contradictions to pull you apart: *if Jane Oxford intended to kill James and Lauren Rose, why did she spend ten thousand dollars buying them false identities, booking airline tickets and arranging for them to stay with Mr and Mrs La-de-da in Toronto. And so on.*'

'But why would she try to kill us?' Lauren asked. 'We never did anything to hurt *her*.'

'I suppose she thought you might have talked if you were ever recaptured,' Theo said. 'You knew about Etienne and the Little family. She clearly wanted you dead the second Curtis wasn't around to see it happen.'

'Heartless bitch,' James said, shaking his head. 'We helped her own son escape and her only thanks was to try and kill us.'

'It figures though,' Warren said. 'Oxford hasn't evaded the law for twenty years by being sentimental.'

'We can speculate all we like once this is over,' John said tersely. 'Right now, I suggest we put our heads together and concentrate on working out where we go from here.'

'I think we'd better call an ambulance for Eugene first,' Theo said. 'Things are starting to look a little gooey over there.'

'Apart from that, all we can do is make sure we don't lose track of Curtis,' Warren said. 'We've got agents on standby at Dallas airport and in Brazil. Hopefully Jane will show her face wherever Curtis ends up. Trouble is, she'll run a mile if she finds out that everything here just went pear-shaped.'

Theo's cellphone rang. He grabbed it out of his jacket and had a brief conversation with Marvin.

'You're not going to believe this,' Theo groaned. 'Bill got a phone call while he was on the airport bus. When they arrived, Marvin got off and hung back to follow Bill and Curtis, but Bill told the bus driver he'd left something back at the hotel and they're staying on for the ride back.'

'Is Marvin still with them?' John asked.

Theo shook his head. 'It would have been too suspicious if he'd re-boarded the bus. Curtis and Bill should be back at reception any minute now.'

32. MOTEL

The shuttle bus only took fifteen minutes to ride between the hotel and the airport.

'So here's what happened,' John said, thinking as he spoke. 'Eugene tried to kill James and Lauren, but got his comeuppance. Once they realised Jane Oxford wanted them dead, James and Lauren grabbed the money and valuables and left the hotel in a big hurry.'

Warren pointed at Eugene, who was still unconscious on the bed. 'What about him? He needs an ambulance.'

John shrugged. 'He was about to kill the kids, so forgive me if I haven't got a lot of sympathy for him.'

Theo leaned over the bed and inspected Eugene's injury. 'It's behind the windpipe and he's not losing much blood. With the Biro still bunging up the hole, I believe he'll be good for a few hours, at least.'

'OK, let's grab the valuables and clear out of here sharpish,' John said.

Theo pocketed Eugene's wallet, while Lauren grabbed the briefcase with the money and passports. They were almost out of the door when the phone rang.

John made a split-second decision. 'James, you answer that.'

'Hello,' James said, as he frantically grasped the receiver and stumbled on to the bed.

'Eugene? Is that you?' Bill asked.

'It's James.'

'Oh,' Bill said, sounding exceptionally surprised. 'I didn't expect you to still be around. Is Eugene there?'

'He's been locked in the toilet for ages,' James said, trying to sound cool. 'I don't know what he's playing around at in there.'

John gave James a smile and thumbs-up for his quick thinking.

Bill sounded angry. 'You tell Eugene to get his sorry old ass moving. Tell him I've checked Curtis in for his flight, but I'm on my way back here to find a certain car and I'll meet him at the motor lodge this evening.'

'OK, I'll pass that on,' James said. 'Thanks very much for helping us out, by the way.'

Bill sounded stunned. 'Um . . . that's OK, James, it was a pleasure.'

The call went dead.

'What did he say?' John asked.

'Something about being on his way to find a car, but he said he'd dropped Curtis off at the airport.'

John shrugged. 'I guess he said that for your benefit.'

'It's classic Jane Oxford, again,' Theo said. 'She has Bill set up with a passport and an airline ticket. Then she pulls the plan at the last minute and sends him off on a car journey.'

'But why wait until he gets to the airport, then send him

back here?' Lauren asked. 'Wouldn't it have been better to send him to pick up the car somewhere else?'

'I guess Bill was running early,' Theo said. 'Jane probably thought he was still here.'

'Judging by that phonecall, Bill and Curtis won't be coming back to this room, which makes our lives easier,' John said. 'We've got to get downstairs and make sure we don't lose them when they get off the airport shuttle and try to find this car.'

'Someone will have to stay here and deal with Eugene,' Theo said. 'We can't leave him for the poor maid to find.'

'OK, Theo,' John said. 'You stay here and deal with that, but don't call for an ambulance until after you see us leave. Warren and I will go down to the car park, see what car Bill and Curtis get into and chase after them.'

'What about me and Lauren?' James asked.

John thought for a second before digging out his car keys. 'You can navigate and operate the radios. It's a black Chrysler, parked in row F. Get in, start the engine so that the car's ready to pull away as soon as I get there, then belt yourself into the passenger seat.'

Warren dangled his keys in front of Lauren. 'Blue Volvo, parked next to John's. Make sure you keep down if you see Bill or Curtis.'

James and Lauren raced five floors down the back stairs, out through the fire doors and into the car park. They found row F and were climbing into the cars as the Airport Shuttle stopped in front of the lobby. A rumble of static burst out of the police radio in the dashboard, as James started the engine and climbed over to the passenger seat.

Curtis and Bill both disappeared inside the lobby. James

looked across at Lauren in the next car and shrugged, hoping that they weren't changing plans again.

Warren's voice erupted from the loudspeaker. 'I'm in the lobby and I think we're OK. They've both gone into the bathroom. Curtis looks a little green around the gills.'

James spotted them emerging through the revolving doors a couple of minutes later. Both kids dropped down in their seats, so they were out of sight, as Bill led the way out into the rows of cars. He stopped when he reached a shabby yellow Nissan that looked like a retired taxi. He stepped back to read the registration plate, then fumbled around under the front wheel arch until he located an ignition key.

James was feeling tense. He jumped out of his skin as John opened the driver's door beside him.

'Look in the glove box,' John said, as he slammed the door and pulled his seatbelt across his chest. 'Get the best map you can find. Try to keep track of where we are and remember the names of shops and landmarks as you pass them. In any pursuit, you must be able to accurately relay your position to other cars.'

James nodded, as he rummaged through the glove box for a map. As John pulled away, he passed Warren walking briskly towards the other car.

Theo's voice broke out over the radio. 'I'm looking out of the hotel window. I see a yellow Nissan pulling right. Over.'

John pointed at the microphone. 'You work the radio, James.'

James picked up the plastic microphone and looked unsure what to say.

'Just tell him we're on it,' John said.

*

By the time Marvin had sprinted across Boise airport to the taxi rank and arrived back at the Star Plaza, an ambulance crew was on the scene to deal with Eugene. Marvin hurled money at the cab driver, and rushed off without getting change. As he pulled his car out of its spot, Marvin asked for a fix on Bill and Curtis over the radio.

'This is car F. We're eight miles ahead, on route sixteen, heading southwest,' James replied.

Bill clearly didn't want to risk getting pulled over for speeding and kept the yellow Nissan dead on the limit, enabling Marvin to catch up with John and Warren.

Marvin and Warren had been trained in pursuit driving on the opposite side of the Atlantic to John, but the basic technique is the same wherever you learn. The lead car kept the yellow Nissan in sight. The second car held back between a quarter and half a mile, ready to continue the chase if the suspect made a sudden manoeuvre and fooled the driver of the first car. The third car followed another mile behind that. To minimise suspicion, the cars switched positions every fifteen to twenty minutes.

An hour and a half after leaving Boise, they'd passed into the state of Oregon and were travelling northwest on a busy section of interstate towards Baker City.

Lauren's voice broke across the radio from the lead car. James was dead impressed by how professional she sounded. 'Yellow Nissan is off at Rouge Court Motor Inn. That's Rouge Court Motor Inn. We have passed the exit, but can come around if needed.'

'Negative,' Marvin answered. 'Pull up somewhere a few

miles ahead and keep the engine running. We might need you later. I'm gonna pull in after them. John, I need backup. I want you to pull up short and try to cover me from the side.'

A mile and a half sounds a long way to hang back, but at seventy miles an hour it only took John a minute to reach the Rouge Court. The motel formed part of a strip, along with a burger joint, diner and gas station. John rolled up in front of the diner. They jumped out of the car and crouched behind some bushes overlooking the Rouge Court parking lot. James had nothing but a T-shirt covering his top half, so he tucked his hands under his armpits to ward off the cold.

'Have you still got the Glock?' John asked.

James nodded, as he pulled it from the elastic of his tracksuit pants. John swapped it for his revolver. 'I might need the extra firepower.'

Bill stood in front of a locked glass door, ringing a buzzer to try and get into the motel reception. Marvin couldn't get out of his car, in case Bill recognised him from the airport shuttle ride. Curtis sat in the front seat of the yellow Nissan, with his elbow resting on the ledge of the open window.

James heard the door of one of the motel rooms clunk shut. The woman who emerged was dressed in a pink T-shirt, with big glasses and a towel around her hair, like she'd just washed it. Her mules scraped along the damp pavement with every step she took.

She was almost level with the yellow Nissan, when James recognised the glasses from the photograph he'd seen in the visitors' room at Arizona Max.

'It's her,' James whispered, nudging John excitedly. 'Jane Oxford.'

'I don't think so,' John said, shaking his head.

By the time John had finished denying it, Curtis had jumped out of the car and wrapped his arms around her.

'Holy *cow*,' John stuttered, grabbing his walkie-talkie out of his jacket. 'Warren, Marvin, I'm eyeballing Jane Oxford *right* now. Get over here.'

A shout came at James and John from behind. 'Hey, what you hidin' down there for?'

It was the cook from the diner, a greasy man dressed in an even greasier apron. Curtis and Jane both turned towards the shout. It left John with no option but to move immediately.

'Cover the door of her motel room,' John said urgently. 'She might have backup in there.'

James clicked the safety off the revolver. John leapt out of the bushes and fired a shot into the back of the yellow Nissan to make it clear he meant business.

'FBI, *freeze*.'

John closed Jane and Curtis down, looking nervously from side to side, with the gun held in a two-handed grip.

Marvin and Bill both heard. Bill pulled his gun from its holster and headed around the corner to Jane's rescue, not realising that an FBI agent was emerging from a car behind him. Marvin had never struck James as the kind of man who stood any nonsense and he proved it by pulling his gun and shooting Bill twice in the back, without even bothering to shout a warning.

Marvin snatched Bill's gun, as he stepped over the bleeding man and rounded the corner to the yellow Nissan.

'This is turning into a real good morning's work,' Marvin

grinned, unhooking the set of handcuffs on his belt as he closed in on Jane.

James kept one nervous eye on the door of Jane's motel room, and the other on Curtis, trying to read his face. No sane person would make a run for it with two guns pointing at them from close range, but that didn't take account of Curtis' suicidal tendencies.

While John covered him with the Glock, Marvin made Jane Oxford take her hands off her head and fixed a set of cuffs over her wrists.

'Look at that,' Marvin said smugly, as he squeezed them on. 'Perfect fit.'

Jane lashed her head around and spat down the lapel of Marvin's suit. Marvin furiously lifted Jane into the air and thumped her down on the hood of the Nissan. While pinning Jane with one hand, he unhooked a can of pepper spray from his belt and held it in her face.

'Don't make me use this,' Marvin said firmly.

Angered by what was happening to his mother, Curtis made a sudden lunge towards John. James' heart jumped, knowing John only had to pull on the trigger to tear Curtis apart. But John had no intention of using a gun on an unarmed fourteen-year-old. Instead, he wrapped an arm around Curtis' waist and bundled him backwards on to the damp tarmac. The boy thrashed around, letting out a giant moan, as John zipped a set of disposable plastic cuffs over his wrists.

By the time Warren rolled on to the forecourt, Jane and Curtis were cuffed up in the back of Marvin's car. While Warren leaned over Bill and used his cellphone to call an ambulance, James crept around the bushes and climbed in the back of the Volvo behind his sister.

Lauren glanced over her shoulder. 'It looks like Jane's crying.'

'Good,' James said sourly. 'She wanted us dead. I hope she burns in hell.'

'I feel sorry for Curtis though.'

'Poor sod's not all there, is he?' James said. 'Those drawings he ripped up were fantastic.'

Lauren clambered over the armrest between the two front seats and crashed next to James in the back. She rested her head against James' shoulder as he put an arm around her back.

After all James and Lauren had been through, the scene they overlooked was an anti-climax: a quiet car park, three cops, two suspects cuffed in the back of a car and a man lying unconscious on the ground. When the manager of the motel emerged from reception, he had the resigned look of someone who'd seen it all before.

'Are you OK?' James asked, pulling his rather sad-looking sister a little tighter.

'My tummy still hurts, from earlier,' Lauren said. 'It's all a bit of a let-down really.'

James looked confused. 'We caught Jane Oxford, what more do you want?'

'I don't know . . . I guess I was expecting a big shoot-out, or something.'

'Fancied some blood and guts, eh?' James smiled. 'Helicopters chasing us down the road firing machine guns, and cigar-chomping mercenaries with strings of ammo around their necks.'

'Yeah,' Lauren giggled. 'And it all ends up at Jane Oxford's mountain lair, where we find the stolen weapons and blow them all up. Diving out of the way seconds before a ball of flame erupts from the mouth of a cave.'

James nodded. 'And I get to rescue a whole bunch of hottie cheerleaders, who Jane was holding hostage. The two best looking ones give me their cellphone numbers . . .'

'Trust *you*,' Lauren tutted. 'Of course, my hair would remain perfect throughout.'

'If only we lived in the movies,' James sighed, straightening up his grin. 'Seriously though, the only thing that matters is that we captured Jane without any good guys getting hurt.'

Lauren nodded. 'Do you think they'll find the missiles, now they've caught her?'

'Hopefully,' James shrugged. 'We've done our bit. I'm just looking forward to going home and chilling out. Kerry should be back by now.'

'Will you tell her about Becky?'

'Not if I can help it. You know what her temper's like, she'd break my legs.'

'Oh,' Lauren said.

James sounded anxious. 'You're not gonna spoil everything by grassing on me are you?'

'I suppose not,' Lauren sighed, 'seeing as you're my brother. But I still think you're a dirtbag. You don't deserve someone as nice as Kerry for a girlfriend.'

33. CAMPUS

After twenty hours of cars, aeroplanes, airport terminals, a train into town and a mini-bus ride to campus, James was a wreck. His joints ached, like every drop of liquid had been sucked out of his body and replaced with chewing gum and he was so desperate for sleep his eyes felt like lead balls.

Lauren made the journey worse. She pulled off her usual trick of sleeping effortlessly, while James twisted in his economy-class seat, suffering through two dreadful romantic comedies.

It was past noon when they arrived back at campus. James ignored Lauren's exuberant pleas to help her unpack the boxes that had been piled up in her new quarters for nearly a month. He went to his room, stripped to his boxers, buried himself under his duvet and fell asleep inside two minutes.

*

James woke four hours later with muddy fingertips sweeping across his cheek.

'I thought I'd better wake you up,' Kerry said softly, as she sat down on the edge of James' bed. 'If you sleep for too long now, you won't be tired tonight and you'll still be jet-lagged tomorrow.'

James yawned, as he sat up in his bed. 'What time is it?'

'Quarter to five. I just finished football practice.'

James rubbed his eyes and couldn't help smiling as he took his first proper look at his girlfriend in three months. Kerry had done some growing up, and even with shin pads and streaks of mud on her legs, James thought she looked beautiful. He leaned forward and they exchanged a long kiss.

'I smell all sweaty,' Kerry said, when she eventually pushed James away.

'I don't care,' James said, moving in for another kiss. 'I like your smell.'

'Well, I don't much like yours,' Kerry said, with a tiny hint of sharpness. 'You smell like that horrible air freshener they spray on aeroplanes.'

'Do I?' James asked, raising his arm and sniffing his pit. 'That's pretty nasty, actually.'

'You're a class act, James,' Kerry grinned as she stood up. 'Oh . . . You didn't notice,' she added, pulling her T-shirt down over her football shorts.

James stared at Kerry's breasts bulging out of the T-shirt. 'Of course I noticed, they're miles bigger than they were before.'

Kerry stepped forward and whacked him across the shoulder. 'God, is that all you boys ever think about?'

James grinned guiltily. 'Pretty much.'

'What about my T-shirt?' Kerry said indignantly. 'The *colour* of my T-shirt?'

'Oh,' James gasped. 'You got the navy T-shirt, congratulations!'

'Thank you,' Kerry grinned sweetly as she headed for the door. 'I'm gonna have a shower, then I'll see you downstairs for dinner.'

*

The dining hall was packed when James got downstairs. He passed Lauren and Bethany, who were sitting amongst a group of the youngest grey-shirt kids, making a racket. James queued up and picked spaghetti Bolognese, salad and chocolate trifle, before heading across to the tables where his friends always sat.

Gabrielle and Kerry were the only ones there. James sat opposite them.

'Where is everyone?'

'Callum, Connor and Shakeel are still away on their recruitment missions,' Gabrielle explained. 'Bruce is on a mission in Norfolk and Kyle's over at the back of campus, up to his waist in slurry.'

'And *I've* got a bone to pick with you,' Kerry said, folding her arms seriously.

James grinned as he crammed in a fork-load of spaghetti. 'Oh, that *does* make a change.'

'I hear you've been cheating on me while I was away.'

James inhaled two hundred strands of spaghetti as he gasped. He couldn't believe that this had happened after Lauren had promised not to tell.

'Listen . . .' James coughed. 'Whatever she told you, it's not true.'

Kerry shook her head slowly, as James hacked chewed-up pasta into a serviette.

'Don't lie to me, James. Bruce and half a dozen other guys saw everything that happened.'

Now James was seriously confused. '*Bruce?*'

'I'm OK with it,' Kerry said. 'You know, if you ever feel that you want to explore your gay side . . .'

'My what?' James gasped, shaking his head. 'What are you on about?'

'Look,' Kerry giggled, 'I just wanted you to know that if you ever feel the urge to snog Kyle again, I won't be holding any grudges.'

James felt like a five-billion-ton weight had lifted off his chest as the pieces fitted together. This had nothing to do with Becky. Kerry was winding him up about the time he'd kissed Kyle as a joke after fitness training.

'Yeah, me and Kyle,' James groaned, as he desperately tried to recap everything he'd said to make sure he hadn't accidentally given the game away. He realised the pasta had probably saved him. He dreaded to think what he might have blurted if he hadn't been choking. 'Real funny . . . Did I hear you say Kyle's on punishment cleaning out ditches again?'

Gabrielle nodded. 'That boy is *so* dumb.'

'Why?' James grinned. 'What's he done this time?'

'You remember the little DVD production line he was running?'

James nodded, his mouth too full to speak.

'I think the staff were prepared to turn a blind eye while he was running off the odd movie for his mates,' Gabrielle explained. 'But he started getting greedy.'

'How come?' James asked.

'Kyle started getting more orders than he could handle by himself, so he employed Jake Parker to help burn the DVDs and put the labels on.'

James nodded. 'I know Jake, he's Bethany's little brother.'

'Jake thought it would be funny to mix up the labels.'

James broke into a smile. 'That's *not* good.'

'No it wasn't,' Gabrielle said. 'Especially not when a bunch of six-year-olds ended up at a sleepover with a copy of *The Texas Chainsaw Massacre* instead of *Harry Potter*.'

'Classic,' James yelled, banging on the tabletop and howling with laughter.

Kerry kicked him under the table. 'It's not funny, James. One poor kid peed her nightie.'

'I guess it's not really funny,' James said, before erupting into a fresh round of hysterics.

Kerry was struggling to keep a straight face herself. She leaned across the table and stared into James' eyes. He wiped the Bolognese from his mouth and kissed Kerry on the lips. It was good to have her back.

EPILOGUE

JANE OXFORD did not cooperate with the FBI. She refused to answer any questions, except to acknowledge her name. She faces charges for murder, racketeering and weapons smuggling and can expect to spend the rest of her life in prison. The complexity of the charges against her mean that a trial is unlikely to take place for several years. In the meantime, she remains on remand at the federal supermax prison in Florence, Colorado.

After Jane's arrest, the FBI used information in her possession at the time to uncover homes and assets she controlled around the world. As more secrets were unveiled, it became clear that Jane Oxford had changed the focus of her operations from stealing weapons, to stealing the technology underlying them. She then used front companies, such as Etienne Defence Consultancy, to sell this knowledge on to other weapons manufacturers.

With the global armaments industry turning over half a trillion dollars a year, Jane found this business far more lucrative than selling arms to terrorist groups and poverty-stricken third-world governments. The FBI has already uncovered assets belonging to Jane Oxford worth more than $1.4 billion. Not only is this figure well in excess of what the FBI had expected to find, it is more than Jane's relatively modest lifestyle would ever have required. It seems that, true to her psychological profile, Jane Oxford carried on her criminal activities purely for the thrill of it.

So far, no specific information has been found about the PGSLM Buddy missiles. The FBI now suspect the missiles were stolen to order on behalf of a rival weapons manufacturer. However, until concrete evidence is found, there is no way to be certain of this. The possibility remains that the weapons have fallen into the hands of terrorists or even that Jane Oxford did not steal them at all.

CURTIS OXFORD was reclassified as an escape risk and returned to a single cell inside Arizona Max, after forty-eight hours in the hole.

A few months later, Curtis' Las Vegas based 'uncles' discovered that the psychiatrist who recommended he be sent to the Arizona-based military school was being investigated for accepting money in return for recommending his patients to the school. They instructed a lawyer to appeal Curtis' case, on the grounds that the murders he committed were a result of the inappropriate advice given by the corrupt psychiatrist.

On appeal, the judge accepted the arguments of Curtis' lawyers, stating that: 'Curtis Oxford has a long history of mental health problems. While Curtis must clearly still accept some responsibility for these very grave actions, this new evidence shows that it was inappropriate to try and sentence him as an adult.'

Curtis' original convictions for first-degree murder were quashed. Charges relating to the death of Scott Warren and the subsequent escape were also dropped. Three weeks later, Curtis pleaded guilty to four counts of the lesser charge of manslaughter in an Arizona youth court. Following a detailed psychiatric evaluation, he received a sentence of seven years, to be served in a medium-security young offenders institution. The families of the three people Curtis shot appeared on a local TV station saying that they were appalled by this decision.

It has also emerged that Jane Oxford had set up a trust fund for her son, thought to be worth more than $30 million. This money has been thoroughly laundered through the international banking system and FBI sources believe it will be impossible to prove that it is the proceeds of criminal activity. When he is released from prison in 2012, Curtis Oxford will be an extremely wealthy young man.

Among the other prisoners, ELWOOD and KIRCH both turned eighteen and were moved into the adult section of Arizona Max shortly after the escape. The brothers STANLEY and RAYMOND DUFF fully recovered from their injuries and returned to cell T4 once the riot damage had been repaired.

The Arizona Department of Prisons has a long-standing policy of naming cellblocks after officers who died in the line of duty. The SCOTT WARREN memorial cellblock is due to open soon in a new prison complex east of Phoenix. The inquiry into the escape made several recommendations for tightening up security inside Arizona Max. These included replacing the oversensitive doors and issuing all correctional officers with personal attack alarms that activate automatically when an officer is knocked down. A lack of money means these recommendations are unlikely to be implemented.

WARREN REISE (a.k.a. Scott Warren), quit his job as an FBI special agent so that he could spend more time with his wife and three young children. THEODORE MONROE and MARVIN TELLER remain on the FBI team investigating the legacy of Jane Oxford's criminal activities.

PAULA PARTRIDGE was questioned by police in California and Arizona. They saw no reason to doubt her story about being held hostage. She later received an undisclosed compensation payment from the Arizona Department of Prisons and $7,000 from a news agency for an interview about her 'Terrifying ordeal at the hands of ruthless teenage killers'. The article appeared in more than one hundred newspapers and magazines across the United States and around the world. The money enabled Paula to move out of the trailer park and make the down payment on a small house. She also took her daughter, HOLLY PARTRIDGE, for an overnight stay at Disneyland.

VAUGHN LITTLE's ranch was searched by the FBI and a significant cache of illegal weapons was found. These included Glock machine pistols, mortar rounds and sniper rifles. Vaughn and his wife LISA LITTLE were charged with harbouring a fugitive and possession of unlicensed firearms with intent to sell. Vaughn was sentenced to eight years in prison while Lisa received a term of four years. The ranch and Arabian horses had to be sold to pay legal costs and REBECCA LITTLE (Becky) moved to live with her eldest sister in California.

EUGENE DRISCOLL recovered fully after the Biro was removed from his neck. WILLIAM BENTLEY (Bill) similarly recovered from the gunshot wounds inflicted by Marvin Teller. Police checks indicated that the two men had been working together as contract killers for more than forty years. They were wanted for thirty murders, in eleven US states and two Canadian provinces.

After the two men had recovered, the FBI transported them to Texas. Following a three-week trial, they were found guilty of six counts of murder and sentenced to death by lethal injection. The lengthy appeals process means it will be several years before their death sentences are carried out.

DAVE MOSS was quietly removed from his guarded room in the Arizona hospital and arrived back at CHERUB campus a few days after James and Lauren. He resumed light physical training shortly after returning and was declared fully fit two months later, when ultrasound scans showed that the blood clot on his chest had dissolved.

A detailed report is written on every CHERUB mission. The report on the prison break congratulated all participants for the overall success of the mission. However, JAMES ADAMS was severely criticised for his reckless crashing of the Toyota and Dave Moss for falling asleep and almost allowing James to be stabbed by Stanley Duff.

Only LAUREN ADAMS escaped without rebuke. The report described her as 'Courageous, clear thinking, co-operative', and as a 'young agent with massive future potential'. After reading the report, Dr McAfferty decided that her role in the mission justified giving her the navy T-shirt, making her one of the youngest ever to wear it.

While the staff at CHERUB had some reservations about the performance of their young agents, over in America the CIA and FBI were delighted with the capture of Jane Oxford. Four weeks after James returned to campus, Dr McAfferty received a package from CIA headquarters. It contained three boxes made of highly polished piano wood, one each for James, Dave and Lauren.

James wondered what was in the box when he came up to his room after lessons and spotted it resting on his pillow. He pulled open the tightly sprung hinge and stared at the gold disc, with the head of an American eagle at the centre of a five-pointed star, before reading the inscription beneath it:

The Intelligence Star is a medal
awarded by the United States for a
voluntary act, or acts, of courage
performed under hazardous
conditions, or for outstanding
achievements or services rendered
with distinction under conditions
of grave risk.

James couldn't help grinning as he turned the medal over and read his name engraved on the back.

CHERUB IS SEARCHING FOR TALENTED NEW RECRUITS ...

Join CHERUB today to receive special mission briefings from the CHERUB Campus
(and exclusive CHERUB stickers)

Plus the chance to win the ultimate prize:
You could feature as a character
in a CHERUB book!

See **www.cherubcampus.com**
to continue your training

CHERUB: The Recruit

by Robert Muchamore

So you've read CHERUB: *Maximum Security*. But how did James Adams end up at CHERUB in the first place?

CHERUB: *The Recruit* tells James' story from the day his mother dies. Read about his transformation from a couch potato into a skilled CHERUB agent.

Meet Lauren, Kyle, Kerry and the rest of the cherubs for the first time, and learn how James foiled the biggest terrorist massacre in British history.

CHERUB: *The Recruit* available now from Robert Muchamore and Hodder Children's Books.

www.cherubcampus.com

CHERUB campus is the essential internet destination for anyone who enjoyed reading CHERUB: *Maximum Security*.

Packed with exclusive content, you can see in-depth biographies of all the CHERUB characters, read out-takes and bonus stories, preview chapters and all the latest news about forthcoming CHERUB titles.

CHERUB: Class A

by Robert Muchamore

Keith Moore is Europe's biggest cocaine dealer. The police have been trying to get enough evidence to nail him for more than twenty years.

Now, four CHERUB agents are joining the hunt. Can a group of kids successfully infiltrate Keith Moore's organisation, when dozens of attempts by undercover police officers have failed?

James Adams has to start at the bottom, making deliveries for small-time drug dealers and getting to know the dangerous underworld they inhabit. He needs to make a big splash if he's going to win the confidence of the man at the top.

CHERUB: The Killing

by Robert Muchamore

When a small-time crook suddenly has big money on his hands, it's only natural that the police want to know where it came from.

James' latest CHERUB mission looks routine: make friends with the bad guy's children, infiltrate his home and dig up some leads for the cops to investigate.

But the plot James begins to unravel isn't what anyone expected. And it seems like the only person who might know the truth is a reclusive eighteen-year-old boy.

There's just one problem. The boy fell from a rooftop and died more than a year earlier.

Look out for CHERUB: *The Killing*, coming soon from Robert Muchamore and Hodder Children's Books.